BRIA| THE PADDED DOOR

M000195493

BRIAN FLYNN was born in 1885 in Leyton, Essex. He won a scholarship to the City Of London School, and from there went into the civil service. In World War I he served as Special Constable on the Home Front, also teaching "Accountancy, Languages, Maths and Elocution to men, women, boys and girls" in the evenings, and acting in his spare time.

It was a seaside family holiday that inspired Brian Flynn to turn his hand to writing in the mid-twenties. Finding most mystery novels of the time "mediocre in the extreme", he decided to compose his own. Edith, the author's wife, encouraged its completion, and after a protracted period finding a publisher, it was eventually released in 1927 by John Hamilton in the UK and Macrae Smith in the U.S. as *The Billiard-Room Mystery*.

The author died in 1958. In all, he wrote and published 57 mysteries, the vast majority featuring the super-sleuth Antony Bathurst.

BRIAN FLYNN

THE PADDED DOOR

With an introduction by
Steve Barge

DEAN STREET PRESS

"The hangman with his gardener's gloves
  Slips through the padded door."

INTRODUCTION

"I believe that the primary function of the mystery story is to entertain; to stimulate the imagination and even, at times, to supply humour. But it pleases the connoisseur most when it presents – and reveals – genuine mystery. To reach its full height, it has to offer an intellectual problem for the reader to consider, measure and solve."

BRIAN Flynn began his writing career with *The Billiard Room Mystery* in 1927, primarily at the prompting of his wife Edith who had grown tired of hearing him say he could write a better mystery novel than the ones he had been reading. Four more books followed under his original publisher, John Hamilton, before he moved to John Long, who would go on to publish the remaining forty-eight of his Anthony Bathurst mysteries, along with his three Sebastian Stole titles, released under the pseudonym Charles Wogan. Some of the early books were released in the US, and there were also a small number of translations of his mysteries into Swedish and German. In the article from which the above quote is taken, Brian also claims that there were French and Danish translations but to date, I have not found a single piece of evidence for their existence. Tracking down all of his books written in the original English has been challenging enough!

Reprints of Brian's books were rare. Four titles were released as paperbacks as part of John Long's Four Square Thriller range in the late 1930s, four more re-appeared during the war from Cherry Tree Books and Mellifont Press, albeit abridged by at least a third, and two others that I am aware of, *Such Bright Disguises* (1941) and *Reverse The Charges* (1943), received a paperback release as part of John Long's Pocket Edition range in the early 1950s – these were also possibly abridged, but only by about 10%. These were the exceptions, rather than the rule, however, and it was not until 2019, when Dean Street Press released his first ten titles, that his work was generally available again.

The question still persists as to why his work disappeared from the awareness of all but the most ardent collectors. As you may expect, when a title was only released once, back in the early 1930s, finding copies of the original text is not a straightforward matter – not even Brian's estate has a copy of every title. We are particularly grateful to one particular collector for providing *The Edge Of Terror*, Brian's first serial killer tale, in order for this next set of ten books to be republished without an obvious gap!

By the time Brian Flynn's eleventh novel, *The Padded Door* (1932), was published, he was producing a steady output of Anthony Bathurst mysteries, averaging about two books a year. While this may seem to be a rapid output, it is actually fairly average for a crime writer of the time. Some writers vastly exceeded this – in the same period of time that it took Brian to have ten books published, John Street, under his pseudonyms John Rhode and Miles Burton published twenty-eight!

In this period, in 1934 to be precise, an additional book was published, *Tragedy At Trinket*. It is a schoolboy mystery, set at Trinket, "one of the two finest schools in England – in the world!" combining the tale of Trinket's attempts to redeem itself in the field of schoolboy cricket alongside the apparently accidental death by drowning of one of the masters. It was published by Thomas Nelson and Sons, rather than John Long, and was the only title published under his own name not to feature Bathurst. It is unlikely, however, that this was an attempt to break away from his sleuth, given that the hero of this tale is Maurice Otho Folliott, a schoolboy who just happens to be Bathurst's nephew and is desperate to emulate his uncle! It is an odd book, with a significant proportion of the tale dedicated to the tribulations of the cricket team, but Brian does an admirable job of weaving an actual death into a genre that was generally concerned with misunderstandings and schoolboy pranks.

Not being in the top tier of writers, at least in terms of public awareness, reviews of Brian's work seem to have been rare, but when they did occur, there were mostly positive. A reviewer in the Sunday Times enthused over *The Edge Of Terror* (1932), describing it as "an enjoyable thriller in Mr. Flynn's best manner" and Torquemada in the *Observer* says that *Fear and Trembling* (1936) "gripped my interest on a sleepless night and held it to the end". Even Dorothy L. Sayers, a fairly unforgiving reviewer at times, had positive things to say in the *Sunday Times* about *The Case For The Purple Calf* (1934) ("contains some ingenuities") and *The Horn* (1934) ("good old-fashioned melodrama . . . not without movement") although she did take exception to Brian's writing style. Milward Kennedy was similarly disdainful, although Kennedy, a crime writer himself, criticising a style of writing might well be considered the pot calling the kettle black. He was impressed, however, with the originality of *Tread Softly* (1937).

It is quite possible that Brian's harshest critic, though, was himself. In *The Crime Book Magazine* he wrote about the current output of detective fiction: "I delight in the dazzling erudition that has come to grace and decorate the craft of the 'roman policier'. He then goes on to say: "At the same time, however, I feel my own comparative unworthiness for the fire and burden of the competition." Such a feeling may well be the reason why he never made significant inroads into the social side of crime-writing, such as the Detection Club or the Crime Writers' Association. Thankfully, he uses this sense of unworthiness as inspiration, concluding: "The stars, though, have always been the most desired of all goals, so I allow exultation and determination to take the place of that but temporary dismay."

Reviews, both external and internal, thankfully had no noticeable effect on Brian's writing. What is noticeable about his work is how he shifts from style to style from each book. While all the books from this period remain classic whodunits, the style shifts from courtroom drama to gothic darkness, from plotting serial killers to events that spiral out of control, with Anthony Bathurst the constant thread tying everything together.

We find some books narrated by a Watson-esque character, although a different character each time. Occasionally Bathurst himself will provide a chapter or two to explain things either that the narrator wasn't present for or just didn't understand. Bathurst doesn't always have a Watson character to tell his stories, however, so other books are in the third person – as some of Bathurst's adventures are not tied to a single location, this is often the case in these tales.

One element that does become more common throughout books eleven to twenty is the presence of Chief Detective Inspector Andrew MacMorran. While MacMorran gets a name check from as early as *The Mystery Of The Peacock's Eye* (1928), his actual appearances in the early books are few and far between, with others such as Inspector Baddeley (*The Billiard Room Mystery* (1927), *The Creeping Jenny Mystery* (1929)) providing the necessary police presence. As the series progresses, the author settled more and more on a regular showing from the police. It still isn't always the case – in some books, Bathurst is investigating undercover and hence by himself, and in a few others, various police Inspectors appear, notably the return of the aforementioned Baddeley in *The Fortescue Candle* (1936). As the series progresses from *The Padded Door* (1932), Inspector MacMorran becomes more and more of a fixture at Scotland Yard for Bathurst.

One particular trait of the Bathurst series is the continuity therein. While the series can be read out of order, there is a sense of what has gone before. While not to the extent of, say, E.R. Punshon's Bobby Owen books, or Christopher Bush's Ludovic Travers mysteries, there is a clear sense of what has gone before. Side characters from books reappear, either by name or in physical appearances – Bathurst is often engaged on a case by people he has helped previously. Bathurst's friendship with MacMorran develops over the books from a respectful partnership to the point where MacMorran can express his exasperation with Bathurst's annoying habits rather vocally. Other characters appear and develop too, for example Helen Repton, but she is, alas, a story for another day.

The other sign of continuity is Bathurst's habit of name-dropping previous cases, names that were given to them by Bathurst's "chronicler". *Fear and Trembling* mentions no less than five separate cases, with one, *The Sussex Cuckoo* (1935), getting two mentions. These may seem like little more than adverts for those titles, old-time product placement if you will – "you've handled this affair about as brainily as I handled 'The Fortescue Candle'", for example – but they do actually make sense in regard to what has gone before, given how long it took Bathurst to see the light in each particular case. Contrast this to the reference to Christie's *Murder On The Orient Express* in *Cards On The Table*, which not only gives away the ending but contradicts Poirot's actions at the dénouement.

"For my own detective, Anthony Lotherington Bathurst, I have endeavoured to place him in the true Holmes tradition. It is not for me to say whether my efforts have failed or whether I have been successful."

Brian Flynn seemed determined to keep Bathurst's background devoid of detail – I set out in the last set of introductions the minimal facts that we are provided with: primarily that he went to public school and Oxford University, can play virtually every sport under the sun and had a bad first relationship and has seemingly sworn off women since. Of course, the detective's history is something not often bothered with by crime fiction writers, but this usually occurs with older sleuths who have lived life, so to speak. *Cold Evil* (1938), the twenty-first Bathurst mystery, finally pins down Bathurst's age, and we find that in *The Billiard Room Mystery*, his first outing, he was a fresh-faced Bright Young Thing of twenty-two. So how he can survive with his own rooms, at least two servants, and no noticeable source of income remains a mystery. One can also ask at what point in his life he travelled the world, as he has, at least, been to Bangkok at some point. It is, perhaps, best not to analyse Bathurst's past too carefully . . .

"Judging from the correspondence my books have excited it seems I have managed to achieve some measure of success for my faithful readers comprise a circle in which high dignitaries of the Church rub shoulders with their brothers and sisters of the common touch."

For someone who wrote to entertain, such correspondence would have delighted Brian, and I wish he were around to see how many people enjoyed the first set of reprints of his work. His family are delighted with the reactions that people have passed on, and I hope that this set of books will delight just as much.

The Padded Door (1932)

The hangman with his gardener's gloves
Slips through the padded door,
And binds one with three leathern thongs,
That the throat may thirst no more.

The Ballad of Reading Gaol, Oscar Wilde.

ENTER Inspector MacMorran. The amateur sleuth in classic detective fiction often has a regular sparring partner – Poirot has Detective Chief Inspector Japp, Sherlock Holmes has Inspector Lestrade – and Anthony Bathurst has Chief Detective Inspector* Andrew MacMorran. However, these allies in sleuthing are often not as ever-present as the casual reader might think. Lestrade only appears in two novels and eleven of the short stories (his nearest rivals Inspectors Bradstreet and Hopkins only amass three appearances each) whereas Japp only features in seven of the Poirot novels and several short stories. Previous to this story, Bathurst had dealt with a number of different police detectives, notably Chief Inspector Baddeley, but from hereon, Inspector MacMorran becomes his almost-regular sidekick when the police are required.

It's an odd partnership as they are clearly friends, a friendship that develops across the books, more by familiarity than by any particular action, yet while Bathurst is quick to start

* While the title is now formally Detective Chief Inspector, it seems that the order of words was more flexible in the early twentieth century.

referring to MacMorran as "Andrew", I have yet to find an instance of MacMorran using any form of address other than "Mr Bathurst" or "sir" – as is common in detective fiction, MacMorran is very much there to represent the common man, whereas Bathurst, for all his charms, is very much not. Some of the interplay between the two characters are highlights of the later books – Bathurst's attempt to extol the virtues of rugby to the football-loving MacMorran in *The Swinging Death* (1949) is a delight, especially MacMorran's rant about everything wrong with the former. MacMorran is not the comic relief, however; he is a very capable police detective, just lacking the insight of Bathurst. The Padded Door (1932) is MacMorran's first full appearance (he appears briefly at the end of *The Mystery Of The Peacock's Eye* (1928) and gets a couple of other namechecks in other books) and after a few more books, becomes a regular fixture in the tales.

The Padded Door is a great example of Flynn's ability to turn the tables on the reader's expectations. The tale of a presumably innocent man on trial for a brutal murder has, I believe, a genuine surprise at the halfway point, where the plot suddenly shoots in a completely unexpected direction. Bathurst is originally brought in to find evidence for the defence, despite the only indication of innocence being the accused's character – even then, it's acknowledged that he very likely would have killed the victim, but being an honourable man, he wouldn't have hit him from behind. Not something that would stand up in a court of law . . .

We also get to see another example of Bathurst ruining a woman's life by his general unawareness of how charmingly wonderful he is, as a character falls head over heels in love with him – "What other man could she ever love after this secret idolatry?" – joining a list of women from previous adventures. For the reader curious about the unnamed woman – "the story of whom may one day be told" – previously alluded to in *The Orange Axe* (1931), you do not have long to wait to find out more, as she will make an appearance in *The Edge of Terror* (1932), the very next book.

There is so much more I could say about *The Padded Door*, from the nature of Bathurst's chronicler to a surprising fact, to me at least, about Stilton cheese in the 1930s, but I would hate to spoil the tale for you. *The Padded Door* has, we believe, never been reprinted since its initial appearance over eighty years ago and it is a real pleasure to be able to bring it back onto your bookshelves.

Steve Barge

CHAPTER I
THE MURDER AT PERRY HAMMER

THE true facts of the mystery surrounding the Perry Hammer murder and its astonishing sequel as it affected Mr. Justice Heriot, may now be told to the world. I saw Bathurst the other day und he withdrew the embargo that he had previously placed upon the telling. The death last week of one of the most prominent figures in the drama has cleared the air considerably, and little, if any, harm can now be done by giving publicity to the full details.

Of all the cases that Anthony Bathurst, in the course of his eventful career, had been called upon to handle, this may be said to have been the one most influenced by considerations of human psychology. Also, he was forced by circumstances to work in the dark a great deal. Called to the scent when it was comparatively cold, Fate for a very long time resolutely averted her face from him. In contradistinction to almost all of his previous investigations, there was, in this case, little of pulsating thrill. There was, however, on the other hand, an appreciable amount of dour and dogged perseverance. Upon several occasions during his following up of details, the venue would be suddenly changed, and this, too, with scarcely the hint of a warning. The ways to the light were twisted and labyrinthine. Little was there that was clean-cut. There were two trails to be followed—neither of which could be neglected for any length of time, without the running of a serious risk. Moreover, it was necessary that they should be followed more or less simultaneously, which fact added difficulty to doubt and flung many weapons against that sure shield of his—the science of deduction. Over and above all this, cul-de-sac followed cul-de-sac. Their ugly heads were many. And Anthony Bathurst was compelled to explore every one of them. In spite of all the dangers and difficulties, however, he ultimately succeeded in handing over to Justice a brutal and callous murderer. He succeeded by reason of his qualities of persistence and pertinacity, with the result that the history of the Perry Hammer crime may now be added to the memoirs of this remarkable man.

Leonard Pearson was murdered in his house at Perry Hammer on the evening of Wednesday, April the 22nd. He had been treacherously struck down from behind by a blow or blows from a heavy weapon of some kind and his blood and brains had mingled upon the surface of the table at which he sat. His head had fallen forward on to his left arm. That is how he was found by a servant, Amy Talbot, when she entered his room early on the following morning to carry out the usual tidying up and dusting operations.

Pearson, it must be mentioned, was a man of somewhat unwholesome and unsavoury reputation. His offices in town were ostensibly the centre of money-lending transactions. There, both large and small sums changed hands. But rumour had it that the man who owned these offices was by no means disinclined to ventures that sailed exceedingly close to the wind and lay perilously near to blackmail. Certainly, the headquarters of Leonard Pearson were the market where strange and dissimilar wares passed from one person to another. Many a man and woman, prominent members of society, spent sleepless nights when they knew what Pearson knew of them, and what the rest of the world might know, from documentary evidence that he held in his evil, clutching hands. There were four processes. Pearson bought, assimilated, threatened, and waxed fat. His house at Perry Hammer, which is a village a few miles from Wantage, and in the heart of the Berkshire downs, was a country mansion and staffed by a battalion of the most efficient servants. He had never married, and on the 22nd of April, during the second week following the octave of Easter, he died, as has been described. Few there were that sighed at his passing. Detective-Sergeant Waterhouse, hot-foot on Amy Talbot's discovery, entered Pearson's study on the morning of the 23rd of April, in the company of Dr. Clive, the Divisional Surgeon, and wasted no time in the marking down of what he saw and in the assembling of his facts.

"You needn't stay in this room for the time being, Murray," he jerked over his shoulder to the butler. . . . "If I want you, I'll send for you. So be right handy. First of all, tell Talbot I want her. That's the girl's name, isn't it? The girl who found your master dead, I mean?"

Murray nodded, and the maid materializing a few moments after his departure, Waterhouse proceeded at once to question her.

"You're Amy Talbot, aren't you? Yes? Good, What time was it you found your master dead?"

Amy Talbot, white-faced, retained her nerve and some, at least, of her composure.

"When I came in first thing to dust the room. About half-past six this morning, sir."

"What did you do then?"

"Screamed first, sir. I'm sorry, but I just couldn't help it. Then I ran for Mr. Murray—that's the butler."

Waterhouse was curt. "I'm aware of that. You didn't touch anything, by any chance? Or move anything? Curious-like, eh?"

Talbot shook her head emphatically. Dr. Clive looked up from his examination to speak to Waterhouse.

"Been dead about ten hours, I should say, Waterhouse. That's as near as I can get it. Fracture of the skull. There's considerable tearing of the brain. Look here at this nasty, lacerated wound at the back of the head. Whoever hit him, hit him with terrific force."

Waterhouse faced the now trembling Talbot. "Any visitors here last night? Any callers?"

"I don't know, sir. But I shouldn't know that, you see. I was in the servants' quarters all the evening, sir."

Waterhouse summarily cut her. "Who would know, then, if you don't?"

"Either Mr. Murray, sir, the butler, or one of the other maids. Knowles is the maid who would have—"

Waterhouse pressed the bell. Somewhat to his surprise, Murray answered it himself. It was evident that he had obeyed his instructions literally, and remained very handy.

"You've a maid on the staff here named Knowles. Send her in here, will you?"

When Knowles arrived, she proved to be the antithesis of the other girl, Talbot. Talbot was fair, tall, and heavy. Knowles was a little dark thing, whose quick black eyes, full of intelligence and alertness, darted here, there, and everywhere. Waterhouse was a firm believer in rapid and sustained attack.

"Oh, Knowles, that's your name, I believe, your master, Mr. Pearson, is dead. We're very much afraid that he's been murdered." The girl went white, as her predecessor had, and swayed ominously. "You needn't look over there," continued Waterhouse, more mercifully, "and there's no need to get scared. All the worrying in the world won't bring him back. All I want you for, is to answer a question or two. Understand?"

Knowles gripped the back of a chair to steady herself, and nodded. "I think so, sir. What is it you want to ask me?"

"I'm asking you because I'm told you're the right person to ask. Can you tell me if your master had any callers here last evening?"

"Yes, sir. He did."

"Ah! That's interesting. I thought so. Do you know who they were, by any chance?"

Knowles shook her head. "No, sir, I don't."

Waterhouse frowned. "Come, now. Did they call by appointment?"

"I don't know that, either, sir. But one was a young lady who arrived about a quarter-past eight; the other was, I think, a gentleman, who came shortly after nine o'clock. I say that because I heard a man's voice in conversation with my master. Beyond that, sir, I can't tell you anything."

"They came separately, then?"

"Yes, sir. That is to say, the lady came in the first place by herself. As regards the gentleman—"

"Had the lady gone when the gentleman arrived?"

"Yes, sir. I think, if it would help you, the butler, Mr. Murray, would be able to tell you the exact time it was when the lady left."

"What makes you think that, eh?"

Knowles hesitated for a second, and stole a glance at her colleague. Waterhouse permitted himself to encourage her. "Yes . . . what is it?"

"I think I'm right in saying, sir, that Mr. Pearson sent for him just before the lady took her departure. But you could ask him, sir, and then you would be able to make sure."

Waterhouse pursed his lips.

"I take it, Knowles, from what you said to me just now, that you don't know either this lady or the gentleman who followed her, by name, eh?"

"No, sir."

"Had you ever seen either of them before?"

"The lady was a stranger. I never saw the gentleman."

"Sure?"

"Certain, sir. Positive."

Waterhouse caught the eye of Dr. Clive, and turned again to the maid whom he had just questioned. "All right, Knowles, you and Talbot can go now. Tell your Mr. Murray that I want to speak to him at once."

The butler was soon back. He listened to the detective's remarks with calm imperturbability. "What Knowles has told you is quite true," he assented. "The lady that she mentioned had an interview with my master, and left about ten minutes to nine. I think that I have seen her here before. I should imagine that the gentleman came about a quarter of an hour after her departure. But I didn't see him come in. Also, I did not see him go."

Waterhouse seized on the admission with avidity. "What? What do you mean?"

Murray remained impassive and unruffled. "My master's instructions are—were—habitually, these. The whole house is bolted and locked up, as you might say, under my supervision, at eleven-thirty, but if my master is engaged in here at that time, on work of any kind, I am never allowed to disturb him. I have specific instructions to that effect. When the time comes that he thinks fit, he closes the room himself and goes up to bed." Murray paused, and then seemed to realize the position. "Or rather, that's what he did."

"Supposing he has a guest, a visitor?"

Murray shrugged his shoulders. "I have never known him keep a visitor in here after the hour that I have mentioned."

"Do you always, then, see a guest off the premises?"

"Not always. Usually—yes. But sometimes my master would conduct a guest to the front door himself. Just as he must have let this gentleman both in and out, when he came and went."

"Did you hear anything of this gentleman's interview with your master?"

"Yes, sir."

"What did you hear?"

"I passed the door of the room about twenty minutes past nine, and I heard a man's voice raised in anger. I may remark that there is not the slightest doubt of that. He was uttering what I would describe as a *threat*." The substantive was heavily stressed.

Waterhouse became impatient.

"Why, in the name of all that's wonderful, didn't you let on about this before?"

"As far as I am aware, I was not asked. You seemed to attach more importance to the maids' information than to mine. I make it a rule never to tell the police anything until I am directly questioned. That was also a rule of Sir Randall Bowers, my late master. I should have said—er—my previous master. It saves a good deal of time and a great deal of bother. In fact, that has been my experience throughout my career. I came to Mr. Pearson from Sir Randall Bowers. Prior to that, I was with a judge of the High Court," Murray sighed. "Sir Randall was a gentleman."

Waterhouse struggled successfully with his emotions. He choked back the exclamation that was almost on his lips. When he spoke, his voice had become very quiet.

"Tell me the nature of the threat that you say you heard uttered."

Murray fingered his chin reflectively. "The words were these, to the best of my memory. And my memory is distinctly above what I may term the average standard. 'Pearson, you blasted swine, if you aren't careful what you say, I'll smash you as you sit there. The world will be a thundering sight better place to live in, when you're in hell.'"

"What did your master say?"

"I heard no more," replied Murray, majestically. "It is not my practice to go eavesdropping."

"What did you do?"

"I retired to my own room and ruminated on my decline in the social scale. I think that I mentioned that I was previously with Sir Randall Bowers, and before that with—"

"You never heard the name of the man who came?"

"No, sir. Nor the lady's, either."

Waterhouse tossed his head and glanced round the room before turning again to the butler. "Did this man carry a stick, I wonder?"

There was a far-away look in Murray's eyes as he contributed his opinion. "Very possibly. The same idea has occurred to me. Some little time ago, in fact. A strong man, wielding a heavy stick with a knob on it, would have been capable of delivering a tremendous blow." He looked at Dr. Clive almost as though in an invitation for acquiescence. Instead of this being forthcoming, however, Clive pointed to the two doors that led out to the garden.

"Here you are, Waterhouse," he declared with dry emphasis. "Don't neglect the obvious. Here's where your man got out."

The detective walked across to them and pulled back the heavy portière that hung in front. As he did so, he whistled softly. "Open, by Jove! Been open all night, I'll bet a fortune." He swung round to Murray almost fiercely. "These doors haven't been tampered with? Since Talbot came into the room first thing this morning, I mean?"

"No, Mr. Waterhouse. Certainly not. As soon as Talbot gave the alarm, I 'phoned down for you and Dr. Clive. As far as I know, the room is exactly as it must have been when my master was murdered. Certainly, nothing whatever has been touched since I myself was called to it. You can absolutely rely on what I say. I know my duty even in circumstances of this nature."

Waterhouse made his way to the table. Upon it, to the right of the dead man, was a small mirror of the kind that stands like a photograph-frame. Waterhouse looked at it and then picked up an ash-tray that was on the table, close to the dead man's left arm. It held four cigarette stubs. Waterhouse picked them up, one by one, and examined them. Two were of one brand and two of another.

"Look here, doctor," he said to Clive. "There have been four cigarettes here. Two Turkish—Mourakis. Two ordinary Virginian. The Turkish must have been put down because the smoker had let them go out, or else deliberately put them out. Otherwise, they would have burned to ash. Been put out, I fancy. The others have been smoked right down to the bitter end. Now I wonder if I can discover which—" His eyes made a quick survey of the room and were instantly rewarded. On the mantelpiece was a silver casket, obviously used to hold cigarettes. Three quick strides across the room put Waterhouse in possession of it. He opened it. What he saw inside it, pleased him. He advertised his pleasure.

"There you are, doctor! There's first-hand evidence for you. Pearson smoked Virginian cigarettes. The Mourakis belonged to one of his evening visitors. It's a thousand to one on it." Taking a cigarette from the silver box, he compared it with one of the smaller stubs and held the two out on the palm of his hand for Clive's inspection. "Absolutely identical, doctor! Same paper. Same tobacco. No doubt about that, is there?"

Dr. Clive took them and made a similar comparison. "I think you're right, Waterhouse. So you're trying to prove to me that one of Pearson's visitors smoked Turkish, eh?"

Waterhouse smiled. "Yes. *One* of them, doctor. And the man at that. All the evidence points that way."

Murray took a step forward. "I am in a position to confirm some of what Mr. Waterhouse is putting forward. If I may be allowed to do so, of course. My master never smoked Turkish cigarettes. I've heard him say many times that he couldn't stand the smell of them. I mean the—er—aroma. Whoever smoked those two Turkish cigarettes there, wasn't Mr. Pearson. I can verify that. That's as sure as night follows day."

Waterhouse ran his eye over the butler. "Where did Pearson keep his correspondence? Any idea?"

Murray, the ever-ready, pointed to the right of the table. "In that top right-hand drawer. But first of all, let me explain. It is quite likely that in this matter I may be of some real assistance. More than I have been up to the moment. Most of Mr. Pearson's correspondence was, no doubt, sent to his London offices. Very little, I should say, would be addressed here. Stray, isolated cases, perhaps, but no more. But everything that went to the office, and everything that came here that was important, and, as you would say, affected my master personally, was filed and eventually found its way into the drawer that I have indicated. My master always kept the key of that particular drawer on his person. Usually in the top right-hand pocket of his vest—er—waistcoat. It might even be there now. Would you mind—?"

Waterhouse looked at Murray, considered for a moment, and then felt in the pocket of the dead man's waistcoat that Murray had named.

"Here's a key here, certainly," he declared. He held it up for approval. Murray inclined his head gravely. Waterhouse tried the lock of the drawer. The key fitted. He turned it in the lock and pulled the drawer open. It contained, as the butler had foreshadowed, several files of correspondence. Waterhouse selected the most recent. He turned over a dozen or so letters. Little came his way that he regarded of any special significance or importance. They were, without exception, letters that concerned the lending and borrowing of money. Not one of them suggested, for instance, that the writer had a grievance against Pearson. Not one of them contained anything in the nature of a grumble, criticism, or a threat. And none contained the slightest reference to the evening of Wednesday, the 22nd of April. He tried the remaining files, with no better result. Waterhouse replaced them reluctantly.

"Murray," he said, "I asked Knowles a question which she couldn't answer. Perhaps I may have more success with it with you. Have you any idea whether this man who called on your master last evening did so by definite appointment?"

Once again Murray proved admirably adequate.

"As it happens, I think I can answer your question. My master kept an appointment diary. In fact, I constantly noted appointments in it for him. Mr. Pearson has often asked me to do so. Confidential appointments, as you might say. There was nothing in it for the evening of yesterday. I saw the diary as late as half-past four in the afternoon and the space against the date of the 22nd April was entirely blank."

Waterhouse furrowed his brow. Noticing his indecision, Murray proceeded to drive his point home.

"Look for yourself. You will find the diary that I mention, Mr. Waterhouse, in the top left-hand drawer. Then you will have the evidence of which I speak, absolutely first-hand."

Waterhouse opened the drawer in question almost mechanically. His mind was considering a point of view that had only just occurred to him. The diary lay close to his hand. He took it out, somewhat unintelligently, but immediately his eyes glanced down to it and took in what they saw written there, all the fine flower of his intelligence returned and bloomed amazingly.

"Is this your master's handwriting?" he demanded of the butler. Murray, surprised for once from his imperturbability, looked keenly at what Waterhouse held out to him.

"Yes," he exclaimed.

"What luck," cried Waterhouse. "What stupendous luck. Pearson made this entry after you saw the diary at half-past four in the afternoon. Come here, Doctor Clive, please." His voice rang with excitement.

On the diary, against the space for the twenty-second of April, were scrawled a few words in pencil. "Phone 4.40.—9 p.m., Captain Hilary Frant."

Waterhouse looked at the doctor and repeated the name aloud. Almost hungrily. "Captain Hilary Frant."

CHAPTER II
CAPTAIN HILARY FRANT

CAPTAIN Hilary Frant, with stick in hand and blazing hatred in his eyes, looked at the figure of Pearson and decided to make his exit from the house at Perry Hammer in the most convenient manner—by the french-windows that gave immediate and easy access to the garden of Pearson's house. As far as he knew, he had entered it unobserved. That is to say, by any of Pearson's servants, and he hoped to make his exit in an equally unobtrusive manner. He pushed open the two doors gently and quietly, and stepped out noiselessly on to the beautifully-kept grass lawn that spread its green carpet in front of him. It was a dark night. The stars in their courses were fighting for him. What moon there had been, during the earlier hours, was now obscured by a heavy bank of clouds, and Hilary Frant, for once in his life at least, heartily welcomed the silent darkness.

Keeping on the grass for as long as he was able, he carefully made his way down the garden until he reached the wall that bounded it. He gave this wall a quick glance, threw his stick over impetuously, and, within a second, had commenced to scale the barrier. He was an active, athletic man who had represented Sandhurst with distinction on more than one field of sport. On this occasion, moreover, there was an impetus that moved him, which was far in excess of the ordinary. Within the space of three-quarters of a minute he had reached the eminence of the wall and had dropped lightly to his feet on the other side. Pulling his hat hard on to his forehead, he ran swiftly round to the front of the house, where, within the distance of a hundred yards or so, and with its lights out, his car was waiting for him. Another five minutes saw him well clear of Leonard Pearson's house at Perry Hammer and of all the unpleasant memories it held for him. Once away, he drove hard and fast. Two hours and a half passed. A few minutes over that time, after only one deliberate stoppage on the journey, Frant halted his car before a house in

Lancaster Gate. The girl who opened almost immediately to his ring, was agitated and apprehensive.

"Is that you, Hilary?" she asked, as she peered into the comparative darkness.

"Yes. It's me all right, Pamela," he answered, a trifle jerkily. "And what's more, everything's all right, too. You'll sleep to-night, my cherub, for the first time for weeks."

"Did you get them?" she questioned, breathlessly.

"I did. I went to get them. Wild horses of the old and original mustang breed wouldn't have stopped me. Let alone a fellow of the Pearson kidney." There was a hard, forced note in his voice, and the girl to whom he spoke, scanned his face with eager anxiety.

"What do you mean, Hilary?" she demanded nervously. "What do you—?"

Hilary Frant pushed a packet into his sister's hands and turned impulsively away.

"No questions—no pack-drill. Take these, Pamela, and thank God for them. Let the whole thing rest there. It leaves too nasty a taste in the mouth to be a subject for conversation. I'll run the car round, shove it in the garage and come back. I shan't be half a jiffy. Is the guv'nor in?"

Pamela nodded. "He's in bed. Hasn't been out all the evening. Had dinner and went to bed early. Lady Stapleford's op. is at a quarter to twelve to-morrow morning. So we mustn't disturb him on any account. Take the car round, as you said you would, and I'll wait for you."

Captain Frant ran quickly to the car and his sister closed the door very softly behind him. Motionless almost, she pressed the precious packet to her breast and awaited the reappearance of her brother. But had anyone been intimate enough, he would have seen something closely akin to thankfulness in her eyes. She was not destined to wait there over-long. A matter of a few minutes and she heard her brother's quick step on the pavement outside. She opened the door again to admit him. His face was paler even, she thought, than it had been before. He was worried, she felt sure.

"What *is* it, Hilary?" she asked.

"I'm annoyed about my stick—you know the one I mean. I told you why I was taking it when I went down there. Now I've been and lost the damned thing somewhere."

"How?" she asked, wonderingly. "Where? I don't see how you could—"

"I'd have sworn it was inside the car when I came in just now. When I got to the garage and opened the door of the car to take it out, it had vanished. Do you think somebody could have lifted it during the few minutes I was in here?"

"They might have done, I suppose, come to that," she returned consideringly. "But are you certain that it was in the car?"

"Pretty well certain, Pamela. When I left Pearson's, I'm sure that I remember chucking it—er—into the car. So it must have been there. Stands to reason, doesn't it?"

"Somebody must have taken it, then. Looked through the window, I expect, and saw it there. You know what people are, nowadays. What a shame."

"Ah, well, it can't be helped. It's no use crying over spilt milk. If it's gone, it's gone, and that's the end of it. All the same, I don't understand how it happened, and it's rather worrying."

"Tell me, Hilary," she said. "I don't want to keep pestering you, but I must know. What happened at Perry Hammer?"

His fair, boyish face, with its clipped toothbrush moustache and light blue eyes, took on a strength and purpose that was rarely seen there, but which she, as his sister, knew of old and recognized. Then he laughed; the laugh, however, held more than a trace of nervousness.

"I told the hound a varied selection of home-truths illuminated by lurid adjectives. But his hide is so thick that I question very much if any of them reached its spiritual destination. All the same, Pamela, he'll never put his filthy paws on anything to do with you again. You can lay a pony to a peanut on that."

Her eyes searched his face rather relentlessly, as though endeavouring to drag the truth from him, at all costs. He evaded her direct glance and turned away.

"I'm going to bed, Pamela. I'm dog-tired, old girl. I don't suppose you want me to tell you that. I'll just have a spot of Scotch and then I'll clear off up. I drove back from Perry Hammer hell for leather. Only stopped once. Thinking of your peace of mind, I suppose. Night-night, my dear."

His sister went across to him and put her hands on his two shoulders.

"Good night, Hilary, darling." Pulling his face down to the level of hers she kissed him twice, eagerly. "I can never thank you enough, dear, dear Hilary, for what you have done for me tonight. And though it may sound a desperately silly and paradoxical thing for me to say, I am sure Dick would thank you just as much as I."

He kissed her and then held her away from him at arm's length. For a little while he watched her face. He spoke: "That reminds me—talking about Dick, Pamela, are you absolutely positive that Lanchester knows nothing at all?"

"Why?" she returned doubtfully. "How can he? Whatever makes you—?"

"Never mind. Stick to the main road and answer my question. Are you sure that he doesn't?"

"As far as one ever can be sure of matters of that kind—yes. Now answer *my* question. I've answered yours. Why do you ask me that about Dick?"

He shrugged his shoulders as he drew away from her. "Don't know quite. Perhaps I am inclined to imagine things sometimes. I've thought one or two of his remarks lately, a trifle cryptic, that's all. Still, let it sweat. Night-night, Pamela. See you in the morning."

She watched him go up to bed, with a wistfully affectionate expression on her face, and within a minute, switched off the electric light and turned to follow him.

Sir Robert Frant's breakfast-table on the morning following this last-recorded conversation lacked something of its wonted light-heartedness and badinage. Hilary Frant looked tired and worn. His adventure of the previous evening at Perry Hammer had, temporarily at least, left its mark on him. His father, silent as always, was quick to notice it and rallied his only son, a few moments after the morning meal commenced. Almost coincidentally with Detective-Sergeant Waterhouse showing Dr. Clive the all-important entry on Pearson's appointment diary, miles away at Perry Hammer, Sir Robert Frant turned to Hilary with a smile playing round the corners of his mouth.

"Late again last night, Hilary?"

"A little, sir. Nothing to speak of. If you think so, I'll apologize now. Did I disturb you?"

Sir Robert winked at his daughter. "If I'm disturbed, my boy, believe me, it's not on my own account. It's on yours. There are two ends of the candle, you know, and combustion should only be at work at one of them. You can't cheat Nature, my boy. The oysters are eaten, Hilary, and no doubt thoroughly enjoyed, but they are also put down on the bill. The date of the bill's presentation varies, that is all. I commend the consideration of that fact to your careful notice."

Hilary Frant smiled at his famous father. "'Pon my soul, I might be one of your distinguished patients, Guv'nor. You'll be asking me for a hundred guineas next." His smile became a laugh. "I'll take you on your own terms, sir, too. You've missed a point. Besides the date of the bill's presentation, there's always another point that comes up for consideration. In the words of Mr. Samuel Travers Carter to Lord and Lady Mickleham (I think you were quoting him, weren't you?), it does not necessarily say on *whose* bill. I may eat the oysters, for example, and Pamela here may be called upon to foot the bill. Or even you yourself. Agreed, sir?"

The eminent specialist for malignant diseases of the throat acknowledged the adroitness of the thrust with a bow of mock seriousness. It was one of his greatest assets that his charm of manner had never been known to desert him. Neither that, nor his genial tolerance. His face was lean, but the features were strong. His nose was prominent, his chin delicate and his mouth large and humorous. This was the feature, perhaps, in which he most resembled his even more famous brother, Maddison Frant, the actor-manager. Sir Robert's eyes were humorous, too, grey and rather deep-set. His hair was grey. It was the particular shade of the grey of distinction. The result of all this, added to his height, was, that he looked scholarly-earnest, but yet, at the same time, humorously-human and pleasantly-strong, an impression which was all the more confirmed when one heard his voice. It held a tang of authoritative asperity that seldom offended and nearly always pleased.

"*Touché*, Hilary," he admitted cordially. "I, of all people, should realize the truth of what you say. For all I know or anybody else, come to that, the sins of the fathers and of the grandfathers are paid for in the bills that are paid to me by sons and grandsons." He turned to his daughter.

"Lanchester coming in this morning, Pamela?" It was obvious from the tone in which he addressed his daughter that Sir Robert intended to change the subject. Whenever he thus signified his intention, his son and daughter, loyal subjects always, took up the cross of their obedience and philosophically accepted the altered situation.

"I think so, Daddy. At any rate, I'm expecting him. If he changes his mind he'll ring me up, he said. Otherwise, I'm doing some shopping, and after that we're lunching at Claridge's."

Sir Robert nodded and put down his cup. "Good. It gives promise of being a delightful spring morning. April at an exercise of virtue, for once in a way. The virtue that Browning must have known so well. You know where I'm due, of course?"

"Yes; 11.45, isn't it? Is she pretty bad, Daddy?"

The easy smile left her father's face and was replaced by a look of gravity. He shook his head ominously. "Left it too late, I'm very much afraid. And I fancy Stapleford thinks the same way himself. That's my greatest handicap. People put things off, and go on putting them off; then when they send for me—well—" A shrug of the shoulders seemed to complete his sentence for him. He rose from the table. "Well, cheero, you two. Tell Hall not to worry about luncheon for me. Take it that I shan't be back in time. No doubt Stapleford will ask me to lunch there and I should be eternally false to my Highland ancestry if I refused him. Also—as I loathe the slightest suggestion of the curmudgeon—I won't run the risk of the accusation." Before he could reach the door of the breakfast-room, the telephone-bell rang.

"There you are, my dear Pamela," he announced with boyish abandon, "there's your call from Lanchester, I expect. Don't keep him waiting—he's an impatient young man, as I expect you've noticed. One can't very well censure him, however."

Pamela smiled and unhooked the receiver, to discover immediately that her father's playful vaticination was wrong. She frowned involuntarily as she answered the voice that spoke at the other end. "Yes. This is Sir Robert Frant's. Yes. No—it's Miss Frant speaking. Who? Captain Frant? Captain Frant is here. Yes. Who is it? Very well, then. If you'll hang on, I'll ask Captain Frant to speak to you now. Very good. Yes. I understand. Chief-Inspector MacMorran."

CHAPTER III
CIRCUMSTANTIAL EVIDENCE

CHIEF-Inspector MacMorran was actually at work on the case of the Chigwell Hill "snide" shop on the morning of Thursday, April the 23rd. Although he knew he had a clean-cut issue and that the arrest of Lew Friedlander was a mere matter of time, there were many of the more intricate details that still required working out from headquarters. He had just determined on a raiding force of five men, with himself at the head thereof, when his 'phone rang insistently at his elbow. MacMorran scratched his rather prominent nose vindictively, almost as though to spite his face. He cursed softly but scientifically.

Sir Austin Kemble's voice at the other end of the line had the effect of altering his external presentation but nevertheless left unchanged his point of view. He smothered his curse soon after birth, and answered the Commissioner in, what for him, were mellifluous tones. "Very good, sir. I'll be along to you in a couple of minutes, sir." Replacing the receiver with a look of seraphic and martyred resignation, he proceeded along the corridor to report himself to Sir Austin without a moment's delay. The Commissioner gestured him to a chair.

"Sit down, MacMorran," said Sir Austin, upon his subordinate's entrance. "I'm sorry to trouble you and all that, because I know you're up to your eyes in it. Hand that Chigwell affair over to Henson at once. Something's come through to me that's bigger than that, and I want you to take it over."

MacMorran breathed a prayer of internal gratitude and endeavoured to look interested. Sir Austin proceeded:

"There's a call come through from Perry Hammer—that's in Berkshire, if you don't happen to know. Pearson—the Leonard Pearson, of Fenchurch Street—you know him, no doubt, MacMorran, has a place down there, near the Berkshire Downs. Well, he's been murdered."

"Murdered," echoed MacMorran.

"Yes. Murdered. No doubt about it whatever. Last night, some time. Head battered in. Found at a table in his own room. A local man's on the case, naturally, and from what I can gather from what he said to me on the 'phone, he appears to be well above the average and on top of the case generally. Waterhouse, by name. Moreover, he's had the exceptional sense to call in the Yard. Well, to cut a long story short, MacMorran, Pearson's reputation is by no means angelic, as you know. Very much the other way, in fact, and this fellow, Waterhouse, has got something on a Captain Frant, son of Sir Robert Frant, the distinguished medical chap in Lancaster Gate. Here are the facts, as Waterhouse has them, and as I've jotted them down. I want you to go along and see this Captain Frant at once. See what he has to say. Go slow, of course. But check him up, with what Waterhouse tells you here, and see if you can make anything of it."

Sir Austin pushed over the notes that he had made of Waterhouse's telephone conversation, and Chief-Inspector MacMorran picked them up, glanced them over and then pocketed them. Once free of the Commissioner's subduing presence, he went through them again, formed his own conclusions as to Waterhouse's line of investigation and repaired hopefully to the telephone directory. Sir Robert Frant's designation and description had been of such a character that they had halted him a little from the exploitation of a usual routine and what he saw in the directory only served to impress him even more. Leaning forward on his own desk he caressed his chin slowly and thoughtfully, before he decided to unhook the receiver. Somewhat to his relief, it was Pamela Frant who answered him. Captain Frant himself, however, came to the 'phone a minute or two later. Was it MacMorran's imagination or did the speaker's voice waver a little as it spoke the opening words of the first sentence? The Inspector said what he had to say. He listened again for the reply.

"Thank you, Captain Frant," returned MacMorran eventually. "That's very good of you. I'm greatly obliged. I'll step right over at once and have that word that I want with you. Very many thanks indeed."

Captain Frant was as good as his word, and met MacMorran in the big room downstairs. His sister, white-faced and tight-lipped, was with him. The C.I.D. man looked askance at the lady, but Frant interpreted the glance and attempted to explain matters.

"That's all right, Inspector MacMorran," he declared rather icily. "This is my sister, Miss Frant, who answered you on the 'phone in the first instance. You can say what you like in front of her. In fact, I'll prefer that she were here. After all, the interview can't be very important. That is, from my standpoint. I won't presume to judge yours." He smiled at MacMorran to give additional point to his words. "What a consoling thing a clear conscience is," he supplemented.

MacMorran, as befitted his descent, was habitually cautious.

"That's as maybe, sir. Perhaps I've never suffered from one. But that's neither here nor there. To get to my business straight away. You know, of course, that you needn't answer my questions unless you choose to. But you promised me I could drop over and see you, so here goes. Do you know a man named Pearson—Leonard Pearson?"

MacMorran flicked back a page of his note-book preparatory to noting Frant's answer. As he did so, he heard Pamela Frant's quicker breathing, and drew pertinent conclusions therefrom. Careful of procedure, as always, he remembered the judges' rules in regard to the use of evidence. "You don't mind me taking notes down," he said.

Captain Frant's reply, when it came, was guarded. "I suppose not. But just a minute, Inspector. I don't quite know what you're getting at. First of all let me see where I stand. I know what you police Johnnies are. Do you mean 'know' him, or 'know of' him?"

"Either or both," responded the laconic MacMorran. "Please yourself."

"I see. I know—of him, then, but don't know him."

"I see. 'Know's' a bit elastic, sir, I agree. Ever met him?"

"I may have done. Never to my certain knowledge, though."

"That means to say never by appointment, doesn't it, sir?" MacMorran cast his net and knew now, without the shadow of a doubt, that Pamela Frant's mental disturbance was increasing.

"Of course," returned Hilary. "But why do you ask me all these things, Inspector? Out with it, man. I hate subterfuge. What's the point behind all this?"

MacMorran came to a quick decision. He chose his words with care.

"Leonard Pearson was murdered some time last evening at his own house at Perry Hammer in Berkshire."

He heard the girl's quick gasp, but the look of incredulity on the man's face seemed real and sincere.

"But what on earth has that got to do with me, Inspector? I tell you, I don't know the man."

MacMorran eyed him most directly. "That's very strange, then. Your name, Captain Frant—note carefully what I say—was found scribbled on Pearson's appointment diary for an appointment at a time during last evening."

Frant paled. The statement had shaken him badly. Of that there was no question.

"That's most extraordinary, Inspector. But it's quite absurd and ridiculous, and, after all, if I may say so to you, it proves absolutely nothing. Nothing whatever. The man may have seen my name somewhere—anybody could have written it there—there may be any one of a hundred or so of the most simple explanations—"

"Of course, Captain Frant," assented MacMorran, with unwonted cheerfulness, "you are absolutely right; you have only to inform the authorities where you were yesterday—and yesterday evening—and everything will be cleared up, with regard to that. But please yourself, of course. You've no objection, have you, to telling me of your movements?"

Hilary Frant hesitated. He had been dreading the question for a few moments now and the realization had come home to him that he would have little time in which to answer it. If he refused to answer there and then, as he had every right to do, he feared greatly that it would strengthen the suspicion that had obviously taken possession of MacMorran's mind. From whichever angle he looked at it, the whole situation was double-edged, He lost his head and decided to fall back on a story foundationed on false generalities. Within the space of a moment he had crossed the Rubicon.

"I've no objection, whatever, Inspector, to doing what you suggest. Why should I have? I fancy that I can account for the whole of my movements yesterday with very little difficulty indeed. I'll begin at the beginning. With my sister here, and my sister's fiancé, a Mr. Richard Lanchester, I attended the Epsom race-meeting. Lanchester—who is the eldest son of the Lanchester of tobacco fame—had a horse running in the big race, the City and Suburban, and very naturally we were all anxious to see how it shaped. We left the course before the programme finished— the last two races on the card had no particular interest about them for any one of us—and we motored straight back to town. I drove the others in my car." He paused. Pamela watched him.

"Yes," said MacMorran, encouragingly, "and the time then, would be about—?"

"About a quarter past six, I should think, Inspector."

"Thank you, sir. And then—?"

Captain Frant proceeded with commendable smoothness, but the pace at which he spoke was a trifle slower than before. The difference was infinitesimal, but the difference was there and MacMorran's discerning ear noticed it. He remembered that the only two materials of speech are words and ideas and that true fluency consists of having a ready supply of the former with which to clothe the steady output of the latter for their presentation to the world. Captain Frant was undoubtedly feeling his way. Just a little. Hardly perceptible, perhaps, but feeling it, nevertheless.

"Well—we dined here, Pamela and I, with my father, Sir Robert Frant, after dropping Lanchester at his place, and then my sister tootled off to get ready for a dance to which she was going with her fiancé. I was at a loose end, more or less. Didn't feel like a dancing crush. So at the last moment I decided to go to a show."

"Good!" remarked MacMorran. "That's pretty definite, at any rate, and clears the air considerably. Where did you go, sir?"

"Oh—er—to the Whitehall. *Good Losers*. I'm rather keen on Hackett's stuff."

"Stalls?" MacMorran poised his pencil over his note-book.

Frant saw his danger and drew back. "Er—no. I hadn't booked—you see. I didn't even trouble to 'phone the box-office. I just took pot-luck. I very often do, as a matter of fact. Crawled in just before the curtain—got a seat in the circle."

"You'll appreciate my point, Captain Frant, I feel sure; but I am bound to verify all this as far as possible. For your sake, if for nobody else's. Can you remember what row you sat in?"

"Oh—er—the last row of all. Right at the back. I was probably lucky to get there even. It's doing pretty good business, you know."

"H'm," observed MacMorran, "and you returned home at—when shall we say?"

"About half-past eleven, Inspector. Anything more you want to know?"

Before MacMorran could answer, Pamela Frant intervened impulsively. "There's this one point, Inspector. Something about which I wouldn't wish there to be any misunderstanding. I can confirm my brother's story in almost every detail, but there's just this fact. I don't want you to labour under any misapprehension. Actually, I didn't attend the dance that he just mentioned. My fiancé, Mr. Lanchester, 'phoned through during the evening, that he wasn't feeling up to the mark, and would rather that we didn't go after all. Naturally, in the circumstances I fell in with his arrangements and spent the evening quite quietly here. Had I known of Mr. Lanchester's indisposition, say half-an-hour earlier, I should have gone to the theatre with my brother."

MacMorran expressed his understanding of the situation with a benevolent nod.

"Thank you, Miss Frant. And you, too, Captain Frant. I think that I understand the position pretty well. Let me see now. I don't think that there's anything more for me to ask you. If I want to have a further word with you I'll let you know."

The C.I.D. Inspector rose on the point of departure. He then delivered himself of what seemed to be an afterthought.

"I suppose you didn't meet anybody on the way to the theatre, or in the theatre itself or . . . on the way back . . . anybody, let us say, who could absolutely corroborate what you have . . ." His glance and gesture were each eloquent of his meaning. Hilary Frant assumed an air of supreme nonchalance.

"I'm afraid that I didn't, Inspector. Nobody that I know of . . . whom I could absolutely pin down, as it were. . . . you see, I hadn't the knowledge that I have now and wasn't keeping a particularly keen look-out. Still, I'll put a 'feeler' round . . . perhaps I shall be able to chance on somebody whom I didn't spot at the time but who may have spotted me."

"Thank you, Captain Frant. Care to sign the notes I've made? Read them through first, of course."

Brother and sister watched the emissary of the law depart, and directly the coast was clear the girl turned to her companion with a complete epitome of interrogation in one word. "Hilary . . ." He held out his hands to her . . . They were out of his control . . . shaking.

The inquest on the body of the late Leonard Pearson took place on the following Saturday morning in a small room attached to an alleged place of worship within the hamlet of Perry Hammer itself. The coroner, a Dr. Rendlesham, was a medical practitioner who was noted in the district over which he held jurisdiction, for efficiency, kindness of heart and a large fund of native wit and shrewdness. Strangely enough, the affair excited but little local interest. It may have been that the inquest on the victims of the terrible Reading cinema fire that occurred on the night after the murder had pushed it away from its anticipated place of prominence.

Dr. Rendlesham cleared his throat and addressed the twelve members of the jury very briefly. He wagged his head and warned them that the case was far from an ordinary one, and far removed, indeed, from those that usually came their way and his. What little evidence there was, at his disposal, to call and place before them, he hoped, or rather he *knew*, would be reviewed by them with ungrudging interest and care, in order that they might be guided to a true and eminently proper verdict. Fortified by Dr. Rendlesham's confidence in them separately and severally, the jury heard the evidence of Amy Talbot, John Murray, the two members of Pearsons' household most directly concerned with the finding of the body, Sergeant Waterhouse and Dr. Clive. Sergeant Waterhouse then caused a certain amount of excitement. He called Edna Revallon, who described herself as an actress and danseuse, employed at the present time in the chorus of the Diadem Theatre. This last witness—a tall, dark, handsome girl, with face unnaturally pale—deposed that she had visited Mr. Pearson during the evening of his death and had left him, hale and well, as far as she could tell, somewhere in the region of a quarter to nine. In reply to a member of the jury, she said she knew of nothing that could possibly help in the investigation of the murder. Her visit was not a business one. Rather the contrary, in fact. She was an intimate friend of Mr. Pearson. Two months ago, on the 11th of February, to be exact, he had offered her marriage. As he was considerably her senior, she had asked for time to think it over, and when she had last seen him on the fatal evening, it had been with regard to that offer. In answer to the coroner himself, who put the question to her with extreme delicacy, Miss Revallon informed the gathering that she had still been undecided in the matter, and had informed Mr. Pearson to that effect. He had asked her to come to a final decision within another month. Miss Revallon then showed signs of acute distress. Dr. Rendlesham, directly he observed this, became a model of sympathetic understanding and discreet commiseration.

Eventually, after a sitting of two hours and a half, the jury filed back to their places and through their foreman, returned the verdict which had been expected by the majority of those present. Sensation on this occasion, to use an extremely hackneyed phrase, was conspicuous by its absence. For the verdict of popular anticipation was the time-honoured one of "Wilful murder by some person or persons unknown".

The moment of the sensation-seekers, however, was yet to come. For, a little less than a month following the open verdict returned by the coroner's jury at Perry Hammer, Chief-Inspector MacMorran of Scotland Yard called at the house in Lancaster Gate which he had visited on the morning of Thursday, the 23rd of April, and arrested Captain Hilary Frant for the wilful murder of Leonard Pearson. Sir Robert Frant wilted under the shock, but Pamela Frant, his daughter, forewarned by the horror of knowledge, had sought to nerve herself for the ordeal for some time . . . ever since the Inspector's first visit. Captain Frant rigorously respected the usual warning when MacMorran punctiliously gave it to him, and went with his captor, head erect, white-faced and very quietly. He squared his shoulders almost instinctively, as though to fend off a blow which, he seemed to sense, must inevitably come to him. Pamela turned appealingly to her father in the stark stress of her emotion and demanded from him the alert activity of attack.

"What are we going to do, Daddy? Whatever are we going to do?"

"What *can* we do, Pamela?" returned Sir Robert, listlessly. "I don't know what the case for the Crown is . . . but you can rest assured that it's a damnably strong one, otherwise they'd never have dared . . ." His voice trailed into the resignation of silence.

She, knowing more than her father, knew also, therefore, the heavy weight of his words. It gave the impetus to immediate decision. "The case for the Crown . . ." words pregnant with horror and dread and of more unspeakable horror yet to come perhaps . . . it was for her, too, that Hilary had gone there . . . her personal responsibility surged violently in her and threatened to overcome her.

"If that's so," she said steadily, and the even tone of her voice amazed her, "Hilary must have all the help that it's in our power to give him. Every atom of it. And the best help, too."

Sir Robert nodded. The nod held just a tinge of hope.

"I'm with you, my dear, of course, all the way. Who is there whom we can have?" he asked. "Have you anybody special in mind?"

She considered for a moment. When she spoke the words came slowly.

"We must have Sir Gervaise Acland for the defence—he's easily the best, now . . . and besides him we must have Anthony Bathurst."

Six weeks elapsed, however, before Sir Robert was able to get in touch with Mr. Bathurst.

CHAPTER IV
MR. BATHURST AND A BLANK WALL

MR. ANTHONY Lotherington Bathurst had read of the Perry Hammer case in the columns of the *Morning Message* and had read also from between the lines of the later Press announcements, without surprise, that an arrest was moderately imminent. When the definite news came through, therefore, of the apprehension of Captain Hilary Frant, it was not altogether contrary to his anticipation. His surprise came later. This condition was reserved for the occasion of the visit to him of Sir Robert Frant and his daughter, Pamela, somewhere about the middle of July. They wasted no time in the formulation of their appeal to him. He listened attentively. It was the lady who ultimately decided him. But not for the reason, shall we say, that would have swayed many men in a like situation. Sir Robert had told him that he had wanted him six weeks ago. Anthony had explained the mission that had taken him to Milan—the affair of the Cardinal's agate . . . it was a great compliment to him, he said, that Sir Robert had been content to wait for his return. The critical moment of tension had come when the lady had leant forward and touched Mr. Bathurst on the forearm.

"Mr. Bathurst," she said, "I'm well aware that the case is horribly black against Hilary. That's one of the reasons why we have come to you. But I'm his sister and I'll tell you something."

Attracted by the purpose and sincerity that revealed themselves in her eyes, Anthony listened more keenly. After all, he said to himself, there must always be the psychology of a crime to be weighed in the balance and assessed accurately.

"I *know* my brother is innocent. He did not kill Leonard Pearson. Shall I tell you why?"

"Please, Miss Frant. From what I've already seen of it, I shall want all the help I can get, you know."

"Yes. Listen to this, Mr. Bathurst," contributed Sir Robert Frant. "What Pamela's about to tell you is absolutely true, and unless something like a moral revolution has taken place within my son's mind during the last months, it can be implicitly relied on. Listen to her, and then you'll see what she means and what I mean, besides."

"Proceed, Miss Frant, please."

Pamela's eyes were bright now with all the glittering justice of her cause.

"Do you remember *how* Pearson was killed, Mr. Bathurst?"

"By a blow on the head, wasn't he?"

"From *behind*, Mr. Bathurst, mind that. From *behind*! The blow was a *treacherous* blow. All the evidence is in that direction. The murderer must have crept stealthily behind Pearson and taken him all unawares—unsuspecting. That is as utterly unlike my brother Hilary as deliberately kicking a horse would be. Just as I know that he is totally incapable of the latter, so do I know that it is equally impossible for him to have done the former. Isn't it, Daddy? You *know* that's true, don't you?" She appealed to Sir Robert.

"My daughter is right, Bathurst. Perfectly sound in all she's saying. My boy couldn't have done this thing."

Pamela proceeded to amplify the point.

"Hilary might have faced Pearson and shot him even; might have killed him in temper or as the result of a violent struggle. He would never have done the thing with which he is charged. *Wouldn't*—because he *couldn't*. And even you can't think of a better reason than that, Mr. Bathurst. Can you?"

Her eyes were as eloquent as her voice, and Anthony Bathurst looked into the violet depths of them and delivered into them his trust. His instinct told him that he had nothing to fear.

"I'm converted. Count me on your side, Miss Frant," he answered quietly. "It would be presumption on my part to range myself opposite to the side that included both you and your father. And he who is not with you must be against you. I'm with you, therefore." He drew his arm-chair a trifle closer to her, leant forward towards her and took hold of her right hand. Pamela's eyes met his and wondered. Her condition of wonderment was short-lived.

"And because I am with you, Miss Frant," continued the insistently quiet voice of Anthony Bathurst, "please tell me the truth. The truth of *everything*. Remember that I cannot fight your enemies properly if I am handicapped by the lack of *anything*."

Pamela Frant sat straight up in her chair, combative, semi-indignant; only, however, for a mere moment. Suddenly she relaxed again into her former position.

"You are right, Mr. Bathurst. How did you know?"

"The name Pearson, when pronounced by you, always carried with it a halo of dread. This halo was a trifle smaller when you heard the name spoken by somebody else, but it was still there. You spoke it four times. On each occasion, your eyes, your hands, and your voice all told the same story. Their combined eloquence was unmistakable. You hated the name. Why? After all, the man has been brutally murdered! Which should, in the ordinary course of events, exhort sympathy from a young lady like yourself. A little boy of my acquaintance considers that to be murdered gives you an immediate passport to Heaven. I argued to myself that you hated the *name* because you hated the *man*. That argument is usually fairly sound. And you hated the man, I suggest, because you feared him. You see, Miss Frant, I know a little of the late Master Pearson's life and habits. Words and music. There are many whose feelings towards him were on a par with yours." Bathurst gestured to her to continue the story from the point where she had left it. After a glance in the direction of Sir Robert, she did so.

"You are right again. It's all been a horrible mistake, right from the first. Forgive me, Daddy, for I fear the fault has been mine."

Sir Robert regarded her with amazement. Pamela continued. She ignored the incredulous look that came from her father, and her voice took on a tone that was cold, hard, and passionless. "Pearson had some letters of mine. I was only a girl when I wrote them. They were imprudent—nothing more, I assure you. The man to whom I wrote them was many years older than I was and entirely unworthy of the things that I said to him and of the things that I offered him. Let me explain it all by saying that I was infatuated. Anyhow, it's all over and done with now. If I were to tell you the man's name, you'd be astounded—as I'm not going to, it doesn't matter. Let me tell you one thing. He occupies a very high and important position. Dick Lanchester wouldn't like those letters. Still less would I care for him to see them." She began to rock herself impatiently—backwards and forwards. "Pearson's price for those letters was £1,000. My brother went down to Perry Hammer to pay it. That's all. Nothing more whatever. He brought back my letters that night . . . but when he left Perry Hammer, Pearson was alive. I have Hilary's word for that, and that's good enough for me."

Sir Robert Frant rose and confronted his daughter. "And he's attempted to foist on Scotland Yard a counterfeit alibi? Why, in the name of Heaven, haven't you told the truth before?"

Pamela bowed her head and nodded an affirmative to her father's first question. Frant turned to Bathurst. "You hear that, Bathurst? This is a pretty kettle of fish, to be sure."

"Tell me of this alibi, Miss Frant, that your father mentions."

Pamela obeyed. When she had finished, Anthony Bathurst rose and paced the room. "Tut-tut, Miss Frant. How incredibly foolish of your brother. Don't you see what will happen? Sir Hubert Kortright will lead for the Crown and will immediately—"

She intervened.

"I had no part in my brother's alibi, Mr. Bathurst. There is no responsibility on me there. I knew it was a mistake from the first. But he had put it forward before I had a chance to stop him. We never discussed it, you see. Never had a chance to. He had no idea that he would be traced to Perry Hammer. He thought that he had thoroughly covered up his tracks."

"What's Acland doing about this, do you know, Sir Robert?"

"He must be told, of course. Hilary's only chance lies in his putting all his cards on the table and being absolutely frank. Even then, I doubt very much if—"

"There's another chance, Daddy. Don't forget that."

"What's that, Pamela?"

"For Mr. Bathurst to find the real murderer." She spoke rapidly. "It's the best chance of all."

"I'll do my best, Miss Frant. But the scent's a bit cold, you know, by now. I shall have to have a consultation with Acland, that's certain. And I must see your brother at once. At Reading, isn't he? I must also see Sir Austin Kemble *re* the necessary permission. Luckily, we're close pals, he and I. Do you think I could see your son to-morrow sometime, Sir Robert? When I've seen the Commissioner, there'll be no trouble about fixing things. But there's absolutely no time that we can afford to lose. Too much, unfortunately, has already been lost."

"I think you can see Hilary to-morrow, if you can pull the strings at the Yard, as you say you can. What's your next step—after that?"

"Perry Hammer itself. All the people round Pearson. There, and in town. The room where Pearson was murdered. I shall have to talk to Sir Austin about that, too. Wonder if I can convince him? Shall have to be at the top of my persuasive form, I expect. When's the trial, Sir Robert?"

"That's some way ahead, thank God. October 13th. At least, it's expected so—a Tuesday. Three or four small cases are down before it, but they'll be disposed of very quickly I expect. And Heriot's got it, too. Heriot, of all people! Would be Hilary's confounded luck to get Heriot, wouldn't it?" He showed signs of imminent departure. "Come on, Pamela, we shall only hinder Mr. Bathurst by stopping here. Any time you want me, Bathurst—or want anything, let me know at once. And spare no expense whatever. My 'phone number's Palatine 8885. Good-bye, my boy, and God bless you. I'm not a sentimentalist or a fatalist, and I think somehow that He will."

Anthony Bathurst saw them out, noted the pallor of Pamela Frant's face and returned to his room. "By Jove," he whispered to himself, "we're properly up against it, all round the wicket. Heriot! Had it been Dalliance, or even Lassiter, it might not have been so bad—but Mr. Justice Heriot—"

CHAPTER V
MR. JUSTICE HERIOT

MR. JUSTICE Heriot, let it be said, was, despite his reputation, an experienced, able, and strong judge. Sentiment and sentimentality left him as cold and unmoved as that Pharaoh of old, who, unskilled in reading the future, hardened his heart and refused to part with the Children of Israel. Heriot hated wickedness with all the genuine hatred that sometimes goes hand in hand with a certain kind of austere righteousness. He applauded the Jehovah who ruthlessly destroyed such people as the Amalekites and the degenerate inhabitants of Sodom and Gomorrah. Had he had his way, the same omniscient and omnipotent God would have continued those practices of extermination that he appears to have exercised in so many places of the Old Testament. In this respect, too, he often felt that he would like to draw up lists of names for submission to an Almighty who was pleased to rely very largely on his judgment. Names of people utterly worthless.

. . . The result was that old lags grossly libelled him, and more than one vitriolic statement had gone the rounds regarding him.

There was no authenticity, for instance, in the story that had emanated from a rate-collector in the service of a certain County Borough, that it was Heriot's habit during trials for murder, over which he presided, to caress repeatedly his thin, stringy neck and at the same time to catch the prisoner's eye during the process, and subsequently hold his entire attention. His neck . . . always his neck.

There was no doubt, however, that he was a stickler for the strict observance of court etiquette, and his meticulously precise elocution of the words of the death sentence was due, not to any excess of sadism, but rather to a due appreciation of what was fitting, right, and proper in regard to ceremonial ritual. His delicately elegant and eminently dignified manner of sustaining the Black Cap was in no sense to be regarded as an ostentatious desire for display.

Here was no playing to the gallery. On every occasion that it had been placed on his head, he had been filled with a fervent wish that the murderer for whose benefit it was worn, should see it well, without the slightest physical difficulty, and realize at the same time, that it was part of the ceremonial of the administration of the King's Justice. Just as his own trumpeters were. Just as his exquisitely precise phrasing of the words "by the neck" was. Mr. Justice Heriot, at the age of seventy-two, the servant of the Lord, lover of little children and all animals, and loved in his turn by those who served him!

Three months before the opening of the autumn Assizes and the trial of Captain Hilary Frant for the Perry Hammer murder, Mr. Justice Heriot was indisposed. In fact, as he said to his maidservant, Angela Mansell, he felt downright ill. His throat had been troubling him for some appreciable time, and ultimately the mischief, whatever it was, went to his voice. Mr. Justice Heriot, a little tired of his own doctor, who as far as he could see was doing him no good, decided to see a specialist in these matters. The renowned Sir Randall Bowers, an old friend of Indian and Canadian fame, also a fellow-Etonian, submitted two names for his consideration, Barrow-South and Frant. For somewhat obvious reasons, Mr. Justice Heriot chose the former. Dr. Barrow-South made the appointment with him by 'phone, and when the judge put in an appearance, was at pains to place his distinguished visitor at his ease.

"How long have you been affected?" said he.

"A matter of months now," replied Heriot.

The eminent specialist examined the judicial throat and became definitely grave. In reply to a further question from the eminent specialist, Mr. Justice Heriot detailed his various symptoms. As he listened, Dr. Barrow-South became graver. "There is mischief in the throat, without a doubt," he asserted. "I will see what an X-ray photograph will tell me, and after that, I shall be in a position to pass that information on to you." He paused and looked at his visitor somewhat pointedly. "I can, of course, be perfectly frank?"

Mr. Justice Heriot, game as ever, showed no signs of quailing. "Of course," he returned. "I have come here for the truth."

"What is your age, my lord?"

"If I live, I shall be seventy-two years of age on the ninth of October."

Dr. Barrow-South toyed for a moment with his ivory paper-knife. "In that case, my lord, it is rendered appreciably easier for a man in my position to tell the truth. I have little doubt, from what you have told me, and from what I have seen, that the trouble is grave. The singularly inflamed condition of the aesophagus is very significant. There is also, I very much fear, a growth of some kind within the throat itself. It may be an ordinary tumour; it may, on the other hand, be malignant. That is what the X-ray may tell us."

For a brief space, the lines of Mr. Justice Heriot's face became more marked. But the old man stiffened his jaws and seemed almost involuntarily to throw back his head, to meet whatever it was, that was coming to him. "Cancer?" Dr. Barrow-South put the affirmative into a nod that was full of meaning. Mr. Justice Heriot attempted to rise from his chair, but the next words that came from the specialist interrupted and dissuaded him.

"But that is looking on the worst side. We will hope, my lord, that the tumour is an ordinary one and that it can be dealt with in the ordinary way."

The old man's eyes glinted in something like rebellion. "The knife?"

"An operation, of course."

"I find the prospect you hold out to me damnably unattractive, in either case. When shall I know?"

"As I said, I shall be able to make a more definite announcement when I have seen the X-ray. Let us say, by the end of the week."

This time the judge succeeded in rising from his chair.

"Thank you, doctor," he said stubbornly. "But I would rather die standing up and in harness, than lying on a wretched bed with two or three of you fellows having a saw at me. Hate hospitals. Loathe nursing-homes. Do you understand?"

"Let's hope that it won't come to that," put in Barrow-South kindly. "Or at all events, let us wait until we know."

The old man grunted. "If the worst comes to the worst, doctor, how long have I got? You needn't be afraid to tell me the truth. I've sentenced a good many to death in my time—it's only common justice, I suppose, that I should have the compliment returned to me." He chuckled to himself. "My own medicine—eh? Well, how long, Barrow-South?—Come man, out with it."

The specialist considered the question.

"Using your own words, that is to say, in anticipation of 'the worst', anything from six months to two years. It's hard for me to say on the knowledge that I have at the moment. On the other hand, however, if the growth be of a simple character, I see no reason why you should not have several more years yet of useful life before you. I make that statement in full cognizance and appreciation of your present age, but your body generally is well preserved and your organs are reaping the benefit of a well-ordered and temperate life."

Mr. Justice Heriot smiled. "That's the most cheerful thing that you've yet said to me, doctor. Let's hope that you're right."

Dr. Barrow-South smiled back evasively.

"Before we see about that X-ray, tell me something. Your case, as you know, interests me tremendously. As you may have, perhaps, heard, I am at work on a brochure dealing with the one hundred and forty-two known affections of the throat. Each case that comes my way seems to add something to my store of knowledge. Now, tell me. Has your voice been much affected?"

The judge nodded. "At times—yes. More than once I have been in a condition almost bordering on aphonia. With the work that I have to do, this is extremely disturbing."

Dr. Barrow-South nodded, with a certain amount of self-satisfaction.

"I suspected as much. Now listen. That condition of which you speak is brought about by semi-paralysis of the vocal cords. Let me explain myself more fully. The growth, such as a tumour, or even an aneurism, shall we say, either presses upon the nerves of the voice, or else those same nerves are in some way involved *in* the growth. Do you follow me? Loss of voice is the inevitable sequel."

At the mention of this, Mr. Justice Heriot became more interested. "I should have thought that the condition you describe would have been chronic. In my case, it hasn't been such."

"Not necessarily chronic. The body, as you know, reacts, more or less, to certain external influences. There may be many reasons for this, all playing their part unbeknown to us. Some days something happens and your voice is definitely improved. The next day something different takes place, and the improvement vanishes. But come along and I'll make arrangements for that X-ray."

Mr. Justice Heriot followed him from the consulting room. "This has come at a damned awkward time for me," he said. "I'm due at Reading during the second week of October, and there are no fewer than five judges on the sick list as it is. Incidentally, I'm stopping at Erleigh with Lord and Lady Madden."

"You'll take the Perry Hammer murder, then?" said Barrow-South. "Young Frant's case."

"I shall," said the judge, with a curious complacency. "The autumn Assizes are for criminal cases only. Looks like being my last, eh, doctor? I shall end in a blaze of sensation. Flags flying to the end." He changed the subject. "I was sent to you, Barrow-South, by no less a person than Sir Randall Bowers. He recommended you. Said it was a case for either you or Frant. I couldn't very well go to Sir Robert Frant, could I?" His old eyes twinkled.

"In the circumstances, I suppose you couldn't," said Barrow-South thoughtfully, "although I don't know that Sir Robert Frant ... By the way, going back a little way, how is Sir Randall Bowers?"

CHAPTER VI
SIR RANDALL BOWERS DISDAINS CONVENTION

SIR Randall Bowers, it may be mentioned, was in the best of health. Consider the following:

Readers of that estimable daily paper known as the *Morning Message*, upon opening it on the morning of October the second were interested, entertained, amused, annoyed, and shocked respectively by a contributed letter which occupied the foremost place in the middle column of the middle page. It had been given this position, no doubt, with editorial malice aforethought. This letter purported to have been signed by Sir Randall Bowers. Sir Randall Bowers, it may be mentioned, had for many years now, occupied a warm place in the hearts of the British public. His two tremendous successes as Governor-General of Canada and Viceroy of India, coming almost on top of each other as they did, and after so many "intellectual" failures amongst his predecessors, had given him a *locus standi* such as is given to the few. The result was that Sir Randall could step in confidently where other men would shiver on the brink. The letter that has just been mentioned had for its heading "The Perry Hammer Incident" and was worded as follows:

Ootacumund Lodge,
Glanmore,
Nr. Mickleham,
Surrey,
Oct. 1st.

To the Editor of the *Morning Message.*

Sir,

A great many of the habitual readers of your valuable paper will doubtless be surprised at the wording with which I have chosen to head this letter. Not "murder", it may be observed, nor "tragedy", but just "incident". For it is that and nothing more. They will be possibly even more astounded when they read a little further on, and discover what I have to say. Within a very few days from now a young officer of our incomparable Army will be called upon to stand his trial for what is known generally as the Perry Hammer murder, but which I have chosen to describe as the Perry Hammer incident. I call it that because I love the truth and have always been able to face facts. Whatever success may have come to me in my career has come, very largely, from those two conditions. I have no doubt in my own mind that, in writing this letter, I am disgracing those terrifying traditions of British justice about which we hear so much, and at the same time breaking all the canons that relate to that most heinous of all misdemeanours known as "contempt of court". Believe me, Mr. Editor, notwithstanding all this, I am left entirely unmoved. *The man who was called was a menace to society and a living violation of all that is clean and decent and British. And Scotland Yard knows it,* as well or better than any of us. I herewith challenge Scotland Yard to deny that fact. I am not concerned whether Capt. Frant killed this man Pearson or not. I am not concerned as to *who* killed him. Why should I be? Why should anybody? Am I disturbed when a cancer is cut from a human body? What I am concerned with is the future of Capt. Frant himself, and I tender my sincere thanks to the man or woman, whoever it was, that removed the excrescence known as Leonard Pearson from our midst. In my opinion he or she had every right so to do. It was very meet, right and a most bounden duty. And let those whom this letter shocks, and who in extenuation of their shock would prate of the sacredness of human life, and the protection of society, etc., and all the other bilge that these things let loose, cast their minds back to the war years of 1914-1918. Blood flowed like water then—"the rich, sweet wine of youth", at that—and few cared! Then, in the name of the good God Himself, why should we be concerned about vermin now? Good luck to you, Capt. Hilary Frant, and may the 16th of October—shall we say—see you a free man. I never did care very much for this hanging business, and in your case I find the contemplation positively appalling. All the same, I've my doubts of your acquittal. I've seen too many muddle-headed juries and listened to too many addle-pated counsels in the past. If I'm hauled up by the scruff of my neck for this letter (which I rather hope will happen) I'll pay the fine willingly, and I also undertake to indemnify the newspaper in which I hope it will appear, against any damages in which this Government of doddering idiots may see fit through their so-called courts of Justice, to mulct it!

I have the honour to remain, Mr. Editor,

Your obedient servant,

RANDALL BOWERS, K.C.B., K.C.S.I., D.S.O.

This remarkable, audacious and sensational epistle achieved, no doubt, the purpose that Sir Randall Bowers intended it to achieve. Without exaggeration, it may be said to have fluttered the dovecotes of the entire country. The Frants, however, Sir Robert, his brother, and Pamela, and also Dick Lanchester, her fiancé, read it with mixed feelings. It must be remembered that in their case the point of view was definitely peculiar.

"I don't like it, Robert," said Maddison—"seems to me that it's just the kind of thing will put old Heriot's back up. He's the worst man in the world for anybody to attempt to influence in this way. This letter, if my judgment's worth anything, will, in all probability, bring his natural pigheadedness and obstinacy to the absolute peak. I can't imagine what prompted Bowers to make such an ass of himself."

His brother agreed gloomily, whilst Lanchester put into words the thought that was passing through the minds of all of them. "What progress is Bathurst making? Have you heard anything from him lately? When I saw Hilary in Reading last week he was particularly anxious to know how Bathurst was faring. He's been down to the prison twice, and has also had a conference with Acland. Hilary had an idea from what he said to him on the occasion of the second visit, that he'd been able to cotton on to something. Hilary didn't know what it was, however, and so I'm none the wiser, either. Any of *you* any idea what it is?"

Sir Robert Frant took it upon himself to answer his prospective son-in-law's question.

"I've not, if you're asking me, Lanchester. That fact, however, need not necessarily indicate bad news. I should say from what I've seen of him, that Anthony Bathurst would be the very last person on earth to raise hopes in our hearts before he was certain of success. Besides having been to see Hilary twice, I can tell you that he's been down to Perry Hammer as well." Sir Robert paused and then, when on the point of continuing, checked himself. Pamela noticed her father's indecision and immediately queried it.

"What were you going to say, Daddy?"

Sir Robert bit his lip before replying. "Well, putting the whole thing into a nutshell, Pamela, I'm far from confident. I may as well be frank about it. More than that, I'm fairly certain in my own mind that Bathurst shares my opinion, and my—er—lack of confidence."

Dick Lanchester looked from Sir Robert to Pamela with undisguised anxiety.

"That's just what I was afraid you were going to say, sir," he ventured. "Bathurst's been on the case some little time now, and considering that he started on it when the scent was almost freezing I think that we've asked him to bite off a pretty tough mouthful. Clever as he may be, and successful as he undoubtedly has been, we can't shut our eyes to the fact that the man isn't a magician, and that the age of miracles is past. We've got to sit tight, put our trust in Sir Gervaise Acland, and hope for the best. Anything beyond that, I think, is so much waste of time."

"I think that Lanchester is talking sound common-sense," contributed Maddison Frant. "After all, as Pamela has always insisted, there is just the chance that the murderer may make a false step, and give himself away. Sometimes the merest slip on his part is sufficient to put the police on the track. Let's hope it will be so in this instance."

"There's not much chance of that, I'm afraid," declared Sir Robert ruefully. "You see, you've got to look at it like this. The police have fastened the crime on to Hilary. Don't forget that point, whatever else you do. They work very much on the assumption that sufficient for the crime is the accused thereof. While they have their hands on Hilary, they're more or less satisfied. They aren't troubling themselves to look for anybody else. It's the Crown versus Hilary Frant, and unless somebody walks into a police station somewhere and makes an absolutely watertight confession, it's going to remain there until the game's been played out. In one respect, however, I differ from Lanchester. I regard Acland as our *second* line of hope. For the first, until the thing's gone right through until the bitter end, I'm relying on the man to whom I went in the first place . . . Anthony Bathurst."

CHAPTER VII
MR. BATHURST TESTS THE WALL

ANTHONY Bathurst, to whom we will hark back, had made, immediately after the visit to his flat of Sir Robert and Pamela Frant, a most exhaustive study of the incidents that surrounded the murder of Leonard Pearson in his own room at Perry Hammer. He read with the most painstaking analysis the various reports of the inquest in all, of what he himself considered as, the more reliable and reputable newspapers. From his survey of the case he collected five points for most careful reconsideration. As his remark to Pamela Frant had illustrated, he had some knowledge of the man, Pearson's, antecedents and habitual operations. Bathurst's comparative intimacy with the workings of Scotland Yard, by reason of his friendly association with the Commissioner of Police himself, Sir Austin Kemble, had brought him into occasional contact with many cases that he did not actually handle himself, and in more than one of these, he knew, from direct evidence that had been placed in the hands of Scotland Yard, that Pearson had figured extremely discreditably. Blackmail, that slow and merciless murder of the human soul, he knew, beyond any doubt whatever, to have been Pearson's most profitable line of transaction. When, therefore, under permit from Sir Austin Kemble, he was shown into the presence of Hilary Frant, awaiting trial, he had definite hopes, that this knowledge which he possessed, properly handled and organized, might eventually lead him to the truth. The man in whose interest he was working greeted him warmly. Mr. Bathurst, whose face the other scanned anxiously, determined to clear the air at once.

"First of all, Captain Frant," he said cordially, "let us begin by understanding one another. That's the best foundation, I think, upon which to start. I will begin by asserting my complete belief in your innocence. Without any real evidence whatever, mind you." He raised his hand. "No—don't thank me. You have your sister and your father to thank for that. Particularly your sister. Belief in the justice of a cause is one of its greatest assets, you know, if only for the reason that it is a sort of spiritual force. It's very much like the voluntary system, shall we say, as opposed to conscription. Mighty life against blind matter." Frant gestured his understanding of the point, and Bathurst, wishing at all costs to avoid irrelevant conversation, proceeded unhesitatingly. "Secondly, I'm going to say to you what I said to your people when they came to me and asked me to help them—I want the truth. Not *part* of it, or *some* of it, but every vestige of it. It is only by being put in the possession of this complete truth that I can have any hope of clearing you. Got that?"

Frant nodded gloomily.

"Of course. I realize now that it must be so. I've been a damn fool."

"You have," responded Mr. Bathurst cheerfully. "All kinds of a thoroughly damn fool. But there's no reason why you should go on being one. To-morrow is also a day, you know. You must tell me everything that you did on the night that Pearson was murdered. I am, I may say, aware of the story that you first told to Inspector MacMorran."

"Sit down, Bathurst," invited Frant. "And I'll tell you. Is it absolutely imperative for me to give you every detail?"

Anthony Bathurst considered the question. "I think I know what you mean. Let us make the following arrangement. When I want details, I'll interrupt you and ask you for them. That suit you?"

"Thank you. That's damn decent of you. I'll get on with the story, then. It was like this. Pearson had some letters of Pamela's, and the swine was putting the screw on her. Just think of that. The poor kid was distressed no end—the worry of it was eating into her, body and soul. Got properly desperate and asked me to get them. . . . You must understand that Pearson was asking a thousand quid for them. On the Wednesday of the murder, April 22nd, we all went to the Epsom Spring Meeting. Lanchester—you've met him, no doubt, by now and know who he is—had a horse running in the big race, the City and Suburban, His trainer, McKenna, reckoned that it was very nearly a good thing. It was absolutely chucked in the handicap and at the weights he had tried it to be a racing certainty. Not that I'd blame Kenneth Gibson for that. Well, to cut a long story short, the horse was 'Buttered Crumpet', and if you're a racing man you'll remember it won with something like a stone in hand. Walked it, in fact."

Bathurst smiled his corroboration.

"I had a thundering good bet (a hundred each way put on in several 'packets')—got 'eights', as a matter of fact, averaging it over the whole lot—and no sooner did I handle the cash than I determined to use it to pull Pamela out of her trouble. It seemed a heaven-sent inspiration to me."

At this juncture Mr. Bathurst made his first interruption. "One moment, Captain Frant, if you please. There's something I'd like to know. Was Miss Frant aware of your intention?"

"Yes—I told her there and then, in Tattersall's."

"I see. Did you tell anybody else? Think carefully."

Captain Frant regarded Mr. Bathurst curiously. "Good gracious, no! Don't you realize that—?"

"I realize more, perhaps, than you imagine I do. I want to be quite certain that Lanchester—for instance—knew nothing of this arrangement?"

Captain Frant shook his head decisively. "Lanchester knew nothing, of course. He was the very last person I should have told. Why, it was the very idea of Lanchester ever—"

"I understand, Captain Frant," conceded Bathurst. "Please proceed."

"Well, I left the course before the others, and before the last two events on the card. Lanchester saw Pamela home. Just outside Epsom I pulled up the car and 'phoned to Pearson from a call-box. I told him who I was—and made an appointment with him for nine o'clock that evening. To be exact I got there a few minutes after that. He let me in himself. That pleased me. I interviewed him, had a row with him, called him most of the filthy names that I could lay my tongue to, got Pamela's letters—counted 'em—and paid him a thousand of the best."

Bathurst cut in with sharp insistence.

"How?"

"All in notes. There were several fifties."

Mr. Bathurst rubbed his hands in appreciation of the point. "Good. What did Pearson do with 'em? Remember?"

Frant looked up. "Do with 'em? What do you—?"

"Where did he put 'em—that's what I mean."

"He counted them in front of me, and put them in a little pile just in front of him."

"Anything round them—or a weight of some kind *on* them. Can you remember? Think!"

Frant reflected. "Yes. Pearson put a rubber band round them. I remember him sitting back in his chair just after he had done so."

"Do you know, Frant," remarked Anthony Bathurst, "I find this little piece of information remarkably interesting. For I have discovered no mention—in what I have read of the case— of any bank-notes having been found on Pearson's table when he was discovered dead."

Frant shook his head. "There's nothing in that. He may have put them away somewhere before he was killed. Probably would do, I should say. Don't build on anything there, Bathurst."

"Leave it for the time being, then. We must. All the same I'm not so sure that you're right. Anyhow the point's decidedly interesting." Bathurst paused and thought for a moment. "It's damnably double-edged—that's the worst of it. If you tell the absolute truth at the trial, which you must, and the notes are gone, as I fear very much that they are, you see where you'll be then, don't you?"

Hilary Frant seemed uncertain. "You mean—?"

"I mean that you're merely strengthening the case for the prosecution, as far as *motive* goes. They'll receive it with open arms and welcome it as a long-lost brother. Call the attention of everybody to the absence of a strawberry mark. They'll insinuate that *you* took them. Don't you see? That you had a double reason for murdering Pearson. Got your letters and then took your price back." Bathurst rose and paced the room. "'Pon my soul, Frant, the whole thing gets worse and worse, the more you see of it. Kortright will seize on every point with crows of delight."

Frant argued: "I can prove that I haven't got them though. My bankers will—"

Bathurst wheeled on him with impatience. "How? In God's name, man, how? There's only one way of doing that and that's going to be precious difficult. It's by proving, *proving*, mind you, that they're in the possession of someone else. The very thing of things you can't do."

Captain Frant shrugged his shoulders and relapsed into silence. Bathurst's next words, however, jerked him back to reality.

"Well—it's no use moaning—what happened next? After Pearson had the notes, I mean, and you had Miss Frant's letters. Did you get away from the place at once?"

Frant, realizing his position more and more, implied almost sullenly. "I told the swine off. Which some of the servants heard, I expect." Bathurst affected the meekness of resignation.

"Go on, tell me the worst. What else did you do to put the noose round your neck?"

"I cleared out. The time would be, I should think, about a quarter to ten. Went out through the french-doors. Nobody saw me. I'm dead sure of that. Climbed the wall at the end of the garden, chased back to the car and drove hell for leather home." Frant stopped precipitately, but he continued almost immediately. "Oh—I forgot. I chucked my stick over the wall before I climbed it."

Bathurst regarded him with amazement. "What stick?"

Frant flushed. "My walking-stick. Took it down to Perry Hammer and carried it into Pearson's room with me."

Bathurst's amazement became incredulity. "What on earth for? What did you take it with you for, in the first place? You were in a car, man."

"That's the reason I took it," explained Hilary Frant with dogged persistence. "It may sound damn silly. I didn't want Pearson's staff to think that I had come by car, if any of them did chance to see me. I was careful and left the car a little distance from the house, I didn't want them to connect me with a car, for instance. See my point? If spotted, I wanted to give the impression that I had walked there. Some part of the way, that is."

"H'm. I see. I began to be afraid that—"

"There's another thing that I ought to tell you while we're on this point," proceeded Captain Frant with increased nervousness. "I lost the stick somewhere on the journey home."

"What?" cried Bathurst. "Lost it? Where?"

"I don't know," responded Frant lamely. "Haven't the foggiest—so that it's not a bit of good of me attempting to explain to you. All I know in that when I got the car to Lancaster Gate, and Pam let me in, the stick had gone. The only explanation I can give is that somebody must have stolen it."

Anthony Bathurst resumed his pacing. "My dear Frant," he protested. "I come to you for light and you plunge me more deeply into the darkness. You pile Pelion upon Ossa. You may, on your own showing, have lost this wretched stick anywhere between Perry Hammer and London, but the Crown, my dear Frant, in the person of Sir Hubert Kortright, will argue that you lost it of malice aforethought. That, in other words, my friend, you deliberately threw it away, *because you had used it on Pearson.* I never, in the whole course of my career, had a worse knot given to me to untie. Of all the precious asses—"

"Don't say that, Bathurst, for heaven's sake. You're my last hope. If you fail me, I don't—"

Anthony Bathurst turned to him with quick sympathy and ready apology. "My dear chap, I'm tremendously sorry. It was unpardonable of me. Please forgive me. I lost sight of your great trouble in contemplation of my own. It was damned selfish of me. Take heart, all the same. A glimmer of light may come to me at any moment, you know. It's astonishing how it does, sometimes. Nearly always, too, when least expected. Good-bye for the present and keep your courage as high as you can."

"Thank you. I'll try to. Where are you going now, Bathurst?"

"To Perry Hammer. Pearson's nephew has the place, I'm told. To the room with the french-doors where you last looked on the late Mr. Leonard Pearson. I have the Commissioner's permission to glance round. You're in luck's way there, Frant, you know. Also, I want a word or two with one or two persons who were in the dead man's personal circle. . . . One of them, for example . . . the butler . . . John Murray."

CHAPTER VIII
THE THREE THUDS

MURRAY surveyed the card that had been presented to him with a supercilious disfavour which he made no attempt to hide. Also, he tapped it rather contemptuously with the edge of an autocratic finger-nail. "I don't know," he said pompously, "that it will be either convenient or possible for you to—"

Anthony Bathurst smiled sweetly. "If you turn the card over," he said suavely, "you will become better acquainted with my *bona-fides*. That's right. On the back of it. That's it—where you're looking now."

Murray read the pencilled words with a frown that was the reverse of prepossessing. "Not the image, I admit," said Mr. Bathurst, "merely the superscription. The superscription of the Commissioner of Police—Sir Austin Kemble—New Scotland Yard. But I'm afraid that it will have to do."

Murray accepted the inevitable and conceded the position with an ill-grace. "If you step this way, sir," he declared, "I will do what I can for you."

"Charmed, I'm sure," murmured Mr. Bathurst.

He followed the butler into the inner parts of the house at Perry Hammer. Opening a door, Murray ushered Mr. Bathurst into a room. "This is the room, sir," he announced with an air. Bathurst almost echoed his words. "The room—" "The room where my late master was murdered."

"Thank you again—this is the room, of course, that I was desirous of seeing." Anthony Bathurst looked round the apartment in which he found himself, with the utmost care. He noted the relative positions of the door, the table, and then again, the french-doors that opened out on to the garden.

"Oh—Murray," he said suddenly. "I wonder if you would be good enough to do something for me."

Murray assumed the countenance of a benevolent deity.

"If it lies in my power, sir. I flatter myself that I know the meaning of tact. You see, I was once with Sir Randall Bowers. What is it that you wanted?"

"Sit down there at that table, in the position—or as near to the position as you are able to remember—in which your master was discovered dead."

Murray surveyed Mr. Bathurst wonderingly and caressed his chin thoughtfully.

"It's all right," added Bathurst encouragingly, "you need have no fear of me. There isn't a catch in it."

The butler checked the reply that had been on his lips, as it were, walked over to the writing-table, took his seat in the chair that was still placed there, and sprawled his head forward on to his left arm. Bathurst regarded his figure attentively and approvingly. He stood there for a little while, hands thrust in pockets. Then, crossing to the french-doors, he measured the distance in steps from them to the figure of Murray at the table.

"I thank you," he asserted, after a period of consideration. "That will do for the moment. Now would you mind arranging the things on the table exactly as they were on the morning your master was found. Can you, do you think? Do you still remember the details?"

Murray nodded curtly. "I think I can do that. Just give me a minute." He moved one or two things slightly. Then he pushed the ink-stand a little distance farther away and brought the ashtray a few inches forward.

"That's about how I think things were," he reflected. "There were four cigarette-stubs in there." He pointed to the tray. "Detective Waterhouse took them away with him."

"You interest me," rejoined Bathurst. "Tell me more, if you can. I could bear to hear full details."

Murray described the points of Waterhouse's find.

"Two of each kind—eh?"

"Yes, sir. Two Turkish—and two of the variety known as 'gaspers'. The latter, sir, had undoubtedly been smoked by my master. They were of the brand that he—er—affected. I informed Detective Waterhouse to that effect."

Bathurst noted the oft-recurring "sir" that was creeping into Murray's address and drew heart therefrom.

"There's one other thing, sir," went on Murray, "that perhaps you'd like me to tell you. There was something else on my master's table that isn't there now. It's been moved since his death. But I know where it is, sir, and could easily lay my hand on it."

"What's that?" queried Bathurst nonchalantly. "Money?"

Murray's face was impassive. "No, sir. There was no money of any kind there. Merely my master's hand-mirror, sir. He made a habit of having one on his table always."

"Get it, please, will you, Murray, and put it in the right place," asked Bathurst quietly.

"In one moment, sir. Will you excuse me?" Murray slipped out silently and almost as silently returned. He placed the mirror in the appropriate position. "There, sir. That's almost the identical spot."

"On the right of the body?"

"Yes, sir. The mirror was to the right of my poor master when he was struck down."

Bathurst looked at it and then back at the french-doors. What he saw in the exercise pleased him. He pointed to the portières that covered them. "Are these curtains here now, the same as were here on the night of the murder?"

Murray shook his head. It seemed almost that he had been anticipating Bathurst's question, "No, sir. The curtains have been changed. The weather then, was considerably colder than it has been lately. That is the reason for the change. The curtains that were hanging there in April were much heavier in texture than these are."

"Who took them down?"

"Knowles, sir. One of the maids. If I might inquire, sir, what is your point?" Murray showed signs of anxiety. Bathurst laughed him off.

"All in good time, Murray. Give me a chance. You mustn't rush me, you know. It's not done. Tends to be disturbing. May I have a word with Knowles, though?"

"Very good, sir. If I ring this bell, sir, Knowles will be the maid who will answer it."

"Excellent. Ring it, by all means, Murray."

Bathurst surveyed the dark-haired little maid with tolerant understanding. Murray made a brief explanation to her to which Bathurst listened with some little amusement. An opportune moment materializing, he seized it immediately.

"Oh, Knowles, I just wanted to ask you something about the portières—the curtains—that were hanging here at the time when Mr. Pearson was killed. You took them down and changed them, I believe?"

"Yes, sir. After Whitsun. The spring-cleaning was done then, sir. It always is, here, sir, about that time."

Bathurst leant forward towards her, and his eyes held that look of eagerness that always came into them when he tested for the first time a newly-formed theory that he regarded as important.

"Can you remember if there were anything like a tear in any part of those curtains?"

Knowles exhibited no hesitation whatever with regard to answering his question.

"Yes, sir. I can give you that information easily. You are quite right. One of the curtains *was* torn. Very little—but torn all the same. And not in a place, either, where a person would have been sure to have noticed it. There was a little jagged tear, so to speak—"

"Before you tell me," intervened Bathurst eagerly, "let me see whether I can correctly anticipate the details even of your answer. The curtain you mention, was torn just a little, shall we say, right at the top, as though one of the hooks that fastened it to the rings of the portière rod had been subjected to a strain or a heavy pull? And it was the left-hand curtain at that. That is to say, the left-hand curtain as one stands and faces the french-doors. Am I right, young lady?"

Knowles regarded him with a look that can be best described as one of dull astonishment. Then she nodded her head slowly but surely. "It *was* the left-hand curtain, sir, and it was torn exactly in the way you say."

If anything, Murray seemed a little disconcerted at the trend of affairs; his disturbance increased when Anthony Bathurst rubbed his hands and glanced in his direction. "Tell me, Knowles," said the latter, turning to her again, "when the house is lit up of a night, are any of the rooms plainly visible from the road?"

The maid hesitated. In consequence of the hesitation, Murray took it upon himself to answer Mr. Bathurst's question. The answer he gave was accompanied by a pompous wag of the head.

"From the road, sir, as you say—only the front of the house is under observation. This particular room, if that's what you mean, cannot be seen. There is only a lane of sorts at the back, and at the end of the garden there is a reasonably high wall."

Bathurst thought of Hilary Frant's story and nodded. "I see. But the house is plainly visible from the front. Yes—that might be the explanation."

Knowles then introduced the element of surprise. "If I might be allowed to butt in, sir, as you might say, I thought of something after the detective had been here that I might have told him if he had thought to ask me. Something that happened on the evening that Mr. Pearson was murdered. A very tiny thing, sir, but all the same it might prove to be—"

"Out with it," cried Bathurst. "A grain of sand may give the vision of a world and eternity may be portrayed within an hour."

His mood communicated itself to Knowles, for when she spoke her words held a ring of triumph. The triumph of heralded discovery.

"Well, sir, it was like this. I was sitting in my room, that's away towards the back of the house, on the night Mr. Pearson was murdered, when I thought I heard the noise of an aeroplane. I said so to the cook, Bassett. So we slipped out into the grounds to see if there was such a thing knocking about. Well, there was one, sure enough. I was quite right in thinking it was that what I had heard. We looked up and saw it—flying away from us in the distance. A small 'plane it was, just like a big bird. Well, this is where the point of my story comes in, sir. As I turned away from cook, who was still watching the 'plane, in order to come indoors again, I thought that I heard a kind of noise inside the house somewhere. I stopped still, just outside the door of our room and listened."

At this stage of Knowles's recital Murray was guilty of a most audible sniff. It was a sniff that contained every kind of contempt. It was obvious, too, from the way that she tossed her head that Miss Knowles strongly resented it. She continued her story with accentuated vigour; the look that she observed on the face of Anthony Bathurst served to encourage her.

"I listened hard, sir, as I was saying, and I felt certain that the noise I heard was coming from somewhere inside this room."

"What chiefly caused you to think that?" Bathurst was keenly interested and made no pretence to hide it.

"From the direction of the sounds, I think, and also the fact that I knew that Mr. Pearson was in here. You know what I mean by that. I knew he was in here, and because of that, I thought of him sort of mechanically—automatically."

"I understand what you mean quite well. It was very natural that you should think as you did. Now, tell me, what was this noise that you thought you heard? Describe it."

Knowles shook her head rather pessimistically. "I don't think that I can."

Bathurst persisted. "Come, what did it sound like, then?"

Knowles inclined her head to one side as she thought it over. "It sounded like thuds. That's the best description I can give to it. Not quite bangs. Thuds." She nodded, as though corroborating her own statements.

Bathurst was frankly puzzled. "Thuds?" he queried. "Can't you be more definite?"

Knowles repeated her previous shake of the head. "I'm sorry, but I don't think I can. I know it's silly of me—but—"

Bathurst closured her, to prod testily at the word that she had used—"thuds".

"What sort of thuds?" he questioned. "Heavy thuds?"

"No-o." Knowles racked her brains. "Not heavy thuds. Not like great weights. Rather the opposite. Not like a heavy body falling, either, or anything like that at all. *Light* thuds, if anything."

Bathurst became critical, "Isn't the term 'light thuds' almost self-contradictory? Surely a thud is a dull, heavy sort of sound produced by a blow or by forceful impact of some kind?"

At this precise definition of the onomatopoeic, Knowles essayed disagreement.

"I know," she said, "but certain thuds *can* sound light, for all you may say, sir. These were light noises—like somebody moving about quickly, as though they didn't want to be seen. And they were quick noises, too. But thuds, all the same."

Bathurst was puzzled. "Quick? How do you mean?"

"They *happened* quickly. Soon after one another, I mean. You know, what you would call—in quick succession."

"Do you really mean—one after the other?"

The maid nodded brightly. "Yes. Like this. One—two—three." She used the numerals quickly.

"Are you absolutely certain that there were three of them?"

"No—not absolutely. But I think so. That was the impression that my mind seemed to get."

Bathurst thought hard. The girl seemed convinced of the truth of her statement. "Three light thuds, eh? What did you hear after that? Anything or nothing?"

"No, sir. I waited for a little while and then, hearing nothing more, made up my mind to come in. After that, I sat talking for about an hour with Bassett and then went to bed."

"Did Bassett hear these thuds, do you know?"

"No, sir, she didn't. I can tell you that. I asked her at the time. She said that she hadn't heard a thing."

"Strange. That you should have heard so well—and that she, your companion at the time—close to you, should have heard nothing?"

"I was standing a little nearer to this room, sir. There's that about it. And sometimes Bassett's a bit deaf, I've noticed."

Bathurst turned and looked at the french-doors. "Do you know, Miss Knowles," he observed to the somewhat flattered maid, "I had rather that you had heard exactly twice as many of your thuds as you did."

"Six?" she queried.

He nodded. "Six—yes. But don't worry over the omission. I think you would have heard the six had you stayed out there long enough." He smiled at her. "I can't be certain, of course."

She shook her head uncomprehendingly. Before, however, she could translate her failure to understand, into actual words, Bathurst was attacking another position.

"Before I go, I want you to tell me something else. A lady called on Mr. Pearson before Captain Frant came. A Miss Revallon. She gave evidence, if you remember, at the inquest on your master. Also, no doubt, seeing the interest that you would naturally take in the case, you remember the substance of her evidence. Now tell me, had you ever seen her before?"

This question was directed towards Murray.

"I have already been asked that question, sir, by Detective Waterhouse. I fancy that Miss Revallon had been to Perry Hammer once before. I would not go further than that."

"She was not, then, anything like a frequent visitor?"

"No, sir. By no means."

Bathurst looked at the curtains with some curiosity. "What was the colour of the clothes that she wore on the evening your master was murdered? The general colour scheme?"

Murray reflected. "Dark, sir. Dark green, I am inclined to say, from the quick glance that I had of her."

"And the colour of the curtains that were taken down?"

"Dark blue," replied Knowles promptly.

Bathurst rubbed his chin. "H'm. That's not too satisfactory. Still, we can't always have things as we want them. For one thing, it wouldn't be good for us, and for another, it would be unpleasant sometimes for other people."

Knowles hastened to agree with him. "That's why we should be thankful for the things that do come our way, sir, and not expect too much."

Which, strangely enough, were the very words that a certain Mrs. Frost had addressed to her married daughter, Rose Stubbs, as far back as one evening during the last week of the month of the previous April. She had nodded her head with prodigious emphasis as she had spoken them. "And what I say is solemn truth," she had added, "and don't you forget it, Rose Stubbs."

CHAPTER IX
THE NOTE FROM THE BLUE

ROSE Stubbs, wife of a certain George Alfred Stubbs, though she live many years past the allotted span of the Psalmist and look back from a considerable distance at that same three-score and ten, will never forget the last week of that month of April that had witnessed the murder at Perry Hammer. For her, it was distinguished by two amazing occurrences. By the first post of the morning of Friday, April the 24th, she had received a letter that bore the Reading postmark. In the ordinary way, the correspondence that arrived by mail for the delectation of Mrs. Stubbs was of such a nature that the question of the postmark failed to interest her. She knew the senders and she also knew what they desired of her. Not always exactly how much, but inasmuch as their demands usually went unsatisfied for a considerable length of time, this matter of inexact knowledge was of small consequence. This letter, however, was different. Radically different. Different in essentials. The handwriting of the address on the envelope was unknown to her. Although she believed that her lord and master, the aforesaid George Alfred, was somewhere in the particular district identified by the postmark, the standard of the calligraphy was far in advance of G.A.'s. By no stretch of imagination could he have been described as a master of the pen. In fact, he hated the pen. The only favourable reminiscence he cherished of it was, that, trained by M. Hartigan and ridden by Clifford Richards, it had won the Cambridgeshire during the previous autumn at the highly-diverting price of 40S., and had turned a shilling each way of "George Alfred's" into the roseate hues of fifty bob. Normally, he arranged that the pen was far removed from the trivial round of his common task.

The contents of this letter, however, excited Mrs. Stubbs far more than its externals. For, wonder of wonders, it contained a note upon the Bank of England. To no less a value than £50. When she opened the envelope and handled the crispness of the note that it held, Mrs. Stubbs speedily dismissed any idea that she might have been hazily fostering that it was her husband who had communicated with her. "Gawd's truth," was the somewhat irreverent greeting that the bank-note received, and the speaker seated herself precipitately in a chair upon the utterance of the words. This was the first of the two astonishing happenings to which reference has been made. An obliging tradesman, surviving a strong sense of shock, changed the note for her, and for the space of a few days the lot of Rose Stubbs had seemed to her to be one with those of the Rothschilds and Rockefellers. At the end of the week, however, there came the corresponding and inevitable debit to this unprecedented credit. It actually arrived in a negative sense; that is to say, there came no George Alfred. Instead of materializing at the end of the week, as had been his truculent wont for years in and out, his home knew him no more.

Days passed and Rose, the wife of his bosom, became first curiously and then acutely uneasy. It was so absolutely unlike him; it was foreign to his nature and habit. As far as Rose could remember, it had never happened before. For a period of over seventeen years now, it had been his invariable custom to come home at some time during the week-end. The week-end in question saw him not! The sudden acquisition of fortune helped Rose to weather the storm of the first few days, but when Wednesday came and George Alfred still did not, she seemed to sense with certainty that the affair was sinister and required investigation. Her first step was the one that she always took in conditions of urgency. She consulted her mother, Mrs. Frost. This lady was therefore called in, and after hearing the story of the unexpected windfall and the subsequent disappearance of her son-in-law, she had made the pronouncement that was likened at the end of the last chapter to that of Knowles to Anthony Bathurst in the room at Perry Hammer.

"Don't expect too much, Rosie," she repeated with unction, "and, after all, say what you like, my dear, you can't grumble, taking it all round. Fifty quid's fifty quid, and your George wasn't everybody's money. As far as I can see, you're well in on the deal. What you could see in him I never could see—although I admit tastes differ. Some like salt butter and China tea—as for me, you can keep both of 'em, say I—"

Rose closured her mother's prolixity. "That's all very well, Ma," she said, "but George was my husband, with all his faults."

"He was," retorted her mother with a kind of grim decision—"you've said it, and I think it sums 'im up very well." She clasped her elbows aggressively.

Rose ignored the implication. "I've got an idea at the back of my mind, Ma, that something dreadful 'as 'appened to 'im."

"It wouldn't surprise me, my dear. It's a long lane that has no—"

"Leave off runnin' 'im down, Ma—now do. None of us is perfect and George never pretended to be."

"Perfect," snorted Mrs. Frost with a derision that was almost majestic in its strength. "I know one thing about 'im—'e's never done a decent day's work in 'is life. He 'ated work as much as any man I've ever known. Which is saying something, too, considering the years I 'ad to live with your father."

Rose's patience became exhausted. She bridled in defence of her missing spouse. "I don't know—when all's said and done. There's more than one kind o' work. There's navvy work and there's brain work. George's work with the organ wasn't child's play, say what you like, otherwise Bill 'Olly would never have gone in with 'im. It might seem easy to some people—but others 'ud find it bloomin' 'ard graft. Ask Bill 'Olly 'imself, if you don't believe me."

"George couldn't 'ave found it that, or 'e'd never 'ave stuck it as long as 'e 'as done." Mrs. Frost delivered herself of what, she was convinced, would prove to be the last word; for a moment or so her daughter remained silent. Her mother's opinions had given her an idea that she found difficult of disposal. Supposing her husband had grown tired of it all; of his precarious mode of life, of her, of their existence together? Supposing the fifty-pound note that had been sent to her at the end of the previous week had come from him, and was the last contribution that he intended to make to her?

She knew that Reading was the centre of a district in which he often moved. Against that, however, wherever could he have obtained such a sum—honestly? The last word stuck in her throat; the contrary adverb swam into her head and took its place silently and menacingly. If she reported her husband's disappearance to the police, she might do him, for all she knew, incalculable harm. It was the very thing against which, more than once, he had solemnly warned her. "Interference is a deadly sin," he would say, "an 'orrible 'abit for anybody to 'ave. It makes me see red." He always took for his example the case of Mahon, the "Crumbles" murderer. "If that bloke's missus 'adn't poked 'er nose into business what didn't concern 'er, the 'busys' would never 'ave pinched 'im. Don't forget that, my gal. A still tongue's the best card a woman can 'ave in 'er pack. You always see you've got it. Otherwise, you and me may 'ave little differences."

Rose reflected on this now. She would never have it said of *her*, by damn good-natured friends, that she squealed, and brought about her husband's downfall.

"Perhaps you're right, Ma," she admitted at length. "I've been thinking over what you've been saying. P'raps George 'as got fed up with me and everything, and cleared off somewhere. You couldn't be surprised. There ain't much for 'im 'ere, after all. Considering, too, that 'e's got the artistic temperament. I shall 'ave to make this fifty quid—or what's left of it—go as far as I can—and then look for some daily work." She brushed a tear from her eye.

The mother, however, took a practical view of the situation as outlined by Rose.

"Cleared off? Away from Bill 'Olly, do you mean? And where, pray, could he clear off to? Who'd 'ave 'im, I'd like to know? 'Andicapped as 'e is, an' all."

Rose felt for her handkerchief and used it quietly.

"'E's pretty nimble, considering. 'E may 'ave gone abroad. 'E's always said that the States and South America appealed to 'im. There ain't no law there, 'e used to say. You could bump anybody off without much of a fuss bein' made of it. 'E's often said to me that's 'ow things should be. P'raps 'e's got on a ship."

Mrs. Frost shook her head very doubtfully. "P'raps not! Look at it like this, Rose," she put forward. "Who could 'ave sent you fifty quid if it *wasn't* George? Look at it for yourself. That's the real problem, ain't it? Get that answered and you'll be able to explain away a lot. That's Gospel, ain't it? See what I mean?"

"Yes, I see what you mean, Ma, but that's all. I don't know nobody who would send me money like that. People like that ain't 'angin' on trees, Ma. Wish they were."

Mrs. Frost surrendered to perplexity. Suddenly she looked up at her daughter and put a question to her. "How did you get rid of the note, Rose? Who changed it for you? Did you 'ave much difficulty?"

"No, Ma, I changed it at the bacon shop round the corner. There was a bit on the slate against me, so the old pot and pan was glad to get it. I'm an old customer there. He knows me well, Mr. Bimson."

CHAPTER X
MR. BATHURST AND A CUL-DE-SAC

MR. BIMSON, it may be remarked, sold best back, collar and streaky at a shop which still retained the external appearance of a dwelling-house, and which served some of the inhabitants of Canning Town. His "corners" of bacon, cheap and satisfying, were renowned from the Iron Bridge to the "Abbey Arms". Canning Town is many miles from Perry Hammer and many millions of people live in, or exist, between the two places. The enterprising shopkeeper mentioned had obliged Mrs. Stubbs in the matter of financial exchange, as he had many times before obliged sundry other of his customers, whose morals and mode of living were no concern of his, but whose financial embarrassments, unfortunately, very often were. Men and women (and their children) must eat. There were times in the year, let it be said, when Mr. Bimson's slate was full to repletion. After all, as he used to say to his wife, when she paused to take breath in between her speeches, "business is business, and a man must live, anyhow". With which admirable statement even Sir Austin Kemble, the Commissioner of Scotland Yard, with his genius for criticism, would have found it difficult to disagree. A month before the trial of Captain Hilary Frant was due to open, Sir Austin found himself listening to Anthony Bathurst, as he had listened so often previously.

"Just a minute," he interrupted with a frown. "I must know, Bathurst, to where I'm getting. I'm perfectly willing to put any information in your way that it's humanly possible for me to do, but I can't get away from the fact that MacMorran regards it as rather a neat job of work on his part. And MacMorran's not a man to blow his own trumpet. Also I must say, in justice to him, that it looks to me like a clear-cut case."

Anthony Bathurst heard him out and stood his ground. "You're entitled to your opinion, sir, of course. On the face of things, I can't quarrel with you. But I'm only asking for help on a matter that I can't very well tackle myself. Single-handed, that is to say. The job's too big. I'll confess what you've already jumped at—that it's connected with the Perry Hammer murder. Beyond that, I really can't say anything. Yet! Because I don't know how it will turn out."

Sir Austin still showed signs of reluctance. Anthony strengthened his appeal by playing one of his best cards.

"I've helped the Yard a good many times in the past, sir, as you know very well. This is about the first occasion on which I've asked it to help me."

The Commissioner sniffed. He was not feeling too comfortable. "You put me in a damned awkward position, boy. I wouldn't have my worst friends accuse me of ingratitude. It's a vice that I absolutely loathe. Almost as much as amateur theatricals. But tell me—you're not asking me to shake up MacMorran?"

"Not in the least," returned Bathurst quietly.

"That's understood, then. No interference of any kind with MacMorran. None whatever! He's had a free hand so far and he must keep it. Now what is it you want?"

His point conceded, Anthony Bathurst settled himself more comfortably in his chair.

"When we worked together, sir, in that somewhat bizarre investigation that has since been handed down to history, I believe, as the affair of the 'Orange Axe', you pointed out to me that the 'Yard' as a machine, with its thousand and one 'cogs', was hard to beat. Those were, I think, the very words that you used. You also drew my attention to the fact that occasionally mere technical routine, as you called it, entered into its kingdom and assumed a place that was peculiar in its value. Well, now, sir, the point is this. I'm asking for the help of that machine. As a machine. Nothing more."

"In what way? Particular way, I mean?"

"I want some bank-notes traced."

Sir Austin looked up critically. Before he could spend himself in declamation, Bathurst was in again. "It's not so bad as it sounds, sir," added Bathurst. "Hear me out and you'll discover that the worst is over."

"How do you mean?" Sir Austin's criticism was still very much alive. It was noticeable in his tone.

"They're £50 notes that I want traced. That's a bit more simple, isn't it?"

"You've got the numbers, of course?"

Bathurst shook his head, and the smile in his grey eyes choked at birth Sir Austin's intended remonstrance. "No, sir. My suggestion would be this. I think it quite possible that one or more of the particular notes that I am after, may have been changed for cash somewhere. Perhaps at a shop or restaurant. I would like an inquiry—a general inquiry—put round the banks, especially the less-important suburban branches, attempting to trace any fifty-pound notes that may have been paid in at any of them, since the third week in April. It is just on the cards that, here and there, we might be able to pick up traces of an isolated note of this kind. What do you think of the chances, sir?"

Sir Austin clasped his hands behind his head and leant back in his chair. "It's possible, I suppose. You're asking me to comb a pretty wide area, you know. Unless I do it by circular letter, it will mean employing a number of men."

Anthony Bathurst rose with outstretched hand. "Thank you tremendously, sir. Your last sentence tells me that you're going to do what I asked you to." He put a paper in front of the Commissioner. "These are my suggestions. I think they will prove to be helpful. Draw a line there and there, sir. Say Oxford on the north and London itself on the south. London and suburbs, of course. Going farther, say the metropolitan ring."

"H'm," grunted Sir Austin. "You're not asking a trifle, are you?"

"You can communicate with the various banks first of all, Sir Austin," recommended Mr. Bathurst sweetly. "And it *might* so happen," he proceeded, "that the news that I'm wanting will come through very quickly. As a matter of fact, I'm inclined to think that it will. I can assure you, sir, that there's quite a fair chance of it."

Sir Austin remained silent for a time, and then used his telephone. "Send Staples to me, will you? Yes, yes, at once."

The man for whom he had sent presented himself almost immediately. Sir Austin beckoned him to come to his side. Taking the sheet of paper that Bathurst had just given to him, he outlined the general position and issued a series of instructions thereon. Staples listened with the keenest attention. It is betraying no confidence, to say that the wish to be called on to assist Mr. Bathurst actively, had always been very close to the man's heart; now that the precious opportunity had come, he determined to leave no stone unturned to justify his personal selection.

"There you are, Staples," concluded the Commissioner abruptly. "I've given you the rough idea of what's wanted. Now get to work at once on it. There's nothing you've on hand that you can't put aside for the time being, is there?"

"No, sir," replied Staples, with prompt emphasis.

Sir Austin nodded profoundly. "I thought so. That was why I picked you out. Organization! Notice that, Bathurst?"

Staples was eager.

"Yes, sir. What men do I use besides myself?"

"Let me see now." Sir Austin reached for a docket. He flicked over half a dozen papers before he answered Staples's question.

"Take King, Merry, and Groves. You can keep the first two until you hear from me again. But Groves must get back on that 'Snow' case not later than Thursday. Understand?"

"Yes, sir. Very good, sir. I'll get the matter going at once."

Mr. Bathurst watched Staples close the door. He prepared for his own departure. "I like your man, Staples, sir," he declared. "He's keen, for one thing, and I should say, intelligent with it." He reached for his hat and stick. "Let me know when you hit on something, sir, and I'll be along to you right away. And very many thanks for your kindness."

"*If* I hit on something, you mean," Sir Austin growled.

"No, sir. I see no reason to alter my choice of word. *When* you hit on something." Waving his hand to the Commissioner, he smiled cheerfully and closed the door gently behind him.

Anthony Bathurst's rather optimistic prognostication justified Mr. Bathurst's optimism. A matter of four days after his interview with Sir Austin Kemble, Staples communicated results. The Reading branch of the Southern and Home Counties Bank reported that a note to the value of £50 had been paid in late in the afternoon of Thursday, the 23rd of April last, to the account of the licensee of the Blue Tambourine Inn. Details were forwarded of the number and series. As far as the bank knew, there were no suspicious circumstances connected with the payment, and the manager of the Reading branch, a Mr. Clinton, knew the man well, into whose account the note had been paid. He was a highly-reputable client in every way. His name was Mark Lane, and he had banked with the Southern and Home Counties ever since he had been established in Reading, which was a matter of over twenty years.

Mr. Bathurst received the information with a pleasure that was most marked and in which he openly exulted. When he 'phoned the Commissioner on the matter, Sir Austin quickly observed the height to which Bathurst's spirits had risen. The town mentioned appealed to him with a considerable attraction. Reading! Within easy distance of Perry Hammer! The place, moreover, where Hilary Frant was destined to stand his trial. His expectations seemed to be approaching something like realization. Things might certainly have turned out very much worse.

He left Paddington on the morning after he heard the news, with a conviction that he was at last coming to real grips with the heart of the mystery. Reading was quickly reached and, fortified by a previous glance at the directory, he made his way to the inn bearing the sign of the "Blue Tambourine". Situated only a few yards from the banks of the Rennet, it presented a rambling, ramshackle appearance in respect of its exterior, and Bathurst halted for a few moments when he first came upon it, so that he might assess more accurately the moral strength of the place to which his steps had been directed. Although the hostelry was open for the purpose of the service of liquid refreshment, there was obviously no boom in trade.

It boasted, he observed, a wooden porch, at one side of which stood part of an old settle. The way in, was over a number of roughish tiles that had evidently been laid by an unskilled hand. Over the porch, there had been fixed a black board on which letters had been inscribed in white paint. Bathurst advanced to the porch in order that he might read the board's announcements with greater ease. Its message was terse and ordinary, and contained nothing in the nature of a superfluity. He had read similar notices many times before. "Mark Lane. Licensed to sell Beer, Spirits, and Tobacco." Comfortable words! Having read the same, Bathurst walked into the porch itself and pushed open the door.

Taking externals into consideration, what he saw within agreeably surprised him. On his immediate left was a homely but very comfortable-looking bar parlour. Its walls held the pictures of nine Derby winners as far apart historically as "Flying

Fox" and "Sansovino". Of customers it was empty. No attendant was forthcoming. Mr. Bathurst announced himself with a
distinctly robust cough. Response was tardy, but eventually a
rose-cheeked maid materialized from the region at the rear and
asked his desires. Anthony issued a normal—and beautiful—
order. "In a tankard, sir—would you like it?"

"Please."

The girl wiped hands on apron, looked a trifle disconcerted,
and disappeared into what was the bar proper. The beer was
good, even for beer, and Bathurst quickly demanded reinforce-
ments. These supplied, he fingered the handle of the pewter for
a moment or so as though in considerable doubt about something, and then, looking up suddenly, caught the wench's eye
and translated the doubt into a direct question.

"Is Mr. Lane about, can you tell me?"

The girl's reception of this very ordinary request staggered
him. She looked at him wide-eyed and open-mouthed, caught
at the corners of her apron with convulsively-working fingers,
burst into weeping, and then turned and fled incontinently from
the parlour. Bathurst checked a frown and set himself a task of
consideration. Here were problems indeed! What smoke had he
started, in the name of goodness? And from what fire? Uncertain for the moment as to what was his best course to pursue, in
conditions so abnormal as those which he was then experien-
cing, he realized that it was imperative that he should exercise
extreme care in the taking of the next step. Where was he? Had
he stumbled into something big? What was there about this Lane
that the mere mention of his name caused his serving-maid to
burst into tears and scatter like a startled faun?

He rose and drained his second tankard; he stood and
listened. All was comparatively quiet within. He could hear no
sound that heralded the man's approach. Very well, Mr. Lane!
If you refuse to come to Anthony Bathurst, there is only one
possible alternative. Mr. Bathurst will go to you! He took a couple
of steps forward, only to meet a stout, motherly person on the
point of turning from the narrow passage into the room where
he had been waiting. Her habitual joviality and serenity of coun-

tenance were marred by an expression that spoke eloquently of worry, anxiety, and sorrow. The face was grief-laden. Bathurst's perception was rapid and vivid. He knew that he looked upon tragedy. He took a tight hold on himself and raised his hat with gentle courtesy. The woman seemed to appreciate the fineness of his understanding, for she stood still in the doorway, saying nothing. Eventually, she raised her head a little and spoke.

"You asked for Mr. Lane. You meant my husband. I can see that you don't know. That you haven't heard." She paused before finishing her sentence. "My husband is dead."

Anthony Bathurst has confessed since, that during the whole course of his career, he had never been more taken aback. The taste of humiliation came to his tongue and he knew its bitterness. What he heard was so far apart from his anticipations. He pulled himself together.

"I am sorry, Mrs. Lane. Please forgive me. But—as you have just said yourself, I did not know. I spoke in entire ignorance. I am intensely sorry to have caused you the pain of explaining to me."

The voice of Mrs. Lane was hoarse with emotion.

"It was a shock—you asking for him. It took me right back to the old days when people used to come in here and ask for him. He was that popular with everybody. And it came on me suddenly, so you must excuse me. I can see one thing, though. You're a stranger in these parts, of course, sir?"

"More or less," replied Anthony. "I certainly don't live in the Reading district, if that's what you mean."

The woman nodded. "It wasn't that I don't know your face that made me say you were a stranger. Don't think that, sir. It was because you asked for Mr. Lane. My husband's been dead nearly five months, and everybody knew him round here. From the Mayor, to the gipsies that camped out at Bracknell."

Mr. Bathurst was conscious of an odd, fugitive sort of thought that darted through his brain. Nearly five months, his informant had stated. That duration of time meant the month of April, which was also the month of Pearson's murder. Nothing in it, perhaps—but still, one never knew. The idea was worth testing.

Decency, however, forbade him from becoming too suddenly inquisitive. He decided that his best plan would be to encourage Mrs. Lane to talk.

"I'm sorry," he said again. "Tremendously sorry. I take it that your loss was sudden? Unexpected?"

Mrs. Lane stared into nothingness. "When a man goes out of a house strong and well at half-past six one evening and is taken from you before that night has run its course, the word 'sudden' even doesn't convey what happens. Do you see what I mean?" she added, with a quaint wistfulness. "An earthquake is 'sudden', but 'sudden' is a silly, tame sort of word to use if you want to describe it properly. It's not big enough, sir. When I looked on my Mark's dead body, I was only able to identify it from little pieces of his clothing that were there. That will show you what I mean. To have him with you at one minute—and then in a little while to know that you have lost him for ever. For ever! Always! Every day." She only whispered the last two words and buried her face in her hands.

Anthony Bathurst reverenced her sorrow and remained silent. When she looked up again, the exquisite pain that had taken possession of her had temporarily passed.

"You see, sir," she said, as though essaying justification, "I'm an old woman. The old find it almost impossible to forget the big things that life brings. It's only the young that can throw off sorrow quickly. Their hearts won't hold pain for very long. They're not meant to." Anthony nodded understanding.

"Your husband's death, I presume, then, Mrs. Lane, was the result of an accident?"

"I keep on forgetting that you don't know all about it. My husband was burnt to death on the evening of April the 23rd, in the big cinema fire. I expect you've heard of that. Don't you remember the 'Anthurium' being burnt down at Reading? Over seventy people lost their lives. They were trapped at the back of the circle—my husband was one of them. There was a panic. A woman started to scream—"

"A mere coincidence of date, after all," thought Bathurst. He remembered, now, how the horror of the disaster had affected the country generally and had, for a few days at least, relegated the Perry Hammer murder to comparative obscurity. The hopes that he had held, that a thread would protrude from the skein and be clutched, were dispelled.

"Terrible. Terrible," he murmured sympathetically. "We will hope that the poor people suffered little."

"I try to whisper that to myself, sir, but sometimes I find it very hard." She paused and groped for comfortable and everyday things again. "What was it that you wanted my husband for, sir? Is it anything that I can do for you?"

"That's very kind of you, Mrs. Lane. To make that offer. Especially considering all the circumstances. And we're up against something rather, extraordinary." She looked startled. Anthony proceeded to make amends. "I've expressed myself rather badly, I'm afraid. The point was in regard to the date. Nothing in it, of course, really. All sorts of things happen on every day, don't they? It's when we run up against them that they impress us. But I'm trying to trace a banknote that was paid into your husband's banking-account on the very day that we've been talking about. During the late afternoon of that day. We want to find out, if we can, the man who paid that note over to your husband."

Mrs. Lane shook her head very slowly. "I couldn't say, I'm sure, but I'll get our paying-in book," she said. "Perhaps that will help me to help you."

Anthony watched her out. Never before, on any previous investigation, had he felt so horribly uncomfortable. It was as though he had been caught tampering with a private letter; he thought of Hilary Frant in a cell, not a great distance away; then of Pamela Frant. Those thoughts nerved him again and steeled him to action. Mrs. Lane was not long away. When she returned she carried in her hand the paying-in book that she had sought to find.

"I must get my glasses," she said, seating herself at the wooden table. She fumbled on her lap. Then, arrayed for the test, she slowly turned over the counterfoils of the book. Back and back. Deliberately. One by one. Anthony held his chin from impatient interruption. June, May and then April. "Here we are," she declared eventually. "This is the one. The last paying-in slip that Mark ever made out. Here's his handwriting." Mr. Bathurst walked across and stood over her. She seemed pleased at his propinquity. Bathurst had a power of sympathetic attraction. "April 23rd," she proceeded. "Here's what you want, I think." Her finger pointed to the details of the payment to the bank on that particular date. Bathurst bent over that he might read them the better. What he saw on the counterfoil gave him a certain amount of satisfaction. There it was—the very entry he had sought. A bank-note to the value of fifty pounds. "That's the chap I'm after," he said. "Look here."

Mrs. Lane nodded. "Yes, I see what you mean. But I don't think that I shall be able to help you, after all. I was afraid that I shouldn't, directly you mentioned what you wanted. You see, my husband paid the money into the bank and he always made out the paying-in book. He might have got this note from *anybody*. If he did change it for somebody, as I fancy he must have done—I shouldn't know. He wouldn't tell me, you see. I never bothered my head about things of that kind." As she made the admission, Mrs. Lane appeared to be genuinely distressed. Anthony himself realized immediately all that it meant to him. With the time at his disposal so very limited, to trace the note now, any farther than the "Blue Tambourine" itself, was pretty well equivalent to running in the "Needle and Haystack" handicap, carrying top-weight. The sudden passing of Lane seemed destined to have more effects than those that had been ultimately anticipated. Frant's luck was undoubtedly dead out. Never before had a case yielded so little.

"I suppose there's no one here on the premises besides you, Mrs. Lane, who could possibly assist me?" Bathurst flung out what was very like a despairing suggestion.

Mrs. Lane's distress, if anything, increased as she repudiated the idea. "No, sir, nobody. In what way did you mean, though?"

"It was just a bare chance. I thought that somebody in the bar might have either seen or heard something of the transaction that involved the passing of the note. But I understand, of course, that I'm asking—"

Mrs. Lane shook her head very emphatically.

"There's only Effie here. We've been carrying on together since our trouble came. She was the only help we had. My husband used to do it nearly all. You can ask her, of course, if you care to." Mr. Bathurst thought that he would. The maid of his arrival, materialized again. Mrs. Lane surrendered control of the affair to him. He put the question. Failure, however, again rewarded him. Effie was ignorant. She had never seen her late master change a £50 note for a customer; neither had she overheard any conversation in any way relative to such a transaction. Anthony Bathurst gave it up reluctantly, and allowed Effie to depart. He could see it was no use expecting any help from her. Shortly afterwards he took his own departure; it may be admitted that he felt very far from pleased with either himself or his efforts. Everywhere he turned, he seemed to be confronted very soon after the turning, with a veritable cul-de-sac. Was it accident or could it, by any chance, be design. On the way back to Paddington, Anthony Bathurst thought matters over very carefully. There were many features of the case that he, an advocate of Frant's innocence, disliked exceedingly. The note that he had just been seeking was only one of many. Where were the others, or, at all events, some of them? Murray's manner was strange, and the dead man, Pearson, after all might have—his thoughts raced off at a tangent. Knowles's story of the three thuds worried him considerably. It held just a hint of the uncanny. After sustained consideration, his theory of the curtains satisfied him, he concluded, and that granted, hope remained extant while life survived. From Paddington, he drove straight to New Scotland Yard and asked to see the Commissioner. Sir Austin Kemble received him with considerable fussiness. "Well, my boy, and what is it this time? Been checking up some of Staples's data—eh?"

Anthony took a chair on the right of the Commissioner. "Took a look at that Reading information of his, sir. Been down there to-day. But it's no good. Luck's dead out this journey. It's been running against me all through the case. Everything's off the edge and nothing on the meat. It's like that sometimes, you know."

The Commissioner chuckled at Bathurst's description. "But it levels up, Bathurst. It levels up in the long run. That's why I hardly ever advocate it as a calculating factor. The only thing is—we *remember* our bad luck and make it a subject of our future conversation. But not our *good* fortune, Bathurst. Oh no, we forget that. It's the short heads *against* us that form part of our reminiscences—not those in our favour. They're relegated to oblivion. When you've heard a bit more news that I've got for you—you'll feel much more inclined to agree with me."

Bathurst smiled tolerantly. "I'm listening, sir. Carry on."

Sir Austin pulled a box file towards him. "There's more here, from Staples. On your work, I mean. Came in early this afternoon. Five more of your blessed notes have been run to earth. But, personally, I don't think much of 'em. However, look at 'em for yourself. There's the report that Staples sent in to me."

Taking the top paper from the file, he pushed it along to Anthony. The first four districts in which the bank branches were situated, seemed to Bathurst to be distinctly unpropitious. They were all West-End and, *per se*, that fact was unattractive, if only for the reason that it failed entirely to fit the half-theory that he had allowed himself to form and to nourish. The names, also, of the people who had paid money in, were considered by him with definite disfavour. The fifth name, however, immediately became docketed in another gallery. It had been supplied from the Canning Town branch of the City and Suburban Bank, and the man who had paid the note in was named Reginald Bimson. The date was about right, too. Against this name was the curt description that Staples had fitted to him. "Small way provision dealer."

Mr. Bathurst tapped the name of Reginald Bimson with his forefinger. "This looks a bit more like it to me, sir. The others, in my opinion, never saw Perry Hammer in their little lives. Canning Town, do you see? Just a little unusual, perhaps, eh? Ah, well, we never know, do we?"

"Going down there to have a look at that one?"

"I am, sir, and I've got a hunch that I shall get on to something that will put up a prolonged 'squeak'. . . . Perhaps the squeak will be so loud and insistent that it will reach the ears of somebody in a high place at New Scotland Yard."

Sir Austin grinned cordially at the pleasantry. "A loud 'squeak', eh, Bathurst? I'm afraid—"

"That it would have to be very loud, eh? That's what you were going to say, isn't it? I quite agree with you, sir. That's why I took the words from your mouth."

The avenue that led Bathurst to the "Blue Tambourine", to Bimson . . . and then to Rose Stubbs, wife of George Alfred Stubbs . . . to the Reading postmark and the date thereon . . . was a straight and moderately easy one. He took hope from each step of the journey down it. He listened to Rose . . . he asked of Rose . . . questions. "After all," he whispered to himself on the way home to his flat, "I'm not done yet. When the 13th of October comes I may have something up my sleeve which Acland may be able to bring down for me. Perhaps. We may, at least, surprise Sir Hubert Kortright."

CHAPTER XI
THE KING AGAINST HILARY DUGDALE FRANT

SIR Hubert Kortright, in his opening speech for the prosecution, the twelve jurors having been accepted by Sir Gervaise Acland and duly sworn, stated that the murdered man, Leonard Pearson, had died in his own house at Perry Hammer on the evening of Wednesday, April 22nd, as the result of violence. It would be the duty of the jury, he continued, to consider at whose hands Pearson had received that violence. At the same time, he would ask the members of the jury to dismiss entirely from their minds, anything that they had already heard or read of the case. He would say no more in reference to a certain discreditable incident that had recently occurred in connection with the daily

Press. Sir Roderick Hope, the celebrated pathologist, would give them the inestimable benefit of his considered judgment, and aver that Pearson had died as the result of a blow at the back of the skull, delivered by a heavy weapon, such as a club of some kind or a knobbed walking-stick. Captain Hilary Frant, the man whom they were about to try, had informed Chief-Inspector MacMorran, of New Scotland Yard, on Thursday, the 23rd of April, that he was nowhere near Perry Hammer on the night in question and in support of that statement, had put forward to the Inspector an alibi that consisted of another statement that he had attended the evening performance at the Whitehall Theatre, London. The prosecution would, however, attempt to prove that Captain Hilary Frant had made an appointment with Pearson, on the evening of the murder, for nine o'clock and had not only made the appointment, but had actually done more. They would attempt to prove that he had kept it. Certain corroboration would be forthcoming from the dead man's own appointment diary and evidence would be called from amongst the staff of servants that had been kept at Perry Hammer, that would attempt to identify the prisoner, as the man who had been heard threatening Pearson in his own room between the hours of nine and ten o'clock. In addition to these facts, there would be further evidence called on behalf of the case for the Crown, which they would hear later. Sir Hubert, at this stage, shifted his bulky body and indulged in his favourite habit of hitching his gown further on to his shoulders.

"I now approach, ladies and gentlemen of the Jury," he said, "that much-vexed question of motive, that we find always operating in cases of this kind. However much misguided people may attempt to argue to the contrary, motive cannot be ignored. It's not necessary, let me tell you, that the Crown should *prove* motive. But in the case under attention, the issue of which will be determined by you, I shall be able to show you what a strong and overpowering motive the prisoner had for the removal of the dead man, Leonard Pearson. It is well known to the agents of the Crown that Pearson moved in circles that might well be described as sordid or even shady. It was believed of him, on excellent foundation," Sir Hubert continued, "that he had even stooped so low as the practice of blackmail. But, even so, conceding the truth of this, he was entitled to a certain amount of protection from the State, and his life was—ahem—as sacred as that of anybody else. It was the proud boast of England, and of Englishmen all the world over, that every one of her sons and daughters, peer and peasant, commoner or courtier, was able to obtain justice. The Prosecution would attempt to show that the accused, Captain Frant, went to Perry Hammer on Wednesday, April 22nd, for the express purpose of recovering certain letters. That whilst there, he quarrelled with Pearson and eventually killed him with blows from a heavy walking-stick. And if," concluded Sir Hubert, "the facts that I have outlined are proved, it will be my duty to ask you, ladies and gentlemen of the jury, for a verdict that Hilary Frant is guilty of the wilful murder of Leonard Pearson."

The eminent counsel for the Crown gave his gown another hitch and resumed his seat.

Mr. Justice Heriot (holding his quill pen between thumb and first finger, and pointing it at the man he addressed): "One moment, please. You alluded, Sir Hubert, to what you called a discreditable occurrence in connection with the daily Press. Before I commence to try the case, I should like further information on that point. Were you referring, may I ask, to the entirely unauthorized statement that appeared in certain London papers on Friday last, that the condition of my health would prevent me from not only going on circuit, but that I had lost my voice so completely that my imminent retirement was inevitable, or were you alluding to that most extraordinary letter that appeared in the Press some little time ago, and was undoubtedly a glaring example of contempt of court?"

Sir Hubert Kortright (rising and bowing): "To the latter, my Lord. If I may say so, the first had never entered my mind. I can only add that I shall be expressing the hope of everybody that your Lordship may continue to—"

Mr. Justice Heriot: "Thank you, Sir Hubert. I understand. Hope—er—from Sir Hubert, is hope indeed. That is all I wanted to know. Thank you."

The case then proceeded, in the normal fashion, with the evidence for the Prosecution. After Amy Talbot had given her evidence with regard to finding Pearson's body, Detective-Sergeant Waterhouse was called, and deposed concerning the entry on the dead man's diary and the cigarette-stubs that he had discovered in the ash-tray on the table. Two of Virginian tobacco and two of Turkish—"Mouraki" brand. He gave more details of his find and of Pearson's tobacco habits, and answered very clearly and intelligently when examined by Sir Hubert Kortright. The cigarette ends ("Exhibits A and B"), were passed up to the jury by the latter, acting upon Mr. Justice Heriot's instructions. Waterhouse was then cross-examined by Sir Gervaise Acland, but the counsel for the defence was unable to shake the detective's testimony to any degree whatever. The witnesses then called were, in order, Murray, Knowles, Dr. Clive, and Sir Roderick Hope. Some sensation was caused in court when the butler, after having told of a telephone call that came through for Pearson just after half-past four, recounted the threat that he had said he heard used to his master about twenty minutes past nine.

Sir Hubert asked him to repeat this threat, word for word. Murray did so, and when Sir Gervaise Acland rose for the cross-examination of this witness, the people in the court, already stirred by the evidence, prepared themselves for a further dose of excitement. The first move surprised them. "Captain Frant," said Acland, addressing the prisoner, "would you mind telling me something, or asking me a question?"

To the utter surprise of the listeners, Captain Frant's response was as follows. Leaning over the rail of the dock, he spoke to his counsel with studied deliberation. "Pearson, you blasted swine, if you aren't careful, I'll smash you as you sit there. The world will be a thundering sight better place when you're in hell."

Murray heard the exact repetition of the words that he had just used, with a look of annoyance and pained surprise. Acland's voice came to him again as though issuing from a cloud high in the heavens. "Are you prepared to swear now, Mr. Murray, that the voice you heard raised in a threatening tone against your master was the prisoner's? Remember, please, that you have had the opportunity and privilege of comparing the exact words that you assert were used."

Hesitation showed clearly in Murray's eyes. Acland pressed for a reply.

"No, sir," responded the butler, at last. "I'm not prepared to swear to it. But I'll say this—there is a strong resemblance in the two voices. I heard one through a closed door, you know."

Acland was inexorable.

"You will not swear to it, however?"

"No, sir."

"The members of the jury will doubtless take note of that fact. Thank you, Mr. Murray."

Acland sat down. The evidence of Knowles, Dr. Clive, and Sir Roderick Hope was both taken and given, smoothly and efficiently. To Frant, in the dock, it seemed to partake of the nature of a relentless procession of accusation. Sir Robert, his father, Maddison, his uncle, Pamela, his sister, and Dick Lanchester, his brother-in-law-to-be, all of whom were present in court, experienced similar thoughts, and when the time came at the end of the day to adjourn until the morrow, the general opinion of those who had heard the proceedings was, that the prisoner wouldn't have a dog's chance after old Heriot had summed up. The rope, they said, was already as good as round Frant's neck. Sir Randall Bowers had also honoured the assizes with his attendance, and with his customary urbanity and hospitality had asked Murray, his old servant, to call on him at the Hotel Sicilian before the trial was over. When, very late in the evening, Pamela Frant was able to obtain a few moments' privacy in her room at the Hotel Sicilian, where her father and she were staying, she turned to Dick Lanchester with a gesture that bordered on both helplessness and hopelessness.

"Dick," she said, "I've got a strong idea buzzing through my brain, that to-morrow's going to be worse even than to-day's been. If it's possible, that is."

He regarded her critically. "How do you mean, Pamela?"

She stared away from him into space. "I mean just this. I feel passably certain, without in the least knowing why I do, that that old fool Kortright has something pretty big and surprising up his sleeve, and it isn't going to come down until the psychological moment."

Lanchester shook his head uneasily. He had seemed particularly uneasy for days. "Don't be unduly pessimistic, my dear. Things are pretty bad, I know. For the Lord's sake don't try to make them any worse by looking for trouble. *Why* do you think so, really? You must have something in your mind to make you talk like that."

Her averted eyes still held the far-away look. "I'm judging the man from his manner. Only that, I admit; but he seems so terribly sure of himself all the time. When he's speaking, and when he's listening, too. Didn't you see it? You *must* have noticed it yourself."

Lanchester replied to her with another question.

"What does your father think of things? Has he opened out at all?"

"He'll be here in a moment or two, Dick. He's gone into the lounge to write a letter. When he comes, ask him yourself."

She stretched herself full length on a divan. "I'm so horribly tired, I can scarcely keep my eyes open. I shall have to use matchsticks in a minute. Here's daddy, I think, coming along now."

Sir Robert entered the room quietly, and closed the door very carefully behind him. Lanchester's greeting was ready and rapid.

"Well, sir," he opened immediately, "what do you think of things as they've gone to-day? Pam here is appallingly pessimistic. Cheer her up, if you can."

Sir Robert shrugged his shoulders.

"It's hard to say, Lanchester. To-day's been the turn of the prosecution. You get their side of the picture all the time pretty well, and as a result, it's inclined to lose its perspective, and assume an inflated importance. Those facts must always be remembered. Wait till the defence has had a say in the matter. That may put a different complexion on things."

Lanchester nodded. "I know what you mean. Pamela's almost given up hope, though. Thinks old Kortright's got something up his sleeve that's going to smash up Acland's case altogether."

Sir Robert walked over and put a comforting arm on his daughter's shoulder.

"Take heart, Pamela girl. Take heart from me, if from nobody else. When you see me in a state of despair, denuded of all my courage, that will be the time for you to give up hope yourself. But not a second before that. Understand?" She nodded. "Then promise me to be brave."

"Where's Uncle Maddison?" she asked.

"Gone back to town," Sir Robert answered. "He had to—he's playing to-night. He did his best to use the understudy, but was afraid to risk it so early in the run. 'Frightened of a "flop",' he said."

"I didn't see him in court," she answered, "but there were so many there, it was difficult to pick people out." She paused before taking hold of her father's arm and pulling him down to her. "What worries me so," she said in an extenuation of the charge that had been levelled against her by her lover, "is that Mr. Bathurst is far from confident. I asked him the question this morning, point-blank. He says that every line of inquiry that opens up to him ends in something like a blank wall. Try as he may, he can get so far—and then no farther! Something happened, he says, the night that Pearson was murdered, that he can guess at, but which he can't possibly prove. Everything seems to have gone wrong ever since. And Hilary stands in the dock—close to the scaffold," she concluded bitterly, "and we, all of us, powerless to help him."

Sir Robert eyed her gravely. "We can, at least, hold our heads up and stand firm, can't we, Pamela?"

She bowed her head, and Lanchester took her hand.

*

The second day of the Crown *versus* Hilary Frant opened with something akin to a sensation as far as the general public was concerned. Sir Hubert Kortright called his first witness: "Stanley Pollard". A tall, long-armed, and loose-limbed youth, whose eyes roamed restlessly round, entered the witness-box. He deposed that whilst walking along Popinhole Lane, the lane that ran along the back of Pearson's house at Perry Hammer, on the evening of the fifth of May, that is to say, thirteen days after the murder, he had noticed something glittering at the bottom of a ditch, fifty yards or so away from the rear of the house. Being naturally curious, he had investigated the matter, and found a silver-mounted walking-stick lying in the ditch (Exhibit F). The initials inscribed on the silver mount were "H.D.F." Sergeant Redvers Brunwin, of the Berkshire Constabulary, followed the youth Pollard into the witness-box, and gave evidence that the stick (Exhibit F) had been brought to him by the previous witness to the police station at Great Perry on the morning of Wednesday, 6th May. Exhibit F was produced in court, and identified by George Alfred Briginshaw, manager of Heath, Mortimer and Co., 27 The Strand, as having been supplied to the prisoner, Hilary Frant, in the November of the previous year. Frederick Clapp, a salesman, attached to the same firm, was called, and was about to give evidence when the learned judge, Mr. Justice Heriot, intervened, and suggested that the witness was not necessary after the previous one. Immediately following Mr. Justice Heriot's intervention, Sir Hubert Kortright rose with a dramatic gesture. "That then, my Lord," he said, "is the case for the Prosecution."

Sir Gervaise Acland was on his feet at once. He spoke very quietly. "My Lord, I call the prisoner."

Sir Gervaise Acland: "Are you Captain Hilary Dugdale Frant?"

"Yes."

"How old are you, Captain Frant?"

"Twenty-seven."

"You are the only son of Sir Robert Frant, the well-known doctor?"

" Yes." Sir Gervaise looked round the court very slowly but very keenly. When he spoke again, he spoke with the utmost deliberation. His delivery was clear and impressive. It seemed to give him control, repose, and a very strong suggestion of reserve. He desired that those who were listening to him should follow him intelligently, and be inspired at the finish of it all with an extreme confidence in him. The confidence, he dared to hope, would dispose them to accept his conclusions.

"Will you, then, be kind enough to tell the Court, in your own way, the story of your actions on the evening of Wednesday, the 22nd of April last?"

It was at this moment, that Sir Hubert Kortright, the counsel for the Prosecution, received his first shock. Hilary Frant spoke softly and easily in response to his counsel's invitation.

"I left the Epsom race meeting somewhere after four o'clock, and when I got well outside the town, I left my car and telephoned from a call-box to the man Leonard Pearson, at Perry Hammer. I spoke to him himself, and made an appointment to see him that evening at nine o'clock at his house. After the telephone conversation, I had some tea, and then drove straight there. In accordance with what he had told me he would do on the 'phone, Pearson admitted me himself, and took me into a room that I should describe as his library. We smoked together and discussed the matter that had brought me down there."

At this stage of the evidence it was seen that Mr. Justice Heriot leant forward in his great chair and eyed the prisoner very carefully, his hands, in the meanwhile, fingering nervously at his stringy looking throat. Frant, unperturbed at the pointed attention that the judge was giving to him, proceeded with exceptional calmness.

"Pearson and I had an unpleasant interview, and although Murray, the butler, was unable yesterday to assert with certainty that I was the man who threatened his master, I can tell him that I *was* the man who used the words that Murray included in his evidence. But that was all. My threats were wordy threats only, and were never translated into deeds. I paid Pearson £1,000 in notes for certain letters that were in his possession, letters that were not his, and to which he had not the slightest legal or moral right. The payment was made to him in notes, chiefly fifties, I forget exactly how many. Pearson put the money on the table at the side of him, and seeing that no possible good could be gained by staying, I cleared out. I didn't wish anybody to know that I had anything to do with a skunk like Pearson—there were others to consider besides me—and seeing that the room where we were, had french-doors that opened out on to the garden, I decided to go out that way, which, I argued to myself, would give me an excellent chance of getting away from the premises—as I believed I had come—unobserved! I picked up my stick, the stick which was produced in court just now, and when I came to the wall at the end of Pearson's garden, which I was forced to climb, I threw the stick over, in advance, as it were. Just as anybody, similarly placed, would have done. Unfortunately, when I landed on the other side, I forgot, in my haste and anxiety to get away from an interview of such unpleasantness, to pick up my stick, and no doubt left it lying there where it had fallen. I did not discover my loss until I had arrived home. That is a full and true account of what I did at Perry Hammer."

Sir Gervaise Acland (examining): "Can you remember, Captain Frant, what time it was that you left Perry Hammer?"

"About a quarter to ten, I think."

"What made you take a stick down there with you, seeing that you travelled by car which you drove yourself? Was it because you wanted to—?"

Mr. Justice Heriot (inhaling the perfume of dark-red roses, in a rose-bowl): "Sir Gervaise, you must not lead here, you know. The witness must answer the question that you have put to him."

The witness: "I wanted to give the impression to the servants, if I were unlucky, and any of them should chance to see me when I was there, that I had *not* come by car. I left my car, you see, some distance from the house, I may say."

Sir Gervaise: "Why was that?"

"As I previously attempted to explain, I did not want to be connected with Pearson in any way. My car, if spotted, might have served to identify me."

Sir Gervaise: "I see. You say that you paid Pearson a thousand pounds in notes, most of which were fifties. From where did you obtain that money?"

"I had won it that afternoon at Epsom. I backed 'Buttered Crumpet', the horse that won the City and Suburban. It belongs to a great friend of mine, Mr. Richard Lanchester. He had told me that it had a great chance, and had advised me and all his intimate friends to back it. I did, and won a thousand pounds."

Sir Gervaise: "Did you, at any time, desire the death of Leonard Pearson?"

"In the sense that you mean—never! He wasn't worth it."

"Did you—and you are on your oath remember, Captain Frant—cause any bodily harm whatever to Leonard Pearson?"

"None! I never raised as much as a finger towards him. When I left the apartment, Pearson was sitting at his table, with his back towards me, looking at the wad of notes that I had just paid over to him. I swear it!"

"Thank you, Captain Frant. That will do."

Sir Hubert Kortright, rising to cross-examine, realized with a sense of acute discomfort, that he had very little upon which *to* cross-examine. *Captain Frant's admissions were manifold.* His evidence was almost all admission. With the exception, perhaps, of one direction. He would attack, therefore, on that line—

"These—er letters—that you state that you purchased from Leonard Pearson at the cost of, you say—what was it?—oh, yes, £1,000—in—er—*notes*—fifties preponderating. Whose letters were they?"

Frant stiffened in the dock. "I don't quite understand what you mean. Do you mean to whom did they belong? Or do you mean who had originally written them?"

Sir Hubert (seeing his two chances, where he had only seen one when he rose): "Er—both. Yes—yes. Both."

"I decline to answer." Frant's reply was curt and crisp.

Mr. Justice Heriot (sternly): "You are entitled, of course, to please yourself. But I would advise you that it would be very much in your own interest to reply to the eminent counsel's question."

"I'm sorry, my Lord, but I cannot alter my previous answer." Captain Frant perceptibly shrugged his shoulders. The Judge interjected a remark, but his voice was hoarse, and broke suddenly in his throat; the result was that his statement was inaudible.

Sir Hubert Kortright: "Why was it that in your first statement to Chief Inspector MacMorran, when he called upon you at your father's house, you concocted a story of your movements on the evening of the murder that you now admit to be false—an absolute tissue of lies? Why this remarkable change of front? What has happened since, to make you change your mind?"

"At that time, I did not wish to be connected with the affair at all. I was absolutely innocent—and did not expect—did not know rather—that the police knew of my visit to Pearson that evening, with any certainty. I will be perfectly frank, Sir Hubert: I tried to bluff them. After all, I was innocent of the main charge—that's really all that matters to me."

"Really? You tried to bluff them. Oh! I see—and it wasn't until you knew that your bluff was called that you became so enamoured of the truth. What might be described as a conversion *de convenance*, eh?"

Captain Frant shrugged his shoulders and remained silent. Sir Hubert Kortright proceeded to follow up immediately the advantage that he had gained. "I put it to you, Captain Frant, that you murdered Leonard Pearson for the possession of those letters, the ownership of which, you refuse to divulge." He drew his body back, and then thrust it forward again. "I put it to you that your payment of £1,000 to Pearson is pure imagination on your part. Fiction, shall we say? A different sort of your stock-in-trade—bluff! Like that visit to the theatre that figured so prominently in your first statement to Chief Inspector MacMorran."

Captain Frant flushed to the roots of his hair, but this was the only indication that he gave that Sir Hubert's thrust had gone home.

"You are entirely wrong in your implication," he replied easily. "When I say I handed that money to Pearson, I am telling the truth. And I never raised a hand against him. I swear it."

Sir Hubert looked at the jury, raised his hands in an eloquent gesture that signified the hopelessness of the answer that had been given, and sat down, a picture of martyred resignation. Acland then called Joseph John Skerritt. A thick-set man, with closely-cropped red hair, blue eyes, and cheerful sun-burned clean-shaven face, with prominent chin, entered the witness-box. He wore a blue serge suit, double-breasted, and looked round the Court with an inquiring sort of look that bordered closely upon the engagingly confidential. He said that he was a turf accountant. More than one member of the jury frowned at the statement. It may be said, though, that the frowns were occasioned probably by the sting of individual reminiscence rather than by any personal dislike the members of the jury felt for the man in the witness-box. It seemed to them, perhaps, that they were regarding a natural enemy of the human race. J.J. Skerritt, oblivious to this visible enmity, proceeded under Acland's skilful examination, to give his evidence. He informed the Court aptly that, in accordance with his custom of many years' standing, he had "stood up" in Tattersalls at the Epsom Spring Meeting, held in April last, and on the Wednesday, the third day of the meeting, "City and Sub." day, Captain Frant had backed Mr. Lanchester's horse "Buttered Crumpet" with him, together with other horses that ran in the earlier events on the card. He had laid Captain Frant eights and twos—£400 to win and £100 for a shop against two fifties. The horse had won, and he had paid over to Captain Frant immediately the "all right" had been called.

Mr. Justice Heriot (as severely as his voice would allow him): "What do you mean by the expressions 'a shop' and the 'all right'?" Skerritt, an amazed look on his face, made the necessary explanations to the learned judge. Sir Hubert Kortright intimated, in a tone of affected nonchalance that conveyed supreme contempt for the value and antecedents of the evidence, that he had no desire to avail himself of his right of cross-examination. Skerritt then left the box, and was followed by three other professional colleagues who told similar stories to that which he had told.

"That, my Lord," said Sir Gervaise Acland, "is the evidence for the defence."

The friends of Hilary Frant shuddered at its meagreness, and at its general likeness to the servant's baby. Anthony Bathurst, in particular, was satisfied that he himself was face to face with a case that seemed, almost certainly, to spell ignominious failure for him. He realized that he must, of necessity, if he wished to give Pamela Frant the full service of his promise to her, take the advice of Simon called Peter, and "gird up the loins of his mind". He heard Sir Hubert Kortright open, and bring to a conclusion, the closing speech for the Crown. He saw the K.C. in question, resume his seat again, and wrap round himself as he did so, a mantle of corpulent complacency. Then he heard Sir Gervaise Acland open the speech for the defence. Considering the materials at his disposal, Acland made what was undoubtedly a masterly effort. A triumph of forensic skill, studded with agile improvisation. Calling repeated attention to Frant's habitual integrity, he finished with an impassioned plea for a verdict of "not guilty". Anthony Bathurst fixed his eyes on Mr. Justice Heriot. Very slowly and very deliberately, that gentleman commenced his charge to the jury. There was a fascination about the whole thing that caught Bathurst and held him. And none listened more attentively than Sir Randall Bowers to the fateful words of Mr. Justice Heriot.

Chapter XII
THE VERDICT

Mr. Justice Heriot's face was a study in impassivity.

"Ladies and gentlemen of the Jury," he opened, "you have already been warned by the learned counsel on both sides as to the manner in which you should contemplate the case that you have been called upon to try. And there is no need, I am sure, for me to remind you of the solemn oath which you have one and all taken, to return a true and faithful verdict according to the evidence. That is to say, upon the evidence which has been presented to you in this Court by the witnesses whom you have heard and, moreover, seen. The prisoner, Captain Hilary Dugdale Frant, has been arraigned for the murder of Leonard Pearson. The learned counsel for the defence, who has pleaded the case for his client, with his usual skill and eloquence, has brought evidence for you to hear, to which you must give your very careful and discriminating consideration. Of its value and of its direct bearing on the case, you alone are the assessors. It will be for you, and you alone, to say whether the evidence of the man Skerritt and of those other witnesses who succeeded him, corroborated to any reasonable extent the statement which the prisoner had made during the course of his own evidence, as to his movements and actions in Pearson's house at Perry Hammer on the evening of the murder. You will judge, upon the facts, whether there are any possible grounds upon which you could arrive at the conclusion of the Prosecution that it was vitally necessary for Captain Frant to kill this man in his own room in order to obtain possession of certain documentary evidence from him. Evidence in the form of letters that may have threatened or incriminated either the prisoner himself or even a third person. You will notice in regard thereto, that the Prosecution has made mention of no actual person who was concerned in the matter of these letters. Neither has the defence. But the defence have, on the other hand, in every other direction, adopted a policy of meticulous frankness. They have almost approached the confines of quixotism. Now, it is a part of my duty—and a part which I cannot possibly attempt to ignore, even if I wished to—to point out to you very clearly and very frankly, that Sir Hubert Kortright, the eminent counsel in charge of the case for the Crown, has . . ."

Mr. Justice Heriot paused to give his throat a much-needed rest, and sipped sparingly from a glass of water that had been placed in front of him. When he proceeded, Anthony Bath-urst found himself listening to his Lordship with feelings that bordered upon incredulous amazement. After a time, he leant forward towards the well of the court and watched the faces of the two forensic antagonists, Sir Hubert Kortright and Sir Gervaise Acland. It quickly became evident to him, as he watched, that they, too, were surprised and astounded at the unlooked-for turn that the learned judge was giving to his summing-up. Truly a remarkable case, all the way through, thought Mr. Bathurst! A tragedy of errors on the part of Frant, the extraordinary contri-bution penned by Sir Randall Bowers, the chaotic finality of his own clue at the Blue Tambourine Inn, at Reading, and now, as a culminating completion, this definitely partisan charge to the jury of Mr. Justice Heriot. Had it not been for Rose Stubbs . . . The minutes ticked by; a quarter of an hour became half an hour. Anthony sought the faces of Pamela and Sir Robert. The former was leaning forward with her lips slightly parted. Sir Robert's face held a strained emotional expression. He had aged considerably during the last week. Hilary Frant himself sat on a chair in the dock, easily and comfortably, with his legs outstretched and his hands thrust deeply into the pockets of his trousers. The half-hour passed into three-quarters. Mr. Justice Heriot's charge was nearing completion. His final words floated into Anthony's ears:

"In conclusion, I leave you to determine whether the evidence in the case satisfies you, beyond any reasonable doubt, that the prisoner took the life of the deceased man under circumstances which can only amount to the crime of murder. If you have a doubt, the scintilla of a doubt even, your decision must be cast in the prisoner's favour. Please do not forget that. I will ask you now to retire and perform the duty which has been thrown in your way by the exigencies of the law. That duty is to find a true verdict according to the weight of evidence and regard-less of what the consequences may prove to be. You have heard my remarks. You have listened with exemplary patience. They should be in the nature of definite assistance to you, and help you to record a true and proper verdict, the future responsibility of which is in other hands than yours. Ladies and gentlemen, you will now retire and consider your verdict! You may take, if you choose to, the various exhibits with you. If there should be anything else that you require, please let me know, and I will see that you are immediately furnished with it." The voice of Mr. Justice Heriot was by now hoarse and strained, and Sir Robert Frant, recognizing the symptoms, from the eyrie of his own personal and particular eminence, turned, and whispered something to Pamela at his side. The members of the jury filed slowly from their places, and as they did so, a warder stepped forward and touched Hilary Frant on the shoulder.

The jury were absent for an hour and twenty-five minutes, and Bathurst drew from the length of their absence the interpretation that the summing-up of Mr. Justice Heriot had fallen on rich soil and borne considerable fruit. At length, there were the usual signs that the jury were on the point of return. As they came back, one by one, Bathurst attempted, as many have done before him, to anticipate the verdict that was about to be pronounced, by carefully scanning the various faces of the people who held the decision. Mr. Justice Heriot entered. He was accompanied by his chaplain and the Clerk of Assize. Bathurst, with an exquisite sense of shock, saw the square of black silk, and once again the fascination of the drama gripped and dominated him. There was a hushed and expectant silence when the Clerk rose and addressed the members of the jury.

The Clerk of Assize: "Ladies and gentlemen of the jury. Are you agreed upon your verdict?"

The Foreman of the Jury (in a loud voice): "We are."

The Clerk of Assize: "Do you find the prisoner at the bar, Hilary Dugdale Frant, guilty or not guilty?"

The Foreman of the Jury: "Not guilty."

There was a pronounced stir in the court as the fateful words left the foreman's lips, and an usher's voice rang through it commandingly, enjoining silence on the people within it. Mr. Justice Heriot leant forward on the ledge in front of him and spoke to Hilary Frant. Frant squared his shoulders in a manner that suggested to Anthony Bathurst that he had failed to hear the foreman's announcement correctly and was still in doubt as to what the verdict had been. Mr. Justice Heriot's opening words, however, quickly reassured him, and his grateful eyes flickered upwards to catch those of his father and sister.

"Hilary Dugdale Frant," said the judge dramatically, "the jury have arrived at a very proper conclusion upon the whole of the evidence which has been laid before them. They have arrived at that conclusion, after what I am absolutely certain, has been a very pertinent and searching inquiry on their part into that evidence. You, Hilary Dugdale Frant, are acquitted and discharged." He turned to the jury. "Ladies and gentlemen, you have been called upon by law to perform an unpleasant and onerous duty at great inconvenience, no doubt, to many of you. If you find the exemption desirable, I will recommend that you be not summoned again to serve in this capacity of citizenship for a period of seven years. Ladies and gentlemen, you are now discharged."

When the court had emptied of most of its occupants, Bathurst, who had waited behind, went to Frant and shook him warmly by the hand. Frant returned the salutation, joyfully vigorous.

"Congratulations, Frant," said Anthony. "I can't tell you how very glad I am."

"And surprised?" queried Hilary Frant.

Bathurst parried the question. "Yes—and no," he replied.

Pamela caught him by the arm with an exclamation of gratitude. "I can never thank you enough, Mr. Bathurst," she cried. "I am certain that it was your cleverness in making Sir Gervaise Acland centralize on that money point that turned the scale in Hilary's favour."

Anthony Bathurst shook his head with a very definite emphasis. "It's extremely generous of you, Miss Frant, to ascribe it to my efforts, but, quite frankly, I must confess that I accomplished little or nothing. All my work ended in nothingness."

Sir Robert Frant rubbed the edge of his jaw.

"I'm satisfied that you did all you could, Bathurst, and no man living can do more. After all, Hilary's been acquitted. That's all with which I'm concerned, I'm afraid. What's it matter how success came, as long as it did come?"

"That's perfectly true, Sir Robert. All the same, 'palmam qui meruit ferat'. I certainly can't claim a single bouquet." Bathurst smiled as he declined the honours. Hilary Frant took a hand.

"You had a devilishly hard job, Bathurst; I realized the truth of that when you came down to see me in prison. There's no occasion at all for you to reproach yourself."

Bathurst's smile broadened at Frant's loyal support. "Thank you, Captain Frant. You are magnanimous to me in my moment of comparative failure."

"Some failures, Bathurst, transcend success. You must reconcile yourself to the fact that the murderer of Leonard Pearson will remain undiscovered."

Anthony Bathurst looked Hilary Frant straight between the eyes, and both Sir Robert and his daughter sensed the condition of "atmosphere" between them. There was a long period of silence.

"On the contrary, Captain Frant," replied Bathurst, "the name of the person who killed Pearson is now known to me. It has been for some days, in fact." He paused and nobody broke the quietude that followed. Bathurst proceeded. "At the same time, however, I doubt whether I shall ever bring that person to justice. Unless the unexpected has happened, I never shall, now."

Pamela Frant intervened eagerly. "Why not, Mr. Bathurst?"

Anthony's grey eyes were steady and resolute.

"Because, Miss Frant, I'm sorely afraid that I, and the wheels of justice, too, have been caught in the fell clutch of circumstance. A clutch from which, in this instance, I fear that there is no escape. Some things that are done can never be undone, you see."

Twenty-four hours later, at about seventeen minutes past six in the evening, a woman returning home from her daily work of pulling celery in an adjoining field, was astonished to find a large cabin-trunk hard against the hedge that skirts the narrow road between the villages of Langley Broom and Langley Marish. Although the evening was a dark one, with rain threatening, she stopped for closer inspection. Attempting to lift it, she found it astonishingly heavy, and its disproportionate heaviness only pointed her natural curiosity. Abandoning her intention of raising the trunk, she decided on another method. After a struggle, she succeeded in prising open the lid. A man's dead body in startling costume was revealed therein to her untutored eyes, and Harriet Polly ran shrieking to the nearest police station. The body, in the robes of Justice, and with the traditional black cap neatly folded across its dead face, was identified before midnight as that of the renowned Mr. Justice Heriot. It was identified as soon as was humanly possible, by the eminent doctor whose visiting-card was discovered resting within the folds of the late judge's scarlet robes. Dr. Barrow-South!

CHAPTER XIII
CHLOROFORM

DR. BARROW-South could give a reasonable, but not an adequate, explanation as to why his personal card should have been found where it had been. He could only suggest, when interrogated, that the murderer, when he had packed Heriot's body into the trunk, had disturbed the card from one of the pockets of the dead man's clothes and that it had fallen and remained between the folds of his robes. Heriot had been a patient of his, he said. Yes—very recently. He would explain further. Not only had been, but actually *was* at the time of his death. Which, he averred, after making an autopsy, was due to poison. The unhappy judge had had administered to him a powerful dose of chloroform. There was no possible doubt as to that, said Dr. Barrow-South. The Sergeant of Police operating at Langley Broom, whom Harriet Polly had aroused from a duty of semi-slumber some hours previously, took the doctor's advice. He immediately placed himself in communication with

Scotland Yard. The hour was late, but "Victoria 7000" pays no attention to that. Some little time after the call was put through, MacMorran listened carefully to what an underling had to say to him.

"Old Heriot, of all people, eh," he remarked. "Whoever would have thought it?"

He was soon in touch with the Commissioner, Sir Austin Kemble. "Go down to this outlandish place yourself, MacMorran," declared the latter. "You'll find somebody having a look round whom you've met before. At least, I'll bet on that, pretty confidently."

MacMorran, lacking comprehension, looked askance at the Commissioner. The latter embarked upon an explanation.

"An old acquaintance of yours, Anthony Bathurst, I mean. He's been on your Perry Hammer case."

MacMorran nodded semi-humorously. "I know, sir. But I don't quite see, all the same, what—"

Sir Austin interrupted him impatiently. "Heriot took the Frant trial, didn't he? Goodness gracious, where are your wits, MacMorran?"

Bewilderment stayed with the Chief Inspector. Observing this condition, Sir Austin proceeded airily: "Bathurst, situated as he is, is bound to be attracted by a new and sensational development like this latest business. Especially when we consider that young Frant got an acquittal. I'm not blaming you for that, MacMorran. Old Heriot didn't hand many out, you know, during the entire length of his judicial career. This is a sequel that can be described in one word only. It's positively amazing." He went on to echo MacMorran's recent sentiment: "Who could ever have foreseen that Heriot would come to an end like this?"

MacMorran's car brought him to Langley Broom shortly before one o'clock. The trunk, after he had taken a look at the lane in which it had been found, was the next thing to occupy his attention. It was the biggest of the kind that he had ever come across, he thought. The local sergeant noted the look of satisfaction that came into the eyes of the man from Scotland Yard.

"Getting on to something, Inspector?" he asked encouragingly.

"This trunk shouldn't be too difficult to trace, Smith," returned MacMorran. "For one thing, it's very distinctive, and better still, for another, it's brand new. Ought to tell us a lot, oughtn't it?" He looked it over carefully. Then he turned to Dr. Barrow-South, who was sitting at the small wooden table in Sergeant Smith's seat. "Chloroform, you say, eh, Doctor? How long's he been dead? Can you put it down for me at all accurately?"

"He was an old man, Inspector. I don't know that I could say within—" The doctor stopped, went over to the body and felt it carefully. "Anything, I should say, from two to three days. Still, we ought to be able to gauge it pretty closely. Let's see, when did the Frant trial end?"

MacMorran thought. "In the late afternoon of the day before yesterday."

"Yes, I thought that was about it. I should say, then, MacMorran, that the old chap must have been killed almost immediately after he left the court. Within an hour or so, most certainly."

MacMorran betrayed signs of more satisfaction. "That ought to help us, too, Doctor. Considerably. Sergeant Smith, what else was in this trunk?"

"Nothing else, sir. The body, in these clothes and robes, that you see here, and this gentleman's professional card. Nothing else at all, sir."

MacMorran's habitual frown reasserted itself.

Before he could say anything, however, the sergeant hastened to correct himself. "Begging your pardon, Inspector, for a mistake that I've made. There was one other thing in the trunk that I forgot to mention. The black cap. The very identical. Here—look!"

Smith handed over the famous black square of silk. MacMorran held it, and stared at it in complete incredulity. "Good God," he whispered, "what's the big idea, man? What were they doing—eh? There's more than one in this, I'll swear. Is it revenge of some kind? A dose of the old man's own medicine, do you think—or—?"

The problem mastered him. He subsided into silence. Smith commenced the exploitation of a theory, but after the first few words MacMorran cut him short.

"I'm going on to Reading," he said, "—now, sergeant—at once. I must find out what happened after the Frant trial was over. Where the old judge stayed during the trial, and so on, and who came in contact with him during his stay in Reading. Also, there's another thing I must see to. I want a photograph of that damned trunk in every London paper. In the first edition, if that's possible. If that brings us anything tangible, as it should, by all the laws of probability, we shall start moving. Good night, doctor. Good night, sergeant. Sorry—I mean good morning."

MacMorran carried out his intentions and found hospitable sanctuary at Waring's Commercial Hotel. Although his hour of retirement had been so late, breakfast brought him down at the usual time. As he removed the cover from the inevitable dish of bacon-and-eggs that a neat-handed Phyllis placed before him, his mind was far distant from the contemplation of savoury meats and country messes. He bethought himself of his last conversation with Sir Austin Kemble at Scotland Yard. He saw Justice Heriot's scarlet robes as they had lain on the table in front of him some few hours previously at Langley Broom; he conjured up also that bizarre harbinger of man's imperfect justice—the black cap. He chuckled to himself as the mirror of imagination caught the light and illumined his thoughts.

"Sir Austin was right," he decided mentally. "I'll give him his due—" The sight of that black cap folded across the dead man's face would have been the last straw for Mr. Bathurst. He would never have been able to resist the intrigue of a touch like that." The Inspector emitted a second chuckle as the tang of an idea came more closely to his senses. As he did so a light tap sounded on the door of the room. Without looking up, and actually scarcely heeding, MacMorran called to it in response. "Come in." The maid entered. Somewhat eagerly, he thought. Evidently she had news of sorts to impart. "A gentleman to see you, sir," she said, almost ecstatically, "a Mr. Anthony Bathurst."

CHAPTER XIV
NEGATIVE EVIDENCE

ANTHONY Bathurst, on the maid's heels, entered to the greeting of a dour smile from the Inspector.

"Good morning, MacMorran. Say you're pleased to see me. Even if you aren't, you know. Say it with bacon. May I sit down?"

MacMorran's smile broadened. "Good morning, sir. Sit down, of course. Over there. You don't mind me going on feeding, do you? As to being pleased to see you, I'm not saying anything about that. If you want the truth—"

"Always," murmured Mr. Bathurst. "Count me, as ever, with the faithful seekers."

MacMorran continued imperturbably. "I was expecting you."

"No! May I ask why?"

"Well, Mr. Bathurst, the Commissioner predicted as much to me before I came down here. Saw a move ahead. It seems he was right."

Anthony Bathurst at once showed signs of interest. "Oh, he did, did he? What was his reason, MacMorran? Did he tell you? I'd be rather interested to know."

MacMorran finessed somewhat awkwardly with a fried egg. "Said you were in the Reading district on the Frant case, Mr. Bathurst, and would dash into this new affair like a common or garden terrier after a piece of liver."

The two men grinned amicably at each other. "MacMorran, you positively humiliate me. You might have given me the rank of Bedlington. Much more imposing, you know. Still, we'll be magnanimous and overlook it, considering all the circumstances." He laid his hat and stick on a couch that was placed against the wall. "MacMorran, your duty is obvious. It stretches out before you like a white ribbon of road lacing a green cliff. Also, I'm perfectly sure that it will commend itself to you intensely. Inasmuch as Sir Austin indicated my presence here to you, I'm sure he intended you to put me in possession of all the facts. All the information that I have at the moment I owe to the enterprise and—er—imagination of the *Morning Message*. I breakfasted before you, you see."

The Inspector nodded with grim appreciation. "I've seen the *Message*. And the *Daily Bugle*. What one of 'em hasn't thought of, the other has. Like a man's wife and his mother-in-law. Mine." MacMorran pushed his plate aside and patted his pocket affectionately for his tobacco-pouch. "I know it will be no earthly good endeavouring to stall you off. The real facts up to the moment, Mr. Bathurst, are these."

The Inspector settled down in his chair and told the story of the find of Harriet Polly in the side road between Langley Broom and Langley Marish.

"A comparatively new trunk, you say, MacMorran?"

"More than that. Brand new, I should say, Mr. Bathurst. If my judgment's worth anything."

"Good Lord. Go on, Inspector."

MacMorran continued until he came to the details of the sinister contents of the trunk. Bathurst pulled his chair an inch or so nearer.

"What did you say, MacMorran? The black cap itself?"

"The black cap itself, Mr. Bathurst! No more and no less. Folded, and laid across the old judge's face."

Bathurst rubbed his hands. "A touch after my own heart, Inspector. And Heriot had been chloroformed, you say?"

"Yes, sir. Dr. Barrow-South was sent for, and motored down to Langley Broom. Got there a couple of hours before I did. He said there was no doubt about it."

Bathurst frowned. "Barrow-South? Why Barrow-South? What made them send for him? Flying high, weren't they? Wasn't there any local man who could have—?"

"I was going to tell you, but you switched me off. Dr. Barrow-South's visiting-card was found in the trunk. The sergeant at Langley Broom told me that it fluttered from the folds of the dead judge's robes when the body had been first lifted from the trunk."

"H'm! Interesting point number three. What explanation did our friend, the eminent throat specialist, give, in respect of the presence of his visiting-card? Did you hear it?"

"Naturally. It was one of my first questions to him when I got down there. His explanation is this. Heriot had been to him professionally. The old man had had throat trouble recently, as you know, and he consulted Barrow-South about it. Was actually still under the doctor's care, as you might say. There was a hint of something of the kind in the Press, if you remember, just before the opening of the Frant trial. Heriot referred to it himself. The doctor's suggestion—and you will admit that it's quite a reasonable one—is that his card must have been retained by Heriot, and fallen into his robes from one of the pockets of the other clothes that he had been wearing."

Bathurst thought hard for a moment. "Tell me this, if you will. What have you done, MacMorran, since you left the police-station at Langley Broom?"

"Slept the sleep of the just, and eaten the breakfast of the hearty."

"I'll remind you that the adjectives are your own, MacMorran, but I'll accept them."

"That's not like you, Mr. Bathurst. Not a bit like you. To accept a statement so easily, I mean."

Bathurst rubbed his hands. For the second time that morning. "Any car tracks in the lane?"

"None." MacMorran was laconic.

"This trunk, MacMorran. Couldn't we—?"

"We could, Mr. Bathurst, and what's more, I have done. There'll be photographs of it in the Press by this time. I'll wager that the bulk of London's already looking at it. If not, it will be, in an hour or so. They know where to find me. Any information that comes through, will be sent on to me immediately. That's been arranged. I'm thinking that trunk's going to help us a lot, Mr. Bathurst. What do you think yourself?"

It was a matter of seconds before Bathurst replied, and his answer surprised his questioner. "On the whole, I'm disposed to disagree with you, Inspector. Without having seen the actual article, that is."

MacMorran knitted his brows and regarded his pipe doubtfully. It was clear that he was surprised.

"What are your reasons for that statement, Mr. Bathurst?"

"It's too good, Inspector. Too juicy. Too much like ripe and luscious fruit ready to fall from the tree into our greedy mouths. In fact, quite candidly, MacMorran, the more I see of this case, the less I like it. All the roads that branch out from it seem to lead nowhere, and I've explored a few, I can tell you."

MacMorran queried his choice of words. "The *more* you see of the case, Mr. Bathurst?"

"Yes, MacMorran. The more I see of the case all through. The murder of Pearson, the trial of Frant, and now this last astounding development, the murder of Mr. Justice Heriot."

The Inspector drew in his breath. "You think they're all connected, then?"

"They *must* be, MacMorran. In some way, dark though it may be. All the workings of my intelligence lead me to that inevitable conclusion. But how, man, how? That's the question you and I have to solve. Either individually or between us."

"Aye—and I'd be giving a lot to be able to solve it. I was relying a lot on that trunk, too."

"Don't lose heart over that. I've taken a leap in the dark, and I may be proved wrong."

A couple of hours later, when Bathurst and MacMorran were on the point of leaving Waring's Commercial Hotel for the Hotel Sicilian, where it was presumed Mr. Justice Heriot had stayed during the Frant trial, the Inspector received a message which delayed their departure. The same maid who had heralded Mr. Bathurst's appearance, brought the news that MacMorran's presence was desired by a gentleman who called himself Mr. Victor Price, and who would be found waiting in the smoke-room. Bathurst accompanied the Inspector down there. A young man, well-groomed and smartly-dressed, came forward rather impetuously, as the two of them entered.

"Inspector MacMorran," he inquired, "of Scotland Yard?" His eyes roamed from one to the other. "I'll introduce myself. My name's Price," he said. "I'm employed by Messrs. H.J. Orridge, Debenham & Co., Leather Manufacturers, of Twine-maker Street, London. I'm here, as you may guess, now you've heard from where I come, over the trunk that is figuring in the Heriot case. The one that's in the later morning editions—I mean the photograph of it." He smiled as he corrected himself.

The Inspector warmed to him. "The very man I want to see more than anybody; and you're here even quicker than I had anticipated. They've done well. Well, what have you got to tell me?"

Price leant forward eagerly in his chair. "When my governor saw the photograph in the paper this morning, and your name below it, he told me to come down here at once to see you. I presume you're trying to trace the original of that trunk, aren't you, Mr. Inspector?"

"I am that," replied MacMorran.

"I thought so. Well, I'm the man you want. I delivered the goods. I sold that trunk, I'm certain as a man can be, on the afternoon of Thursday, the eighth of October. There isn't a great sale for that kind, they're bigger than the ordinary. This is the biggest made size but one."

"Wait a minute, Mr. Price." MacMorran extended a semi-protesting hand. "How can you be absolutely sure that you're talking about the same one? I want to be absolutely sure of my ground, you know. That sort of big cabin-trunk's much the same all the world over, and one of 'em looks very like another. You couldn't gauge the exact size from the Press photograph. How can you be absolutely sure, Mr. Price?"

Price's eagerness to justify himself had almost launched him into an interruption of the Inspector's statement. His good manners, however, asserted themselves sufficiently for him to allow the sentence to be finished. When this happened, his face beamed with the peculiar satisfaction that often goes hand in hand with the possession of knowledge that is select and secret.

"Listen, Inspector. I'm not going by appearance or from experience of the trade, or from anything like that. Although I'm ready to assert that the evidence from them is satisfactory enough. I'm going from something that I *know*, that's vastly more important than any of the things I mentioned. Something you can't get away from. Supposing I told you the name of the person who bought that trunk from me? Will that be sufficient proof of identification for you?"

Anthony Bathurst could almost hear the Inspector holding his breath.

"It will that, Mr. Price. Out with it. Who was it?"

Price toyed, however, with his supreme moment of triumph. He tapped the cigarette that he had just taken from its case, on the lid of that case, with elaborate and aggravating nonchalance. "The name of my customer, Inspector MacMorran, was Mr. Justice Heriot. Mr. Justice Heriot himself."

CHAPTER XV
POSITIVE EVIDENCE

"MR. JUSTICE Heriot—eh?" echoed MacMorran. "Absolutely sure of it, Price?"

The young man nodded with decisive confidence,

"Absolutely, Inspector."

"How?" MacMorran assumed an expression of intense sagacity.

"He gave his name to me, and not only that, I knew him from his personal appearance. I've seen his photograph too often in the papers and illustrateds, not to know him when I saw him."

"You must have great intelligence, then, Mr. Price," observed Anthony Bathurst, cynically, "or else be congratulated on your choice of literature. The last photograph that I happened to see of myself in the daily Press was actually a picture of a prominent leader of the Salvation Army. The Editor apologized to me and explained the *faux pas* by saying that a junior clerk had made a mistake in indexing. I accepted the apology, but the Salvationist, I believe, was absolutely furious. He is still considering bringing a libel suit, I understand—defamation of character, or something of the sort."

Price shut his eyes to the cynicism, and shook his head. "You couldn't mistake Heriot," he declared stubbornly, "his face was so extraordinarily distinctive."

"He wasn't a regular customer at your place, I suppose?"

"No, sir. Not to my knowledge, that is. I could find that out for you, of course."

"Was this trunk sent to his house?"

"No, sir. He took it away with him. In his car."

"Did you have any conversation with him beyond the ordinary? Try to remember *anything*—the most trivial point possibly—we can't tell at this juncture how important it may ultimately prove to be."

Price furrowed his brows as he attempted to revive the incidents of the past. Neither of his companions, with the knowledge of experience, disturbed him by interruption.

"I think," he stated at length, "that beyond questions of price and quality of the article, all he said to me, was that he wanted a new trunk for the next time he went on circuit. I think he mentioned the Oxford circuit, which he said was to take place very soon.

"Yes, that's true," continued Price, with more certainty, as the details of his reminiscences returned to him, "I do remember that, now. He said that he had been in possession of an old one for several years, and that at last it had worn out beyond the possibility of repair."

MacMorran assimilated the statement, and looked across at Anthony Bathurst. "Do you want to ask this young man any more questions?"

"I don't think so, Inspector. He's given me something to think over, though. We can always find you at Twinemaker Street, Mr. Price, I suppose?"

"Weekdays, nine till six. Saturdays, nine till one," rejoined Price promptly.

"Then I don't think we need detain you any longer. Many thanks for your information."

Anthony Bathurst closed the door behind the retreating figure of Price, and turned to MacMorran with raised eyebrows. "How now, Inspector?" MacMorran rubbed his lips. "I'm sorry if I appear to be saying, 'I told you so,' MacMorran," remarked

Mr. Bathurst softly, "but I was sorely afraid that that new trunk of yours 'protested too much'."

The Inspector grunted non-committally. Bathurst waited for coherent expression. It came at last.

"This murderer interests me," declared MacMorran, "whoever he is. I'm saying deliberately that he's got the touch of the artist. First the black cap, and then to put poor old Heriot into his own trunk. I'm not denying that we're up against something that's a bit out of the common."

"In a way I agree with you—and yet—"

"And yet—what?"

"Well, it's hard to express, perhaps, but there's usually something that's common to the mind of all murderers. I'll call it, for want of a better term, a psychological vanity. That's the point I always think of, and take comfort from, when my cases seem impenetrably black."

MacMorran grunted and put on his hat. "You're taking me out of my depth, Mr. Bathurst, and I'll not attempt to follow you. At the same time, I've no objection to your following me. Come on."

"To—?"

"To the Hotel Sicilian, where we were bound for, when that fellow Price blew in."

The Hotel Sicilian is, perhaps, the most modern and most exclusive of the hotels in that district of Berkshire. Occupying a site that up to twenty years ago was made up of what the valuation lists describe as cottage property, it attracts a good many visitors who are called upon, by business or pleasure, to visit that part of the country. MacMorran's card worked wonders. It brought almost immediate audience of the manager, Mr. Ferrari, and he—a trifle flustered—invited the Inspector and Anthony Bathurst into his private room.

"Seat yourselves, gentlemen," he said, with an excessive politeness that betrayed his Latin origin, "and I am pleased to place yourself—I mean myself—at my—I mean your—disposal."

"You have seen the newspapers, Mr. Ferrari, I take it," opened MacMorran. "To-day's?"

"Yes, yes, of course—but I am just a little at a loss—"

"That's all right. I'll help you. I want to see you with regard to the murder of Mr. Justice Heriot."

The manager paled at the ominous words. "To see me? I don't quite understand—"

"I will explain, Mr. Ferrari. I presume that, in the first place, I am correct in my assumption that his Lordship stayed here during the recent Assizes that concluded with the trial of Captain Frant? I know that it was his habit to use your hotel."

Ferrari spread out hands of denial. "I am very sorry, Inspector, but it is not so! No! It was 'is 'abit to stay here—yes! Always in times past, ever since the 'otel 'ave been here. But this time—no! He never came. Why—I cannot say."

Ferrari stopped—breathless almost, and shot a sidelong glance at his questioner; MacMorran took advantage of the cessation, to intervene.

"But surely his Lordship—?"

"Wait! If you please. I will tell you what it was that happened. I 'ave it 'ere. Wait, please. The correspondence that is 'ere will tell us. I know of it. One moment, Inspector, please."

Ferrari walked to his desk, to fumble hurriedly with a pile of documents. "I will not be long," he said, "it is not so long ago that it took place. The letter I am seeking should be 'ere, not far from the top. I know the Judge's writing, his fist, as you English people say. Ah, what is this?" The two men saw him stop his rummaging, to pick up a letter from the pile, and read to himself the opening words. "Yes—this is it," he cried. "This is the letter from Justice Heriot."

Ferrari passed it over to MacMorran, and Anthony Bathurst rose, to read it over the latter's shoulder. The message it contained was short and very much to the point. Also, it seemed to be in reply to a letter from Ferrari. It was dated the 5th of September. Justice Heriot acknowledged the manager's letter of the 2nd of September, with reference to the reservation of his usual rooms at the hotel during the term of the Autumn Assizes, but replied that on this occasion, owing to the fact that he had made definite arrangements to stay elsewhere, he would not require them. "Yours very faithfully," he concluded, "Clement Clavelle Heriot."

"You see from that letter, gentlemen," expostulated Ferrari, "the Right Honourable Sir Clement Heriot did not stay at the 'Otel Sicilian on this last occasion. I wish that 'e 'ad. It is, I think, a very great pity that 'e did not. Per'aps 'e would 'ave been alive now! Who knows into whose 'ands 'e got? Or what wretched, cheap, second-class 'otel he went to? What food, per'aps—" Ferrari shrugged his shoulders at the enormity of the contemplated calamity.

"You are sure, Mr. Ferrari," said Anthony Bathurst, "that that letter is in the late Justice Heriot's handwriting?"

"But, yes! Look for yourself! Compare it with previous letters that 'e 'ave sent me. I can find some easily. One moment, please."

Ferrari was as good as his word. "'Ere you are. Read."

Bathurst compared one, two, three, and four letters after he had looked them over. There was no doubt in his mind of either the general handwriting or of the actual signature.

"Looks all right, Inspector," he said. "What do you think yourself?"

MacMorran nodded his acceptance of the position and then clinched matters. "What I am thinking, is that Mr. Ferrari is right. It's sound sense. If the judge didn't stay here, well, then, where did he stay? That's what we have to find out." He turned to Ferrari. "I suppose there was no question of dissatisfaction on the judge's part, eh?"

"Dissatisfaction?" Ferrari queried the word with dismay. "Oh, no! That can never be said. Ask anybody. Ask anybody who stays regularly at the Sicilian. They come once . . . they come always. Consider the cooking—it is superb." Bathurst attempted to interpose, but Ferrari, thoroughly wound up, went on in torrential justification. "If you don't believe me, I can and will, if necessary, give you names as references. Names which will be proof in themselves. Consider the gentlemen who stopped here for the recent 'cause célèbre', the Frant trial. Who were they? Sir Robert Frant himself, his daughter, Miss Frant, Lady Camberrigg, and also no less a person than Sir Randall Bowers."

Bathurst pricked up his ears at the information. "Don't you think, MacMorran," he said, "that what Mr. Ferrari has just told us may explain the judge's change of plans?"

"You mean—?"

"I'm referring to those names that Mr. Ferrari has just mentioned to us. Consider—to use Mr. Ferrari's word—one only—that of Sir Robert Frant."

He smiled as he made the point, and the Inspector nodded. "Very feasible, I think. Yes. Had Heriot come here, it would have occasioned a certain amount of embarrassment on both sides, no doubt. *If he knew*. But did Justice Heriot know, do you think, that Sir Robert Frant and his party were due to stay here? That point seems to me to be worth considering. If we could prove satisfactorily that he did have that knowledge—"

The telephone bell rang insistently, and Ferrari moved quickly across to answer the summons. "You will pardon me, gentlemen, for a moment. I think perhaps—"

MacMorran and Anthony Bathurst saw his face change almost immediately after he had unhooked the receiver. Suddenly he brought it away from his ear and looked across at the Inspector. "It's for you, Inspector. Will you answer it?"

MacMorran took Ferrari's place at the telephone, and as he did so, a puzzled expression took possession of his face. "Who knows I'm here, Mr. Bathurst?" he muttered. "Eh? Yes," he answered. "Yes! Chief Inspector MacMorran speaking . . . who is it? . . . oh, yes, sir . . . yes, my lord." Bathurst wondered at his change of attitude and harmonic progression of address. But MacMorran was speaking again. "Come up here, my lord, by all means—with the greatest pleasure. I will arrange it with the manager, Mr. Ferrari, in whose company I am now. Oh, no! Not at all, my lord. On the contrary. Thank you very much."

The Inspector replaced the receiver very quietly and turned to Anthony Bathurst, his face showing signs of excitement.

"We're honoured, Mr. Bathurst. There are two gentlemen downstairs who wish to see me. It appears that they called at Waring's just after we left, and one of the waiters told them that he had heard me say that we were coming on here. Our new visitors are Lord Madden and Sir Randall Bowers."

Anthony Bathurst whistled at the names. "Things are moving, MacMorran. A fluttering in the upper dove-cotes, eh? Why have they come? Were you told that on the 'phone?"

"Information *re* the Heriot case, Mr. Bathurst, which is good enough," said MacMorran rather airily. "Don't know what it is— that will come. If Heriot . . . ssh—here they are."

Ferrari almost fell on the door to admit the distinguished callers. Lord Madden, at this date, was still persisting in his attempts to win the Epsom Derby. This was his chief ambition—in fact, it was his only ambition. With a magnificent estate between Langley Broom and Reading, he cherished his racing-stud with almost feverish industry, grumbled at the price of everything and the increasing burden of taxation, entertained lavishly anybody who was everybody and everybody who was anybody, attended every first night with punctilious ceremonial, officiated frequently at the National Sporting Club, and yet, all the time, failed, with inglorious regularity, to breed a colt or filly, which evidenced at the right time, serious classic pretensions. He was a stout, short, jolly-looking man, undeterred by the will-o'-the-wisp that danced in front of him, whose face creased into smiles when the mood caught him and whose shrewd blue eyes twinkled in mute accompaniment. His companion of the minute, the famous Sir Randall Bowers, looked, in every respect, the English aristocrat. Everything about him spoke of his breeding, reserve, and appropriate nonchalance. Physically, he was the complete antithesis of Lord Madden, tall, thin, and usually pleased with himself.

"You may leave us, Ferrari," he said abruptly. The manager obeyed with alacrity; he had learnt early the habit of instant obedience to those whom he joyfully and thankfully accepted as his superiors. After all, God knew what He was doing!

"You first, Madden," dictated Bowers. "It's your funeral more than mine. Don't think I can put it better than that."

Lord Madden coughed impressively. It was more than a good cough. With him it was a good habit. He always extracted confidence from that cough.

"Well, Inspector," he opened pompously, "the news of the death of Justice Heriot has, of course, reached me. In the papers to-day. And quite frankly, it's been a great shock to me. A very great shock indeed. You see—Heriot and I were old friends. Old cronies, if you like. That will convey a bit more." He paused, and his eyes took on the far-away look of pleasing reminiscence. "Because of that fact, Inspector," he continued, "I am in a position to give you some information that may be both interesting and valuable to you. Knowing that my old friend was due to take the Frant murder trial, Lady Madden and I invited him to stay with us at Erleigh while the Assizes were on. We usually have a house-party of a kind about that time of the year, quite apart from anything else. He wrote and accepted; as a matter of fact, he seemed to be more than ordinarily pleased."

"One moment, my lord," intervened MacMorran. "May I ask the date of Justice Heriot's acceptance?"

"Let me see—it would be somewhere about the twenty-second of July, I think."

"Thank you, Lord Madden. Continue, will you, please?"

"Well, Inspector, arrangements for the house-party proceeded at my place, and I invited several other people to make up a congenial company—including Sir Randall Bowers here. He declined the invitation, however, so we needn't go into that. Well, it came to the very evening before the Frant trial was due to come on. The Judge, according to the letter of acceptance that he had previously sent me, was coming down by train and arriving at the station at six-twenty-seven. I had replied that I would send the car to the station for him." He felt in his pocket and produced a letter. "There, Inspector," he declared—"there's the letter to which I have just made reference. You will be able to read it for yourself. Please note the time. You will see it is as I said."

MacMorran glanced over the letter, nodded his agreement and handed the letter across to Bathurst, who was able to compare the handwriting with that of the letter that Ferrari had shown them. The result was completely satisfactory. There was no doubt, on the face of things, of the authorship of either letter.

"You will be able to judge of my surprise, then," Lord Madden went on, "when a telephone message was received at Erleigh, shortly after four o'clock in the afternoon, from Heriot himself, to the effect that he had been obliged, very suddenly, to change his plans. Lady Madden spoke to him and he was—er—profuse in his apologies for having, as he feared, inconvenienced us. He explained to her, she tells me, that something had transpired that day that had made it absolutely imperative for him to alter his arrangements. She did not, of course, ask him for any particulars, but Heriot volunteered one further piece of information to her." Lord Madden came forward a little on his chair and lowered his voice. "He told my wife that it was a matter of life and death that had caused him to alter his intentions. Those were the very words that he used. . . . What do you think of that, gentlemen?"

"I can comment on it, Lord Madden," remarked MacMorran—"and knowing what you do, you will appreciate my comment all the more. The manager of this hotel, Mr. Ferrari, told us just before you came in that the Judge intended to stay somewhere that may be described as special. Otherwise, he would have expected him to have stayed here. What I mean is this—it's all of a piece with what seems to have been his original intention."

Sir Randall Bowers entered the arena.

"It is my turn now, Inspector, to present you with a little information. Of its value, I will leave you to judge. But there is this to be said about it. It touches the same part of the mystery as Lord Madden's information does. Lord Madden gives you, as it were, one half of the story. I supplement it with the other half. I was present in the court for the whole of the Frant trial, and on each occasion when the court adjourned for the day, Heriot was taken away from the court in a Daimler. A damned smart car, it was, too. Smartly-dressed, good-looking chauffeur, and the whole bag of tricks filled the bill to the last ounce, I can tell you.

I happened to be just on the spot outside the court, on the first afternoon when the car rolled up. I saw Heriot get in. Actually, I spoke to him and he waved back in answer to me, as he took his seat in the car." He paused.

Anthony Bathurst's first question cut across the room decisively. "Sir Randall Bowers, you will pardon my semi-interruption, but I should like to ask you a question."

Bowers frowned. Bathurst ignored the menace of the frown and proceeded imperturbably.

"Did this incident of Mr. Justice Heriot leaving in this car you mention occur on the last afternoon, too? On the afternoon that the Frant trial confided?"

"I thought I made that clear," glared Sir Randall. "I said on *each occasion* when the court adjourned."

"Adjourned—yes," corrected Mr. Bathurst. "My point was, that on the last afternoon the Assizes finished. There was nothing then, strictly speaking, in the nature of an adjournment."

"Have it your own way. You know perfectly well what I mean."

"Thank you, Sir Randall. That is clear, then. You were about to say—?"

"Not very much more, as it happens. I've told you the important part. But let us look at the main point together. What *was* this car? To whom did it belong? Where did it come from? Why was Heriot in it? For one thing, I can tell you that Heriot hated cars. Loathed 'em like poison. He travelled by rail whenever and wherever he could. Were you aware of that, Inspector? Going on to what Lord Madden has just told you—what matter of life and death was it that took him from the court in a car, every afternoon? When we get the answer to those questions that I've just asked, we shall solve the riddle of his death."

"I'm not denying that you're right, Sir Randall," observed MacMorran—"it's up to us to trace that car. A Daimler, you say?"

"A Daimler, Inspector. I'm sorry that I didn't get the number. And a chauffeur in very trim dark-blue livery. Tall, well-built young fellow. Couldn't see his face too well. Each time he wore his cap well over." Sir Randall broke off into a chuckle. "All the same, and though he doesn't know it, I've one clue to his identity. One that will make you chaps sit up and take notice." He took out his pocket-book, and from the book an envelope. With an air of mystery, he shook the contents of the envelope into the palm of his right hand. Then he held his hand out to MacMorran for the latter's inspection. "There you are, Inspector," he cried.

"What do you think of this little lot? On the last afternoon, when Heriot entered his car, I was just behind him. Frankly, I was curious. Had been since the first time I'd seen it occur. As this chauffeur chap closed the door of the car on Heriot and went round to the driving-seat, I saw him toss this cigarette away. Still endeavouring to sift things down a bit, I picked it up, little thinking that matters would pan out as badly as they have done. As you can see, it's been about half-smoked."

MacMorran picked the half-cigarette from Sir Randall's hand and looked at it curiously. But if the Inspector's eyes held curiosity, Bathurst's held an intensity of interest that completely transcended the former quality. For the cigarette at which they looked was a Mouraki! Of the same brand as the two Turkish stubs that had been found on Pearson's table at Perry Hammer, the morning after the murder. Sir Randall translated popular thought into words.

"Yes, gentlemen, actually a Mouraki! You see, I remember the evidence of those two other Mourakis." His face was eloquent of his triumph. Game and set to Sir Randall Bowers!

CHAPTER XVI
THE OTHER TRUNK

"Sir Randall Bowers," interjected Anthony Bathurst, with sudden eagerness. "Will you be good enough to answer me two more questions?"

The man addressed, looked hard at Bathurst without so much as batting an eyelid. "I realized," he said eventually, "when I came here in the first place, that I was laying myself open to something of that kind. Well, the bed is made and I made it. Therefore, I'll lie on it. What is it that you desire to know?"

Mr. Bathurst mellowed his first question with a smile. "Going back a little, sir," he opened, "to the Frant murder trial, which I believe interested you considerably, we find a man giving evidence for the prosecution by the name of John Murray. He was a butler, if you remember, in the employ of the murdered man. I've met this man, Murray. I investigated the Pearson case on behalf of Sir Robert Frant, and had access to the room at Perry Hammer where Pearson was murdered. During my time there, Murray, who showed me round, informed me that he had once been in your service, sir. May I ask you if that statement is correct?"

Sir Randall nodded a nonchalant affirmative. "Absolutely, my dear sir. Murray served me for some years. Though what the devil it has to do with this, I don't know."

"Was he dismissed?"

Sir Randall's smile was of the superior variety. "On the contrary, my dear sir, he rendered me excellent and very faithful service. I was very sorry, in fact, when he left me; we parted on the best of terms. It was a question of his wife's health. She had acute asthmatical trouble. The good lady has, I believe, since died and been gathered to her foremothers."

"I see. Thank you, Sir Randall."

The latter went on airily: "As a matter of fact, Mr.—er—Bathurst, I had lost touch with Murray, and was so pleased to hear of my old servant again that, during the progress of the Frant trial, I sent word to him by one of the constables on duty in the court, inviting him to dine with me at this very hotel where we now are. Murray accepted the invitation, and we spent a very pleasant and enjoyable evening together. Damned good fellow, John Murray. I can tell you frankly, sir, that I've never adequately filled his place."

"I sympathize with you, Sir Randall. Allow me to make a suggestion to you. Perhaps, now that Murray's last employer is dead, you will be able to get him back again."

Sir Randall Bowers stared at the speaker, as though temporarily taken by surprise. Then he appeared to recover himself.

"Gad, sir, but that's a thunderin' good idea. I confess that up to now I hadn't thought of it. What do you think of it, Madden? If I get him, Mr. Bathurst, consider me in your debt."

"On those conditions, I'll take payment for the idea at once, sir, if you don't mind. May I?" Anthony smiled.

Sir Randall wrinkled his brows. "How so?"

"Answer me that other question at which I previously hinted."

"What is it?"

"Very personal, I'm afraid."

Sir Randall's frown developed. "Personal? What do you mean—personal?"

Anthony trod deliberately. He knew that it was now definitely necessary to pick his way with the utmost care.

"Lord Madden told us just now, sir—he volunteered the information very courteously—that he invited you to form one of his house-party at Erleigh this month. May I ask you why you declined that invitation?"

"'Pon my soul, young man, but you've a colossal audacity. I'm a damned good mind to tell you to mind your own damned business. What on earth has this to do with poor old Heriot's murder, I'd like to know?"

He paused for a further supply of scorching breath. Lord Madden took advantage of the cessation of hostility, to intervene. He appealed to MacMorran.

"Really, Inspector," he commenced to expostulate. "I must say that I'm in agreement with Sir Randall. I don't see what this young man means, or hopes to gain, by asking a question of that sort. After all, there must be a limit to—"

Before MacMorran could respond to the appeal, Bowers himself took up the cudgels again.

"That's all right, Madden," he growled. "There's no need for you to chip in, even though you mean well, no doubt. I can fight my own battles, thank you. Always have done. Always shall do, I hope." He turned to glare at Anthony, but the glare now held a glint of a more kindly humour. "I'll tell you, young man, why I didn't go to Erleigh this October. And as Madden himself is here, and is going to hear it, he must blame you for it, and not me. His blood will be on your head. But if you want to know, I simply can't stand the appallingly atrocious stuff that he serves up to his guests in the name of liqueur brandy. I've told him of it, time and again; the silly old fool takes no notice of me. It's terrible stuff, fiery as the devil himself straight from hell."

Madden shook his head in protest. "You've a bee in your bonnet over that brandy, Bowers. I've told you many times, that that brandy's been in the cellar over forty years. You won't find stuff like that, if you—"

Sir Randall snorted derision. "In the cellar forty years! Good God! Where's your sense, man? Being in the cellar's no damned good. Age in bottle's no earthly use to a liqueur brandy, you old fool. Age in *cask* is the thing that counts. . . ."

Sir Randall waved his arm in an excess of enthusiasm. Lord Madden rose. The two men confronted each other. . . .

Bathurst was still smiling at the reminiscence of the argument when he was admitted to the late Mr. Justice Heriot's flat in Strathpeffer Mansions by that gentleman's maid, Angela Mansell. Heriot's death in such tragic circumstances had smitten her sorely, for in a strange, detached sort of way she had been very fond of the old man whom she had served for some years now, and whose every taste and foible she had known to a nicety. The investigation of this tall, good-looking young man with the grey eyes which smiled at her so pleasantly and appreciatively, appealed to her strongly, and she found herself answering his questions with an alacrity that was by no means habitual and surprised even herself. If she could have possessed herself of the power of looking into Anthony Bathurst's mind and of reading also what she saw there, she would have understood very quickly that he was intensely interested in two matters concerning her master, the late Mr. Justice Heriot. These were, in order of importance, one, his supply of trunks, and two, his attitude towards the motor-car as a means of transport. Angela answered Mr. Bathurst's first inquiry spontaneously and vivaciously.

"Oh, yes, sir. That is so, sir. The master did buy the trunk that you mention. Just a little while ago, sir. Perhaps a week. Since he went to Reading this last time. I can remember it coming here. Or rather, to be absolutely truthful, I can remember finding it here one evening when I came back after I had been out for a little walk. It was the evening the Frant trial ended. An attendant at one of the other flats had taken it in. They often do little things like that for me, if there's nobody at home here."

The excitement that the words had engendered in Bathurst's brain exhausted itself into a quick, storming question. Here there was something radically wrong!

"One moment, Miss Mansell. Please! Think! Don't you realize the meaning of what you're telling me?"

The maid, failing to comprehend instantly, looked scared at the searching nature of the interruption. "Why, sir, what?"

Bathurst leant eagerly forward. "Why, this! Consider what you have just said to me. Assuming that you are right—if the trunk were brought here since your late master went on his last circuit, it's possible *that your master may have been killed here*. In this flat. That may explain our difficulty in discovering where he had been sleeping during the time he was hearing the Frant murder trial. We never considered the possibility of his having come back here each evening. You see, we found out that he hadn't stayed at the—"

The eyes of the girl opened wide, as she shook her head in immediate denial of his statement. She looked strange. Perplexity and annoyance, and perhaps even a kind of wistful regret, were all present and discernible in the look that she gave to Bathurst.

"But, sir," she cried, "stay a minute. I've been a fool not to realize it before. You've misunderstood me. By my fault, I misled you. My only excuse is that when I heard of my master's death, I was so horrified and so hurt, that my brain couldn't have worked properly. The trunk that you first spoke about—the trunk they put my master's body in—can't possibly be the one that I was telling you about."

"Why not?" demanded Mr. Bathurst, in peremptory interrogation. "I disagree with you. It's at least *possible*. I should say that there's—"

Angela demolished his objection. "*Because that one is in my master's room now.* I am sure it is. You see—it sounds silly and foolish of me, perhaps—but I never connected the trunk I read about in all the papers, with the other one. The one that I thought you were talking about. And your idea, sir, that the judge came back here of a night from Reading, is, if you will pardon me, all wrong. I can assure you that he didn't. Not even after the trial. You can take that from me, sir, as being absolutely certain. I haven't set eyes on him since he went away. Shall I show you the trunk that's here, sir? Would you care to see it?"

Mr. Bathurst, seeing the edifice of the elaborate theory that he had just speculatively commenced to build, toppling gradually to the level, expressed his willingness to view the article mentioned. Angela Mansell led him into an apartment that had obviously been the bedroom of the late Mr. Justice Heriot. Her outstretched finger indicated the trunk of her recent information. Anthony's eyes followed that finger's direction. There in the corner of the room, between the judge's glass-topped dressing-table and the angle of the wall, stood what we may call—the second trunk. Anthony Bathurst walked deliberately to it and then bent over it that he might the more carefully examine it. The girl was right. The description of the trunk in which Heriot's body had been found, which he had given to her during the early stages of the interview, coincided almost exactly, in every detail, as far as he could judge, with the trunk which he now saw before him. A condition of affairs that, at this stage of the inquiry, was merely confusion worse confounded. He would, however, take no chances. He measured the trunk with care. His eyes then comprehended the room. Everything about it was beautiful and in order. There was not the slightest sign of disarrangement of any kind. Normality and regularity were in evidence everywhere. Anthony gestured to the maid to conduct him to the other room.

When there, he thrust his hands deeply into the pockets of his trousers, and to Angela Mansell's unrepressed surprise, began to pace the room . . . up and down . . . backwards and forwards . . . up and down . . . searching for the elusive thread . . . that must be there somewhere . . . and yet where? Suddenly he stopped and wheeled round. The maid's surprise grew when she saw that his eyes were fixed intently on her.

"Miss Mansell," he said, rather sharply, she thought, "start telling me about your master. Everything that comes to your mind. Tell me *about* him and tell me *of* him. His habits, his ways, his circle of acquaintances! Every little whim, trick and mannerism that belonged to him, as you knew him. His hobbies, his likes, his dislikes."

The girl was dumb. Bathurst, unheeding, proceeded even more rapidly.

"His favourite colour, his favourite fruit, his favourite flower. His aversions and dislikes. Was he musical? Did he love the drama? Fond of sport, cricket, football, golf? Racing? Did he ever—?"

Still staring somewhat blankly, but beginning to understand, Angela embarked upon her adventure through the details of description. Bathurst gave way to his habit, closed his eyes and listened to her. It was by this route that he found the path to the most perfect concentration. He heard the girl speak. He heard her continue . . . yes . . . yes, this girl was no fool . . . say what you like . . . that was clear . . . her powers of description were distinctly above the average . . . he could visualize old Heriot the better, now that the brush of her tongue was at work upon the palette of her mind and producing a picture upon which the alertness of his imagination could dwell and feast and understand. Angela, by now, was well warmed to her unusual task. Her fluency increased. Eventually . . . "As for flowers that you mentioned, sir, my master was passionately fond of all of them. Dark red roses, though, were his favourite. The very darkest of all. Like red velvet. Those that are so beautiful and fragrant. I expect you know the kind I mean."

Bathurst nodded, opened his eyes, and immediately interrupted her. "I think I do, Miss Mansell. If my memory serve me correctly, the late Mr. Justice Heriot had a bowl of dark red roses, such as you have just described, on the ledge in front of him in Court, during the whole of the Frant trial." He closed his eyes again to visualize the scene. "Yes—I can see them now." Angela returned his nod with vigorous and corroborative emphasis.

"You're quite right, sir," she said with the vivacity of enthusiasm, "he always had them—at every trial at which he presided. He would pay an awful lot to get them, too, when it was the wrong time of the year for them. Many a time he's told me that afterwards. Talking about trials, sir, another thing has just come to me. I always think it's funny how one thing will bring up another, when you're least expecting it. I've just remembered my master's habit of taking iodine."

Mr. Bathurst looked a trifle puzzled, "*Taking* iodine?" he queried.

"Yes, sir," returned Angela, positively.

"Internally, do you mean?"

"In the spring and early autumn, every morning about half-past eleven, he would take a few drops of iodine in a glassful of water. He picked up the idea, so he told me on one occasion, when I was talking to him about it, from an old uncle of his who had been a doctor in India. Punctual he was about it, too. Like clockwork, you know. He said it had helped to keep him fit for years."

"But his health had shown signs of breaking recently, hadn't it?"

Angela looked grave and troubled. "Yes, sir. It had. And I know my master was very worried about it. He had tried so many things, but none had done him much good. Been to a specialist, too. Not very long before he went away to Reading, he said to me: 'Angela, I've a presentiment that this is the last time I shall go a-judging.' Funny, wasn't it, that he should have said that?"

The tears coursed slowly down the girl's cheeks. Bathurst thought of the testimony of Dr. Barrow-South, and knew only too well that gentleman's world-wide reputation when it came to maladies of the throat.

"Yes, sir," concluded Angela, "he had his little peculiar ways, had the judge, but I'd like to know who of us hasn't? How he loved Stilton cheese! Not a white one. It had to be blue and veined. Always would have it—wouldn't touch any other kind. Said that cheese-making was a lost art in England, and that if he had been a very rich man he would have given a big prize for a new cheese. I remember a young gentleman very much the same as yourself, sir, if you'll pardon me saying so, coming here in the early part of the year to interview him for the *Piccadilly Magazine*. You know what I mean—the kind of thing—'The Lives of Celebrities from Youth to Age'. He confided in me when he was going, that he had come to do the job in fear and trembling—thinking from his reputation that the judge would prove to be a fair Tartar, but that in the end he had turned out to be the very reverse."

Mr. Bathurst rose. "You've given me a lot to think over, Miss Angela," he asserted with some whimsicality. "I don't know that I ever had so many strands to straighten out before. The solution of the affair seems to dance a few paces in front of me, like a will-o'-the-wisp. I reach out, as it were, to grasp something tangible, that I delude myself into thinking that I have discovered, and, lo! it escapes me. Invariably! One moment a theory promises something rich, and I am full of hope—the next moment something else happens. The promise is dissipated, and I am empty, and, if you like, desperate. A detective, you see, is one of those who cannot say, 'it is better to travel hopefully than to arrive.' He *must* reach the rendezvous. Before I leave you, however, I want to ask you something else, if I may?"

"Yes, sir," responded the girl with simple candour.

"Had Mr. Justice Heriot a dislike—let me put it more strongly and say an aversion—to motor-cars and motor travelling generally?"

There was no hesitation now. Angela's answer was ready, rapid and to the point.

"Oh, yes, sir. Unfortunately, sir. He hated them. It was far more than an aversion or a dislike. Hated is the only word that you can use, to do it justice. He used to say that if he could have his way he would abolish them from the roads. Said the public roads were like railways, and without any fences, too. If he had lived to be a hundred and fifty, I am certain sure that he would never have bought a car for himself."

"But yet, I suppose," intervened Mr. Bathurst, "there would be occasions when he would ride in one. Special occasions, shall we say, eh?"

The maid's consideration of the question was pursed in a frown.

"Ye-es," she answered at length, "when perhaps he might be *very* pressed for time for a very short journey, where he couldn't use the train, and might otherwise have to walk. Or—" She hesitated.

"Or what?" prompted Mr. Bathurst encouragingly.

"It's hard to say—to explain properly."

"Let me try to help you. I think you mean that your master would only have consented to use a car when there was some very *urgent* or vital reason for his doing so. Does that fit it?"

"Yes, sir. That would be right, I was trying to put it to you like that."

Mr. Bathurst nodded quietly. "Thank you. I thought I might be able to help you. And for helping me, thank you very much. I expect I shall see you again before very long. There will be many things to do. The judge's affairs will have to be settled up, you know. Still, sufficient for the day—you know the rest, I expect, Miss Angela." He gave her his hand with a smile. "Buy yourself something pretty."

As he walked home from the interview to his own flat, Anthony debated a question with himself incessantly. What was the urgent reason that had caused Heriot to sink his hatred of road travel and enter a motor-car on each occasion, when the Frant trial had adjourned? Where had he been going? What had called to him so insistently? Whose was the car, the chauffeur of which had been observed by Sir Randall Bowers to smoke cigarettes of the quality of Mourakis? Mourakis! A strong coincidence there! Too strong, perhaps, remembering. . . . Stay, though! He had record of yet another occasion when Mr. Justice Heriot had employed a car. There was the evidence of the salesman, Price, of H.J. Orridge, Debenham & Co., Twinemaker Street. He had used it to carry the first trunk home . . . for convenience . . . perhaps . . . it was an awkward object . . . had made no secret of his identity either, when he had purchased the article. But why the second trunk . . . what was Heriot's idea in regard to that? Mr. Bathurst pulled up short in his tracks . . . the embryo of an idea began to breathe vitality and take tiny shape in his brain. Musing, he covered another hundred yards or so of his journey. Then he pulled up short again and suddenly, with one hand, used his stick to clout an imaginary long hop past cover. "Whom can I ask who was present at the trial?" he queried to himself. "Who would have noticed? People whose evidence would be reliable and efficient?" There were, he eventually decided, two people only of his acquaintances, whose testimony he could seek with the necessary confidence. Sir Robert Frant, the accused man's father, and his brother . . . the famous actor . . . who had also been present in court. He remembered either Pamela Frant or her father saying so . . . Maddison Frant.

Chapter XVII
GROPING FOR LIGHT

MADDISON Frant, immaculately attired, received Mr. Anthony Bathurst with his back to his mantelpiece. Since he had experienced the exquisite pleasure (to him) of beholding and hearing himself in his latest talking film, "Red Rust and Ruin", he had considerably developed the habit of standing in the position named. He had used it on several occasions for the screen, and every time he looked upon it, it appealed to him with greater force and afforded him a greater degree of pleasure. With his hands clasped behind his back, he was enabled to square his shoulders so satisfactorily. It helped, too, his tailor. . . . Mr. Bathurst's unexpected visit in a way perturbed him. He was aware, of course, that Anthony had been employed by his brother on his nephew's case, and was prepared, therefore, to grant him the interview that he had desired. Anthony entered the room and bowed to his host. He was courteously waved to a chair.

"This is an unexpected pleasure, Mr. Bathurst. To what am I indebted for the honour? For what I may describe as so signal an honour?"

Mr. Bathurst bowed again, and chose the words of his reply with the most extreme care. "The question that you ask me, sir, is difficult to answer—properly. I will be frank to that extent. It may be, that events will prove that I have wasted my time in coming to you. On the other hand, I may have come to the right person. The decision belongs to the future. We shall see. I want, however, certain information with regard to the conduct of the recent trial of Captain Hilary Frant. I think that perhaps you may be able to give it to me." He paused, and his eyes sought the face of his companion. They met with no immediate response. Maddison Frant, schooled in the imposed silences of the stage, waited imperturbably and deliberately for Bathurst to proceed. Anthony saw this and understood its meaning. He accepted the conditions, and continued—equally imperturbable.

"The astonishing murder of the judge who presided over that trial, may be said to have cast blinding light on the trial itself. Every angle of it is lit up with a relentless glare, and there blazes from it, a flame that will attract the many, and possibly affright the few. It will whet the insatiable appetite for sensation."

Frant moved a pace from his position at the mantelpiece, and seemed on the point of interruption. On this occasion, however, it was Anthony's turn to call the tune. Seemingly oblivious of his host's change of position, he went on:

"And besides the light and the blaze, there will immediately be, I am afraid, something else." He looked up quickly, to find Frant's face fixed intently on him.

"I'm afraid that I don't follow you." The reply was stiff.

"Shadows, sir. Ugly. Grotesque. Not slim shadows, hand in hand, that hold no threat, but sinister shapes of undoubted menace, which worry as well as intrigue me. It is because of those shadows, sir, that I am approaching you for help. Although, as I hinted to you just now, you may not be able to give it to me."

The actor shrugged his shoulders with a gesture of indifference.

"Then why not let sleeping dogs lie, Bathurst? Why rake among the ashes that the flames of which you speak, will leave? As I said, I don't follow you."

Bathurst went on his way calmly and inexorably. "Captain Frant has been tried for murder. Also, and what is more important from your personal point of view, he has been acquitted. But, I submit respectfully, is that all?"

"All?" Maddison Frant repeated the word almost meaninglessly.

"Public opinion is a tremendous force. It is not always easy to ignore it completely. Nor policy, either. Captain Frant will live to realize the burning truth of that. There are thousands of his fellow-creatures who will raise their righteous eyebrows, shrug their sanctimonious shoulders, spread out their Pharisaical palms, and say that a Scottish jury would have returned the bastard verdict of 'Not proven'. 'Lucky fellow, Captain Hilary Frant!'"

"Well? What of it? Hilary must face the plunderers. He won't be the first man compelled to do it. He is not lacking in courage. He must look these traducers between the eyes—his head unbowed."

"Excellent in theory, I grant you. In actual practice, however, it may become a war of attrition. The strongest man's nerves would be likely to fray and then snap under the strain."

Maddison Frant gave way to impatience. "I see your point, but what else can he do, man? Damn it all—I should be delighted to think that there was an option."

"There is." Anthony Bathurst's statement came quietly, but with a wealth of decision. Frant stared.

"I shall be pleased to hear it."

"Perhaps."

"What do you mean?"

"The option to which you made reference just now, can only be one thing. The finding of the truth. The bringing to book of the real criminal. And it's just a chance, it seems to me, that the truth mightn't be as palatable as you imagine it would be."

Frant seemed disturbed at Bathurst's statement.

"I have been told by my brother that you claim to know the name of Pearson's murderer. It is no business of mine to inquire into your justification for that claim. The all-important point to me is—can you clear Hilary?"

"I'm not sure. I don't know for certain, you see, what I shall find on the way. That's why I'm here now." Bathurst caressed his chin contemplatively. "For that, and to ask you a certain definite question."

Maddison Frant turned his head very slowly in Bathurst's direction. "Well—what is it? You've been a long time leading up to it."

"I wanted to make certain of one of two considerations, sir. I looked, you see, before I leapt."

"And yet, that idea cuts both ways—we are instructed also that delays are dangerous. What is it you want to know?"

"I have been told, by Miss Frant, I believe it was, that you were in court during the whole time of the Frant trial? Is that so?"

The actor-manager's face became grim and stern. "You have been correctly informed, Bathurst. I was present *all* the time."

"Good. I was anxious to discover somebody who fulfilled that vital condition, and I immediately thought of you and your brother. If both you and he had failed me, I don't know to whom I should have gone. I also want to ask you a question concerning Mr. Justice Heriot himself. Despite the fact that I was present all the time myself, I find that I am unable to produce an answer that satisfies me. This is my point. Did you watch Heriot at all closely?"

Frant stared, as though bordering on a state of amazement. "I don't understand. Please be more explicit."

"I really don't know that I can, sir. I meant to ask you exactly what I did ask. I will repeat my question. Did you happen to watch the late Mr. Justice Heriot at all closely during the trial?"

"Watch? How do you—er—mean—*watch*?"

When he had spoken Maddison Frant resumed his position by the mantelpiece, and Anthony Bathurst was quick to notice the fact. He was determined to give his host no help. He waited. Frant proceeded:

"I should say that I saw as much of him as anyone else did. The drama of the whole thing appealed to me. Professionally, I suppose. Apart from the fact that the accused man was my brother's only son. Candidly, old Heriot impressed me. I consider that his summing-up was masterly."

"Good. I won't disagree with you there. I'm not in that province, just now. He's been murdered, however, which is evidence, perhaps, that everybody doesn't think as we do. Tell me this, sir. Did you observe the late Mr. Justice Heriot at any time during the trial, drink from a glass that he had, we will say, in court with him?"

Frant replied instantly. "I did, Bathurst. That's easy to answer. What on earth are you driving at?"

"All in good time, sir, please. Did you notice this incident happen each morning?"

"Each morning. At almost exactly the same time. I spotted that all right."

Mr. Bathurst affected a careless nonchalance. "Any idea what it was he was drinking?"

Maddison Frant shook his head with a mixture of sympathy and conscious superiority.

"My dear Bathurst, get that idea out of your head at once. Let me assure you that it won't hold water for a second. For the very good reason that there's absolutely nothing in it. Don't imagine that Heriot was doped in that way. If you want to know, he was drinking plain water with a few drops of iodine in it."

Anthony's rejoinder was quiet but insistent. "How can you be sure of that, sir?"

Frant waved an instructive hand. "My dear Bathurst, I must confess that you surprise me. Heriot's iodine idiosyncrasy is extremely well known. I won't go as far as to say that it's *common* knowledge, but it's almost getting on for that. I've seen the old boy myself preside over several big trials, and if they've been held in early spring or early autumn he's always taken his iodine. I can't recall a single exception. His state of health, I should say, caused him a great deal of anxiety."

Anthony received this last piece of information with mixed feelings. In one way he had hoped for it. In another way, the news disturbed him and caused him to suspect ambushed trouble almost everywhere.

"Almost common knowledge," his host had suggested. "You're asserting then, that his iodine habit was as well-known to people as his passion for dark red roses?"

"Yes." Maddison Frant inclined his head with complete certainty. "To the majority of people—yes. I would assert that, without the vestige of hesitation."

With a look of abstraction in his eyes, Anthony felt for his cigarette-case. He opened it, to find that it was empty.

"Allow me, Bathurst," interposed his host.

Anthony, still wearing the contemplative look, stretched his hand towards the gold cigarette-case that Maddison Frant held out to him.

"Thank you. Careless of me to have let myself run so low."

He took a cigarette and lit it. Then, rising, he addressed Frant again. "On the whole, sir, what you have told me, surprises me. I will admit, quite frankly, that I wasn't prepared to find, that what we will call the late judge's foibles, were so well-known to the *hoi polloi*."

Frant frowned, possibly at Bathurst's form of speech.

"Surely you are familiar with them yourself, Bathurst? I can't believe that—"

"I am. But my knowledge is by no means hoary with age. To tell you the truth, it has come to me very recently. It was supplied by a Miss Angela Mansell. She's a maid who was in the dead judge's employ."

Frant's frown changed into a stare. "It's all very interesting, no doubt, Bathurst, but really I fail to see your drift. What importance, such trifling points as these, can possibly have had on Heriot's murder, I entirely——"

This time it was Anthony who shook his head sympathetic- ally. "If you are able, sir, to attach the adjective-labels 'trifling' and 'important' to this and that point, so lightly and airily, if you will pardon me saying so, you have solved the first secret of successful investigation. Candidly, sir, I find myself in grave doubt—entirely unable to use either of the adjectives with any degree of certainty. For I shouldn't be surprised if the 'trifles' turn out to be the crucialities. They very often do."

Maddison Frant moved his head as though the room in which he stood held a packed gallery of his admirers.

"As you say, Bathurst, who knows? Who, indeed?"

Anthony held out his hand in token of departure.

"Good-bye, sir. Many thanks for your assistance. My mind is certainly a little clearer on one or two points."

"Good-bye, Bathurst, I don't suppose you want any advice from me—only information—eh?"—Maddison Frant smiled— "and still less do I suppose that you'll take it. Let me say one thing, however. Dogs look at their best when they're sleeping. There's an air of repose about them that appeals to me. Good-bye."

A few yards away from the house, Anthony looked very curi- ously at the cigarette that Maddison Frant's case had delivered up to him. It was a Mouraki! The Perry Hammer cigarette was still positively appearing. This was no less than the third occa- sion that it had entered into the arena of calculation. He thought of the circumstances of Heriot's death and of his movements in Reading. The chloroform, the car, the chauffeur, and the ciga- rette. . . . Sir Randall Bowers's statement to him . . . there was something wrong somewhere . . . why had Heriot bought that trunk? Suddenly Bathurst stopped in his paces and turned on his heel. He had come to a sudden decision. He would retrace his steps and call again at the dead judge's flat to see Angela Mansell. Almost at the identical moment that he turned on his way, the man whom he had just left—Maddison Frant, his face troubled und thoughtful—went to his telephone and asked for a number. When he was put through, he spoke very quickly.

"Is that you? It's Maddison speaking. Anthony Bathurst has been here, and has just left me. I don't know exactly what he's after, so I thought I'd tell you all about it at once. At any rate, he's asked me one or two extraordinary questions. . . . What? . . . Yes, yes . . . of course. I know all about that. Very obvious, I think. None better. But listen to this. There happens to be a girl in it with whom he's in touch, and who was Heriot's servant or something . . . by name, Angela Mansell . . . that's right, Angela Mansell. . . ."

CHAPTER XVIII
THE "PICCADILLY MAGAZINE"

ANGELA Mansell looked up and nodded brightly at the request which Anthony Bathurst put to her.

"The *Piccadilly Magazine*, sir? Let me see now. The young man I mentioned, that came to interview the judge, came here soon after Christmas, I should say. About the second week in January, it came out—the interview, I mean—about two months after that. In the March number, I think it was. But I'll find it for you. I know where the copies are kept. That'll be the best way to settle it, won't it? Excuse me just a moment, sir."

Anthony assented, and during the period of Angela's absence strolled round the apartment, his eyes assessing the more prominent features therein. As was to be expected, Heriot's collection of old glass caught his notice immediately. Anthony marvelled at the quality, lustre, and tone. Antique specimens were adjacent to some wonderful examples of comparatively modern glass-making art. An Italian semi-egg-shaped bowl, that had doubtless been pillaged from an Etruscan tomb, was set down next to an exquisite goblet that suggested the Davanzatti Palace at Florence. Anthony was standing gazing at a set of hand-shaped and hand-cut rock crystal pieces of the very earliest period, and noting how wonderfully they retained their pristine vivid hues, when Angela Mansell returned. She carried in her hand, he saw, the April number of the *Piccadilly Magazine*.

"It was April, sir, when the interview with my master appeared—not March. I was wrong."

Anthony contributed explanation. "The April number was probably published some time in March. That is the trade custom with magazines. That's what led you to think what you did. You weren't really wrong. May I look?"

Angela obediently handed over the April issue of the *Piccadilly*. Anthony, seated, opened it, and the girl, in high anticipation, arranged herself at his left-hand elbow. She directed him as he flicked over the pages.

"About the middle of the magazine, sir. There it is." She pointed with some enthusiasm to the article in question. At the top of the first page was a full length photograph of Heriot in his court robes. Subscribed was "The Right Honourable Sir Clement Clavelle Heriot, Justice of the King's Bench Division of the Judiciary of England and Wales."

"A good likeness, would you call it?" questioned Bathurst.

Angela nodded enthusiastically. "Splendid, sir. My master's attitude absolutely, sir. He was always like that when he was in court."

Anthony turned over a page and regarded a second photograph with the utmost care.

"So's that one, sir. A wonderful likeness. Another of his mannerisms, sir."

He saw at once to what Angela referred. The judge's quill pen held between thumb and fore-finger, was extended towards an imaginary counsel or witness, just in the manner that Bathurst had himself seen it on more than one occasion during the recent trial of Hilary Frant. It occasioned further tribute.

"It's life-like, sir," breathed Angela in his left ear.

Mr. Bathurst turned this page over.

"That next one isn't so good," continued the critical Angela. " Not so natural."

This third photograph, to which she was calling attention, showed Justice Heriot seated in the chair of Justice and inhaling the fragrance from a bowl of roses placed in front of him. Mr. Bathurst nodded his own satisfaction, and also his agreement with Miss Mansell's statement.

"I can see very well what you mean. It's pretty good, though, on the whole. It would be unreasonable to expect a hat-trick of perfection. Now, Miss Mansell, I want you to do me a favour. I should like to borrow this magazine of yours and take it away with me. I'll bring it back—or see that it's returned—honour bright."

"Of course, sir." She looked at him with a rare wistfulness. "Do you think, sir, that you will be able to—?" She paused, at a loss for the right word.

Anthony, seeing her temporary difficulty, essayed to help her. "Able to what?" he echoed.

"Find out who murdered my master—that's what I was trying to say to you."

Tears were imminent. Anthony tapped the magazine with the back of his hand. "There are strong hopes, Miss Mansell, that I shall wrest the truth from the facts that I find here. There are some extraordinarily strange features of the case, as you know, and this interview that you and I have just looked at, is going, unless I am sadly mistaken, to play a not unimportant part in my investigation. Say what you like, this interview was very convenient for somebody. It couldn't have happened better, could it?"

He watched her carefully for the possible betrayal of anything. Angela, however, shook her head. The gesture signified her inability to comprehend. "I don't think that I quite understand you, sir."

Anthony smiled at her discomfiture. "Never mind that. Next time I come to see you, I hope to know for a certainty the name of the person who killed your master. Good-bye, and very many thanks for the help that you have given me."

Back in his own flat he found a measure of cheerfulness, and Emily, the maid in attendance there, was destined to discover that fact very quickly.

"Emily," he called to her upon his entrance, "I wonder if you will ever sing sad songs for me? What do you think about it, eh?"

"Sing what, Mr. Bathurst?"

"Sad songs. Roundelays of regret. Plant roses, at my head. At my feet, a cypress-tree. How do you like the idea? Pretty-ish?"

Emily stared, as well she might. "Cyprus, sir?"

"Cypress, Emily. A cypress-tree. When I am dead, that is. In other words, my dear, what will be the measure of your maidenly grief when I am translated to the cold comfort of the grave?"

Emily showed, at the problem that he set her, signs of indignation. "I'm sure, sir, that I should be very sorry, indeed. We all would, sir."

"That's most heartening, Emily. 'And if thou wilt, remember, and if thou wilt, forget.' I was prompted to ask the question of you, because I have been in recent conversation with a young lady who very sincerely mourns a departed master. Most refreshing these days, especially as she is ignorant of the contents of his will. At least, I take it to be so."

Emily bustled out. She always did when Mr. Bathurst talked "that funny nonsense of his". The moment that the door closed behind her, the man who had joked with her sank into his own big armchair and devoted his attention to the magazine he had brought with him from the dead judge's flat. He read through the interview with Heriot from beginning to end—not a single word escaping him. He read with definite method and plan. He was determined to put to the test, a theory that he had formed, and with which he was commencing to coquette. The first part of the interview dwelt upon Heriot's personal appearance.

"Tall and spare, with white hair. Deliberate in every action and in every word. The most wonderfully penetrating eyes I have ever seen." The interview proceeded. Heriot strongly advocated enlarging the powers of the Divorce Court. Then came references to his abode. There was mention of the famous collection of old glass and of Heriot's "penchant" for Burne-Jones. Almost a whole page was devoted to these matters. Heriot philosophized:

"No novel has ever been written—no play or film has ever been produced or put on the screen—that could contain such intensely tragic situations as many of those with which I have been called upon, in the ordinary course of my duty, to deal." He harked back to the accompaniment of a chuckle. "My father knew every actor and actress of note in his time. In those days, you know, most of 'em went through the Bankruptcy Court. Now it's the Divorce Court that attracts them. Gives 'em a reputation."

With regard to his own career, he referred to the case that had brought him fame. "I was a young Q.C. then. Appeared with the great Montagu Williams on behalf of Tatnall's Salvage Association. This was an association formed to furnish under-writers with special protection against fraud. It was a pretty big case connected with the sinking of a ship—the *Joan Mary*, and I helped to send to penal servitude four of the biggest rogues that ever wore shoe-leather. I think that I can remember their names now. Not bad, you know, seeing that it took place over fifty years ago. They were Karslake, Wolff, Bentley, and . . . I forget the fourth . . . had it on my tongue just now . . . a name like Reveley . . . I think it was Reveley; at any rate, that's near enough now." Heriot then entered the confessional. "No . . . I have never married. Perhaps I'm not the right sort. Although I've likes and dislikes, you know. Marriage wants a special temperament."

Mr. Bathurst read the details that followed with avidity. Yes, there was the usual reference to the judge's iodine habit as a means to the promotion of physical fitness. An uncle of his in India was stated to have recommended it to him. Also, beneath the photograph of Heriot with his bunch of dark red roses, was the inevitable explanation of their presence in front of him. The interview concluded with a photograph of Heriot shaking hands with his interviewer.

"Remember," he was represented as saying, "that a judge must be a meticulous student of human nature, and also of the whole ramifications of human psychology. He must be emotional and yet dispassionate—this isn't an easy matter, you know. Mercy is so often the essential characteristic of justice. I can honestly claim to have tried always to remember that, despite what others may choose to say of me. You see, I know about these things. Rumours reach me. What matter? They say! Who say? Let them say."

Anthony Bathurst put the magazine on the table and, returning to his chair, thrust his hands deeply into his pockets. For the first time, perhaps, since he had entered the arena of the Perry Hammer murder, he felt a strong measure of satisfaction. For the details of the interview in the *Piccadilly Magazine*, were exactly as he would have had them, had he been granted the privilege of re-moulding them to his heart's desire. What he had *wanted* to be there *was* there, and, more important still perhaps in his eyes, what he had *wished not to be there* was *not* there. Excellent. Things were shaping at last. He sat and considered his next step. He had it in his mind to see Lanchester, Sir Robert Frant, and one other. Would it be policy to let that part of the investigation wait—in view of the turn that affairs had taken recently? After due meditation, he decided that it would. If he were in luck, and. things progressed smoothly for him, he should be able to establish his theory beyond the scintilla of a doubt. He stood little chance of losing anything and, on the other hand, might gain substantially. Yes . . . he decided . . . that was how matters stood pretty well. He walked across to his book-case and took down the A.B.C. Quick inspection told him that he could be in Reading by a quarter-past ten that evening. It was his intention to seek out Mrs. Lane again, hostess now, by a cruel stroke of Fate, of the inn known as the "Blue Tambourine". There was also a call to be made at the "Anthurium" Super Cinema (or at the remains thereof—such as they might be). There was also . . . all the time . . . that one other, of such vital importance, this last mentioned . . . almost important enough to be seen straight away . . . regardless of the others. If he could only establish this other theory, Anthony felt confident that he would be in a position to link up the two murders in the one possible way that they could be connected. It was so damnably hard to choose from the two alternatives and be sure of having chosen aright.

Mr. Bathurst paced the room. For a time, decision eluded him. Similar problems to these had presented themselves for his solving on previous occasions. He remembered the instance when he had been investigating the murder near Kirve St. Laudus . . . when Eileen Walsingham had been in such deadly peril . . . he had been on the platform at Exeborough Station . . .

forced to decide, in the matter of a few moments, between playing for safety . . . using extreme care . . . and taking a tremendous risk by going straight for the main objective. He had chosen the latter course then, and it had turned up trumps . . . would it do the same in this present instance? The risks, perhaps, on this occasion were not as great as they had been in Eileen's case. Mr. Bathurst continued to pace the room. Suddenly he turned with the impetus of decision. First of all, Mrs. Lane!

CHAPTER XIX
THE CRUTCH

MRS. Lane, these days, lived a patient life of numbed sensation. The blow that had come to her during the previous April, had done its work so completely devastatingly, that partial recovery was doubtful and complete recovery impossible. To her simple mind she was the victim of a monstrous injustice. She had cried most of her feelings away. Nearly all, of what she had retained, that had been unbruised and untorn. Quivering flesh is only sensitive up to a certain point of maceration. The result was that habitual customers came to the "Blue Tambourine", stayed there for their accustomed period of silent and vociferous worship (respectively), and departed on their various ways and errands without the hostess of the inn as much as noticing them. She saw them, it is true, but the physical exercise was completely mechanical, and went no further than that. What they said and what they did, made no lasting impression upon her whatsoever; her mind was as a dweller in the past, and the memories of that past were her only mental sustenance. More than once, this injured and harried mind of hers had groped almost blindly for relief from its incessant pain, and had returned from the quest thereof, with the reminiscence of the tall, lithe stranger who had come to her that day towards the end of the summer, asking for communication with the man who had been taken from her. Her man. Her husband and companion. Ever since that day she had cherished the idea that the tall young man with the grey eyes would return to the "Blue Tambourine", and that, arising out of his return, would come something tangible. It was definitely a little more than a mere idea. It was a lingering, feverish hope that supplied best part of the vision with which she surveyed the remnants of her life. It was, therefore, with no surprise, that one morning she heard his clear, incisive voice again in the doorway. His presence seemed to her to be very meet and right; it would have been wrong if he had not come again to her. The inn had only just thrown open its doors, and Mrs. Lane herself was wiping a row of glasses destined for almost immediate use. Two or three of the faithful had filed in, and the smoke from their cigarettes was beginning to fill the bar. When she heard Anthony Bathurst's voice, Mrs. Lane glanced at the wheezy, tilted old Dutch clock in the corner, and nodded to herself with every appearance of temporary satisfaction. To say that consolation came to her would be an exaggeration; the inevitable was her constant companion. She had lost her world. But she was aroused, to an acuter consciousness of external things, by that voice that she heard close to her, and she journeyed nearer to the things of hope. The figure in the doorway raised his hat, and a light shone lambently in her pale, expressionless brown eyes. Anthony walked across to her, and looked anxiously into her face. He noted its weariness and the heavy lines round the corners of the mouth. He gave her greeting.

"Where can we talk, Mrs. Lane?" he asked. "In the same room as before?"

"Yes, sir. Of course. It may sound a bit strange, but I've been sort of expecting you. Though I couldn't tell you why."

Mr. Bathurst smiled; then he followed her into the inner room. Mrs. Lane pulled out a chair for him. The awakened spirit of the woman, aroused from its long slumber, rose with an eager hunger for this fresh interest.

"This call of mine, Mrs. Lane," opened Anthony, "is really supplementary to my previous one. On the other visit, I asked certain questions, one of which you found yourself unable to answer. That fact, however, was not due to any fault of yours. It was mine entirely. I realize that. I offered you but little straw, and therefore it would have been foolish and unreasonable of me to expect from you a plentiful supply of bricks. This time, though, the position is a little changed."

"Changed?" she echoed. The word he used was a word of which the meaning was now unknown to her. As far as vision was possible, to her, nothing could ever change. She repeated the word:

"Changed? How?"

"In this way, Mrs. Lane. This time I have more straw—more knowledge, than I had in my possession before, so that it is on the cards, shall we say, that I, helping you more, may, in my turn, be more helped by you. Bricks may even result. See what I mean?"

Anthony looked up hopefully. Could he invigorate her? It was vital to his case that he should not fail here. Mrs. Lane made no reply. Anthony, therefore, struck harder.

"I feel, Mrs. Lane, that here in this little inn lies a secret that may throw light on two murders."

She gasped. Here was a word she knew from Mount Sinai, and by tradition, dreaded. "Murders?"

He nodded. "Yes, Mrs. Lane. That is why I have come here, for this is where I can sing my song."

Anthony looked at her quizzically. "Shall I sing the songs of Zion in a strange land? Of course not. They must be sung in their own land. Now listen carefully to me." She turned to him mechanically and nodded her understanding and obedience. "If you carry your mind back, Mrs. Lane, to my previous visit, you will remember that I asked you, and after you yourself, your maid Effie, if you could recall any customer or caller here, for whom your husband might have changed that fifty pound note that I was seeking. Yes?"

The landlady nodded again. "Yes, sir, I remember that quite well. I looked at the paying-in book, and—"

"Good. My point now, in relation to that, is this. Previously, I had nothing at all definite to give you. Now I come armed with certain details. Can you recall a man in this inn, about that time, who had one leg? The other leg, I should say, had been amputated somewhere above the knee. Also, I am confident that he would be using a crutch."

The anxiety that Anthony felt as he asked the question, manifested itself in his eyes. His suspense, however, was but short-lived, and he breathed freely. An answering and understanding look showed almost immediately upon the worn face of Mrs. Lane. Her brown eyes, previously expressionless, now held a keen expression.

"Of course I can, sir. I know that man only too well. Came in here regularly, sir. What's more, he was a man I never liked. I've seen him with more drink in him than was good for him. I told my Mark that, sir—more than once. But he was that easy-going—friends with everybody. That man was in the inn, sir, on the very day that Mark was . . ." Her handkerchief sought her eyes; more words refused to come to her. Tears came in their stead. Anthony, silent for a time, allowed her to recover.

"I thought as much, Mrs. Lane. His name is Stubbs, and he was the man, if you care to hear the news, who changed the note with your husband. I'm as certain of that fact as I am of the coming of to-morrow."

"You know what he was, sir, don't you?"

"You mean—?"

"I mean, what he did for his living. If you could call it a living." She spoke with the contemptuous tone of industry towards art.

"I think I do. But tell me."

"He was a musician of sorts. At least, that's what the wastrel called himself. I heard him talking to my husband one day in the bar. He was telling my husband what he did for a living. As I told you, sir, he was a pretty regular visitor in these parts."

Anthony Bathurst permitted himself to smile. "I fancy that he flattered himself a little, Mrs. Lane. You could scarcely describe him as a musician. If my information is correct, and I don't think I could have found a better source than the wife of his bosom, he was a dancer. That is to say, he put his crutch on the ground and used his one leg to execute a series of ugly, grotesque steps to the notes of a street organ. Sort of 'Peg-leg Joe' or 'Steam-boat Bill'. Considering his infirmity, of course, he must have been tremendously nimble to put up such a performance. In his hands, as he danced to the organ, he used a pair of clappers, which he manipulated in a kind of time and rhythm to his dancing. Also, he affected a sort of scarlet knee-breeches uniform, so that taking everything into consideration, he cut a rather unusual figure. The organ of this artistic combination was played by a gentleman who rejoices in the unseasonable name of Bill Holly. That is to say, speaking at the present time of the year."

Mrs. Lane signified her agreement with Mr. Bathurst's statement. "You're quite right again, sir. I know this second man you speak of, very well indeed. As well as I know that other horrible man, Stubbs. Where one went, the other went."

"Naturally. That would be so. They were inseparable. A business combination." His eyes twinkled.

"This Holly man isn't a beauty to look at by any means. He's a little, thin, peaky, rat-faced man. Sly, furtive eyes. The kind of man you'd distrust, on sight."

"Were they both friendly with your husband, Mrs. Lane?"

"Not what you'd call friendly, sir, in the real sense. Just customers, no more. I told you how easy Mark always was with everybody. It was no good talking to him. He'd never alter. The man Holly has been in here two or three times since Mark died."

"I was hoping that you would tell me that." Anthony showed signs of pleasure. "How long ago is it since you last saw him?"

Mrs. Lane opened her mouth to reply, but suddenly stopped, listening hard. "Excuse me just a moment, sir, if you please. I fancy I'm wanted in the bar for a minute."

Anthony gestured his assent, and the landlady billowed out. Hardly had she departed than she was back with him. Her face was eloquent. "I thought I was right, sir," she whispered. "I never hardly forget a face—or a voice. This time it's a voice I've remembered." She tip-toed across to Anthony, and put her mouth close to his ear. "The gentleman known as Bill Holly is in the bar now. I heard him come in as I was talking to you."

Anthony rose to his feet in some excitement. The ball was at his feet.

"That's very interesting, Mrs. Lane. A very appropriate entry. Couldn't have been better staged of deliberate design. With your permission, I'll have a word or two with Mr. William Holly."

CHAPTER XX
THE CRUTCH AGAIN

MR. WILLIAM Holly looked up from the depths of his tankard with a stare of astonishment. The tall stranger, who had seemingly appeared from nowhere, and addressed him by name, and who now surveyed him somewhat critically, had that indefinable something about him that was invariably and painfully associated by Mr. Holly, with the governing classes. Not exactly with the forces of law and order, but contingent unto them. Anthony repeated his salutation, and added to it.

"Good morning, Holly. Been round Perry Hammer recently?"

Holly's tankard fell to the stone floor with a crash.

"Dear, dear," remarked Mr. Bathurst. "Now, that's too bad. You've spilt quite a reasonable amount of perfectly good beer. Do you know, I've many a time heard my grandfather say that he'd sooner have seen the Houses of Parliament fall down, than a drop of good beer spilt. No admirer of Guy Fawkes, either."

Holly eyed his tormentor with something that approached truculence tinged with fear.

"What's the game?" he demanded.

"Game?" echoed Mr. Bathurst innocently. "I'm afraid that I don't quite follow you. I'm perfectly serious. How's Perry Hammer looking?"

Mr. Holly spat with professional efficiency. It was an action of expression. "I don't know yer," he answered, "and I don't know that I wants to know yer. Put me down as a particular sort of bloke. Also, I ain't answerin' your bloody questions. Got that, young feller-me-lad?"

"'Pon my soul," returned Bathurst, "you're all of a dither. Gone as white as chalk. That comes of spilling your beer like you did. It's upset you. Perfectly natural. So you won't tell me about Perry Hammer?"

"Lay off that tripe, guv'nor. You've made a mistake. That's all there is to it. You think I'm somebody else—that's what's the trouble with you. I guess I'd better be going."

Holly rose from the bench where he had been sitting, in order to put his statement into effect. At the movement, however, Bathurst's voice discarded its note of raillery, and became charged with glittering menace. He held Mr. Holly by the shoulder. The man was helpless.

"I think not, Mr. Holly. At least, for a little while. Be careful I don't put you where you ought to be. It's a matter of ten seconds, I understand. Or, at any rate, very little more."

"What is, guv'nor?" Holly's voice shook.

"The nine o'clock walk, of course. From the cell to the execution-shed. The ceremony's an hour later now than it used to be, I believe. To what did you imagine I referred?"

Holly licked craven lips. "You're talkin' conundrums, guv'nor. Honest now, I don't get yer."

"Don't lie, Holly. How's Mr. George A. Stubbs? Dissolved partnership, have you?"

"I ain't set eyes on that dirty, lousy swine for months. And that's Gawd's own truth, guv'nor. I couldn't alter it, if I wanted to. And if you want to know, I ain't never been near that place you mentioned. Something 'Ammer, wasn't it?" When Bathurst released him, Holly's face worked in nervous emotion.

"Really? I find your statement a little difficult to believe. Very difficult, indeed. Returning, however, to our mutual friend, Mr. Stubbs, is my suggestion that you have dissolved partnership substantially correct?" Mr. Bathurst eyed his victim; patiently he waited for the reply. Holly, however, stuck to his guns. There was no budging on his part.

"I've told you the truth, guv'nor. I said as 'ow I 'adn't set eyes on Stubbs for months now—neither I 'aven't." He shifted his feet uneasily on the stone floor.

"Months?" queried Anthony with direct emphasis. "That's an elastic term, Holly. How many months old is this separation of yours, now? Two? Three?"

Holly affected to consider. "Stubbs left me in the early spring," he replied, sullenly,

"Be more exact," returned Anthony sternly. "Surely the question is easy enough to answer."

Holly's little eyes narrowed even more. "I think it was just after Easter, guv'nor—say about the tenth of April, shall we say. Yes, it was." He brightened perceptibly. "He was with me over the Easter itself, I can remember that. On the Good Friday we was over at Wormwood Scrubs. Terrible day it was, too. One of Old England's best. Didn't take a dollar all the ruddy day. Rained cats and dogs, it did. It was during the week after, that Mr. George Stubbs 'opped it."

His eyes met those of Bathurst. They were unequal to the task of holding them, and wavered almost immediately.

"I'm inclined to think, Holly," declared the latter, "that your memory is one of the convenient type. That third week in April formed a natural boundary mark. It was something from which you determined to keep well away."

Holly laughed a mirthless laugh. "I don't get yer, guv'nor. Honest, I don't. And with all due respect I must be makin' a move. My organ's a few yards down the road, and time's money with me—not 'avin' been born in the purple with a silver spoon in my mouth. Never was one o' the lucky ones." He made a feeble attempt to achieve height, looked shiftily at his questioner, and turned on his heel. Mr. Bathurst, acquiescent in his departure, watched him go—a smile playing round the corners of his lips.

"Twenty-five to one I'm right," he murmured. "And devilish hard luck, all the same. The one chance in a million, and it went against me." He glanced at his wrist-watch, and then, turning, sought Mrs. Lane again. He found her sitting in the room where he had left her. The room in which she would sit for always.

"That was a stroke of glittering luck, Mrs. Lane. To catch that gentleman on the premises as we did. And luck, at that,

that's long overdue. It's about the first piece I've had, all the way through this case."

"Did he tell you what you wanted to know, sir?" Mrs. Lane was obviously anxious, although she herself, had she been asked, couldn't have explained the reason for this anxiety. Anthony laughed lightly at the concern she showed.

"Hardly, Mrs. Lane. If the truth be told, I fancy that I told him considerably more than he told me. I've put myself properly in that gentleman's black books, I can tell you. I had to bluff him a bit, you know, and only time will tell how far the bluff succeeded." After he had talked to her seriously for a time, he held out his hand to her. "Good-bye, Mrs. Lane. You've been more than kind to me. Believe me, I appreciate it tremendously. Always count me as your friend."

She gave him her hand in return. Anthony added a smile to his farewell. A brisk walk brought him into the town, and for a moment he stopped to look at the water of the Abbey mill-stream, that branch of the Rennet known as the "Holy Brook". His immediate destination was King Street—the home of the Anthurium Cinema. He was pleased to observe that the picture-house was in activity again. There were still traces of the disastrous fire of six months previously, but repairs of a kind had been summarily executed, and the Anthurium was offering its usual lurid wares to its patrons. Mr. Bathurst paused on the steps to gaze at photographs of John Longden, Randle Ayrton, Donald Calthrop and Norah Baring that were displayed outside, in "Two Worlds", and, seemingly satisfied, stepped up the palatial entrance that led to the box-office. A resplendent commissionaire announced in dulcet tones that certain priced seats were available. Anthony approached him with a proper measure of awe.

"Do you think," he said engagingly, "that I might have a word with the manager?"

The magnificent gentleman pushed a finger along the side of his nose, and doubted it. All complaints—" he commenced to say—

"It's not that," returned Mr. Bathurst. "I never complain. It's rather more important than that. Perhaps if you glance at my card, it will help you to see what I mean."

The commissionaire inspected the proffered card from an imposing altitude. Suddenly his expression changed. It would be truthful to say that it softened somewhat.

"I will see what I can do for you, sir. Come behind the glass-doors. This way, sir."

Anthony obeyed, and, his companion disappearing, waited. Not for long.

"Come this way, sir."

The manager, as soon as he had assimilated the situation, listened to Mr. Bathurst attentively. At a certain stage of the recital he looked up abruptly. Anthony, seeing this, came to a dead stop. He waited for the explanation.

"There will be no need to see our cashier. As it happens, I can answer your question myself. Thanks to the fire that we had here."

It was borne upon Anthony Bathurst at that moment that the run of his luck, against which he had so bitterly complained, had now definitely turned in his favour. "You can? Oh—splendid. What can you tell me about it?"

"The man that you're inquiring about, was here on the evening of the fire. He paid for two seats—they were one-and-three-penny seats—and he sat at the back of the circle. There is little doubt that he was one of the seventy-four people who perished in the fire."

"But the body was not identified," urged Mr. Bathurst sharply.

"It was absolutely impossible to identify several of the bodies. They were so charred as to be absolutely unrecognizable. For example—to illustrate my meaning—eleven people were identified by tiny pieces of clothing or by blackened and twisted articles that they were known to have had with them."

Anthony Bathurst, schooled by grim experience, was taking no chances. "I am not quite clear. If, as you say, this man's body was never identified, how is it that you are so sure that he was in the cinema?"

The manager smiled a smile of superiority.

"I have two excellent reasons for saying what I did. Although it's a kind of cart and horse business. First of all, the cashier at the pay-office distinctly remembers the man that you describe, paying for two seats—as I stated—at the back of the circle. The question, you see, has been up for consideration before."

"Why?" intervened Bathurst sharply.

"If you don't mind, I'll answer that question in a moment. But you can assure yourself that my cashier is absolutely certain of her ground. The man you are after, was of such distinctive appearance that there is very little chance of her having made a mistake."

Anthony nodded his acquiescence. "I entirely agree with you there. Tracing him is a very different problem from tracing an ordinary, average man."

The manager nodded. "Now I'll answer that other question you asked. As to why this business has been gone into before. Would you like to take a walk for a few steps? Come upstairs with me, will you, please?"

Secretly wondering what the unexpected journey was to bring forth, Anthony Bathurst followed the man up a heavily-carpeted staircase.

"The fire, I ought to tell you, was very much worse on one side of the building than on the other, and the lives that were lost were lost chiefly by reason of sheer panic. Had the people kept their heads, I doubt if there would have been a casualty."

"Where are we going?" asked Anthony.

"I've a private room up here," returned the manager, "just at the side of a small confectionery bar. I've something in there that I'm going to show you. I'll lay a wager that when you see it, you'll be thoroughly interested."

"Depends on what it is," returned Bathurst, laconically.

Arrived at the room of which he had spoken, the manager pushed open the door and at the same time invited Bathurst to step inside. Anthony entered, and his companion walked across to the far corner of the room.

"There you are, Mr. Bathurst," he announced with a strong strain of pleasure. "Take a good look at that thing standing up there in the corner. Going to be of help to you, isn't it?"

It was a heavy crutch of the old-fashioned variety. The arm-rest was of strongly-padded reddish leather, and the wood of it was thick and substantial. Bathurst took hold of it and examined the leather at the head very carefully and critically. This exercise of his, seemed to afford the manager considerable satisfaction. After a short interval, Bathurst replaced the crutch in its position in the corner, and began to pace the little room. He did this two . . . three . . . four times. Then he stopped. A shake of his head accompanied the stoppage. The manager showed surprise.

"What is it, Mr. Bathurst? Can I help you at all?"

Anthony caressed his chin. "What you've been trying to tell me, I take it, is this. Your people here, deduced from the discovery of this crutch, that one of the unidentified victims of the fire was the one-legged man, whom your cashier remembered as having paid for two tickets at the pay-office? Was that the position?"

The manager nodded. "Naturally. And we were perfectly justified in adopting that attitude. Nobody came forward to claim it. Not a single inquiry for it came this way, to my knowledge."

Anthony swung round to him almost aggressively. "But my dear fellow, consider the presence of the crutch. How can you explain it?"

The manager raised his eyebrows. "I'm sorry. I thought that I had made myself absolutely clear with regard to that. Don't you see that it was because of—?"

"Man alive. Look at it for yourself. Why isn't the crutch burned? Cripple burned! Crutch burned!"

"It is. At least, I think so. If you look at the leather part carefully under the light, you will be able to detect a slight—"

"The veriest trifle," returned Anthony. "What might be described as a singe. Hardly anything more than that."

The manager seemed a little discomfited at Anthony's reception of his story. Anthony followed up.

"Doesn't it occur to you as most remarkable, that the crippled man should be burned beyond recognition and his crutch—almost a vital matter to him, mark you, as a means of locomotion—should show scarcely a sign of burning? Candidly, now?"

The man whom he addressed, looked serious. "I suppose it does, now that you mention it."

"Tell me—if you are able, that is—where, exactly, was this crutch found?"

"Come into the auditorium. I'll show you as best as I can."

Anthony was piloted to a stand behind the back row of the circle. The manager leant over the ledge and pointed to the right, and whispered. "Over there, on those side seats, is where the fire was at its fiercest. Do you see where I mean?"

Mr. Bathurst followed the direction of his hand and nodded.

"The people in those seats stampeded in an attempt to reach that corridor that runs along the side as far as the organ. Look."

"Yes. I follow, all that."

"You see where there is the 'Exit' notice. That is the normal exit for people leaving at any time during the performance. There you are, Mr. Bathurst. There's an example to hand. There are some people using it now. Do you see them? They have come from seats near the front and have turned to the left on their way out. But it is possible to turn to the right and go out the same way as you come in—down the staircase that leads to the front of the theatre in the street. If you use the other way, as those people just now did, it brings you out, via a flight of stone steps, in a side-turning at the back of the house. The crutch was found at the foot of that flight of steps."

On the silent way back to the manager's room, Anthony was unable to restrain himself. He rubbed his hands repeatedly. He was about to intervene conversationally when the manager checked him.

"Let me explain the matter a little further. You must understand, that on the evening of the fire, several of the more fortunate people *did* escape that way. The general view here—and it was shared, I may say, by the police authorities—was that the crippled chap got part of the way and was then overwhelmed by sheer weight of numbers. He fell, in all probability, from exhaustion, just the other side of those doors. A heap of badly-burned bodies was found there. His crutch was then kicked, perhaps, or swept along in some way by the other people who escaped, and reached as far as the flight of stone steps. Quite a feasible contingency, don't you think, Mr. Bathurst?"

That gentleman resumed his exercise of pacing the room. Suddenly he turned and launched another question.

"You told me, I think, that your cashier remembers issuing *two* tickets to our one-legged friend. Yes?"

"That is so. There were two tickets sold to him'. The girl is positive on the point."

"Who was the person who came with him? Has she any idea? Was that point ever gone into?"

"It was. But all inquiries led us nowhere. The girl who issued the two tickets was interrogated at the time, but was unable to make any definite statement on the matter. It's like this, you see. There is such a constant stream of people of all ages and of most types, passing in front of the pay-box, that it is a most difficult matter to determine *pairs*, for instance."

"Pairs?"

The manager nodded. "Yes. People that are together, I mean."

"Who is with whom, you mean, and who isn't?"

"Yes."

"I see the difficulty, and I can see also that I can hope for no further help in that direction."

"None, I'm afraid; Mr. Bathurst. If you like, of course, you can have a word with the girl yourself. Give the word, and I'll send for her."

Bathurst considered the suggested arrangement, but ultimately discarded it. "Many thanks for the suggestion. I don't think, however, that I'll act on it. I question its real value very seriously. You say that she could give no accurate information on this particular matter when the affair was young and, therefore, fresh in her brain. It is scarcely likely, then, that she will do any better now. If I attempt to stimulate her brain by putting a series of leading questions to her, I may force a result, that may have every appearance of truth—and yet, in reality, be entirely false. My wish may have parented her thought. Which is the very last thing that I desire to happen. That's a splendid way by which to go astray." He smiled. "I'll ask you another question instead, if I may. Were you acquainted with a certain man of the name of Mark Lane, licensee of a little pub on the outskirts of the town, known as the 'Blue Tambourine'?"

The response was grave. "Knew him a little. By sight only. I never use the 'Blue Tambourine'—it's out of my way—but Lane came here occasionally. He was one of the people burned to death here. But I guess you know that. Otherwise you wouldn't have mentioned his name."

"Yes, I knew that. Mrs. Lane, his widow, told me. But tell me this. Did you know that Lane was in the house before the fire broke out?"

"No. How—er—do you mean? How should I know?"

"It's just possible, I thought, that you might have seen him going in. It's on the cards, surely?"

"Well—yes—come to that, I suppose it is. But I didn't see him beforehand. I can tell you that. My first intimation about him was when his body was identified by Mrs. Lane. Or his clothing, rather."

Anthony spoke resignedly. "That's bad luck. All the same, I haven't done too badly, and I can't expect things all my own way. It was worth trying, though. Keep that crutch in as safe a place as possible. I may want it again before I've finished. How's business in the film world? Looking up?"

On his way back to town, when he, in the comparative quietude of his first-class compartment, was able to assess more accurately the sum total of the knowledge he had gained in Reading and district, he felt a strong degree of satisfaction. The clouds were lifting, And the sky looking much clearer. There wasn't a doubt of it. One of his own great doubts had thinned considerably. Which fact became a pleasing thought. He felt moderately confident that he would be able to effect his *coup* after all. A great change had come over the scene since the position *ante litem motam*. After all the setbacks that had come to him, he was not destined to that unhappy consciousness of talents abused, and opportunities lost, which makes existence so burdensome for the sensitive artist. When his train ran into Paddington, he determined, without delay, to call upon Sir Robert Frant.

CHAPTER XXI
MR. BATHURST EXERCISES PERSISTENCE

SIR Robert Frant held the telephone-receiver to his ear and listened attentively. The remarks that came to him from the speaker at the other end of the line, were punctuated by him by a series of quick shakes of the head. But he still retained his implicit faith in Anthony Bathurst, and the news to which he was now listening filled him with a certain amount of grave disquiet. It was true that his son had been acquitted of the murder of Leonard Pearson, and that, according to English law, he was safe from the consequences of the charge for all time. But, as Bathurst had pointed out to his brother, a verdict of "Not guilty" is not always popularly interpreted as "innocent".

"We must hope for the best," he answered, "and it's no use worrying ourselves. If I hear anything I'll let you know. Good-bye for the present."

Having delivered himself of this statement, he replaced the receiver and walked to his own special chair in his consulting-room, to seat himself therein. To think! To think hard! Why had Fate treated him so scurvily? Why had it placed him in the position that it had?

It was in this same chair and same mood (oft recurring) that Anthony Bathurst (some days afterwards) found him, when, on his return from Reading, he was shown up to the consulting-room.

"Morning, Bathurst," came Sir Robert's greeting. "Don't tell me that you've pulled it off after all?"

"Why not, sir? It would be good news, would it not?"

Sir Robert returned Anthony's smile. "I agree. But after the verdict that acquitted my son had been given, you said a somewhat surprising thing. I've often found myself thinking over it since. Do you remember? Just after the trial finished? That you knew the name of Pearson's assassin, but that it was futile knowledge to you. For the very good reason that you would never be able to bring him to justice."

There was a despairing note in Sir Robert's tone, at which Bathurst laughed cheerfully.

"Perfectly true, sir, and all that. I meant it when I said it, too. Don't forget, though, that a lot has happened since then."

"To what do you refer, particularly?"

"The murder of Mr. Justice Heriot, in itself moderately important, and the finding of a cripple's crutch in a burnt cinema. This second incident, most tremendously important." Bathurst's tone was light, but his eyes were serious.

Sir Robert stared, evidently not too well pleased. "I can follow you in your first statement, but not in your second. What cripple? What crutch? And another thing. Are you certain, Bathurst, that the two murders are connected?"

Mr. Bathurst purposely ignored the first two of Sir Robert's questions, and elected to answer the third.

"I haven't the slightest doubt that there is a connection, Sir Robert. Let me put it a little differently. Let me say that one happened *because* of the other. Without the first, there wouldn't have been the second."

Sir Robert Frant frowned and tapped his front teeth with the barrel of his fountain-pen.

"Which was which?" he demanded. "Are you trying to tell me that a man of Heriot's reputation and standing, had any link with Pearson? I should find that most difficult to believe, my dear Bathurst. The two circles in which they moved were as far apart as the poles."

"I'm not proving anything, sir, at the moment. I have two or three more steps to take before my case is complete and I am in a position to do that. But—in relation to what you say—how much of Heriot's past life is known to you? How does any one of us know the innermost secrets of a man's heart? Or a woman's? I simply content myself with saying that the murders of Pearson and Heriot were as the influences of cause and effect. At the moment, I won't go beyond that."

Sir Robert groaned. "It's all a wretched worry. The heritage of the folly of a young girl. My daughter. My only daughter. The sins of the children, it seems to me, are nowadays visited upon the fathers. We shall have to revise the Commandments if we desire to arrive at the truth." He turned in his chair to give greater point to his words, and as he did so Anthony Bathurst fired another question at him.

"Do you regard, Sir Robert, the consulting-room in the same sacred light as the confessional?"

The doctor answered without any hesitation. "Most certainly, my dear boy. Whatever induced you to ask such a question?"

Anthony replied to him by asking a series of others. "Absolutely? Irrevocably? No matter what the circumstances may be?"

Frant demurred a little. His answer came more slowly than his previous one.

"For the purpose of answering your question—I must reply—yes."

"But *apart* from that particular consideration?" Anthony was merciless.

Sir Robert manifested irritability. "It is impossible to answer a question of that kind with an unequivocal 'yes' or 'no'. Surely you must see that. All I can say to you, is that I should never divulge a secret that came to me in my professional capacity, unless—" He hesitated.

"Unless—what?" asked Mr. Bathurst with soft persuasion.

"No! No 'unless' about it. I was wrong to suggest such a thing," concluded Sir Robert testily. "I withdraw all question of conditions unreservedly. No other course of conduct is possible to a man in a position like mine."

"That brings me, then, Sir Robert, to my own position. You came to me for help. I promised it to you—such as it was and such as it has been. I'm not boasting about it, believe me. Would you, then, deny *me* help if I asked it of you? *As a means to the same end* that brought you to me?" Anthony watched the famous specialist with kind interest. Sir Robert dissembled.

"In a way, Bathurst, your work is accomplished. Surely you feel that. My boy has been cleared. He is free."

"No, Sir Robert. Acquitted! I thought that I had made that plain to you before."

"And again, Bathurst, what possible help can I give you in the matter? Neither Pearson nor Heriot was a patient of mine. Nor anybody else connected with the case, as far as I know."

Anthony's eyes held the fighting look of old. "That statement of yours clears the air considerably. My hands are less tied. I'll put the question direct. What was the disease from which the late Mr. Justice Heriot was suffering?"

Sir Robert's eyes opened in amazement. Did he hear aright? Bathurst's powers were immediately re-valued by him.

"My dear Bathurst," he said with a certain amount of emotion, "I haven't the slightest idea. Heriot never consulted me in his life. You've been ploughing the sands this time, my boy, and no mistake."

Anthony took the implied censure with his usual nonchalance. "Then I'm sorry, sir. Could you suggest to me where I could find out?"

"Find out what?" came the reply imperturbable.

"The nature of the disease from which poor old Heriot was suffering?"

"From nowhere, I should say. From no source that I can indicate. He was under Barrow-South, and you'll extract as much from Barrow-South, I venture to predict, as you would have done from me. Probably a little less. So give up the idea, my boy. Dismiss it from your mind. If you don't, and still cling to it, I'm very much afraid that you'll be doomed to disappointment."

Anthony eyed him with hard resolution. "Let me put it to you in another way. You force me to say this. Suppose, sir, your son's *life* depended upon knowledge that had come to you in the sanctity, as you are pleased to consider it, of your consulting-room? Suppose that that knowledge, in the translated condition of interpreted evidence, had been the one and only means that could have saved Captain Frant from the horror of the gallows? The only life-belt that could have been thrown to him? Would you still have stood aloof and denied him that succour?"

Sir Robert Frant exhibited deep emotion. He bit his lip. "You are asking me a very big question. . . . I should have sought help from a Higher Power. I might not have been strong enough to resist such a tremendous temptation."

"We differ, then, sir," replied Anthony curtly, "as to what is strength and what is weakness."

Sir Robert rose. He remembered his conversation on the telephone of a few days previously, when his concluding exhortation had been to hope for the best, and in very remembrance of it, he drew himself up to his full height.

"To discuss this matter any more, Mr. Bathurst, would be mere idleness. The situation that you have been good enough to depict, never arose. The particular situation that you outlined will never arise. Many thanks for all that you have done. But it has been, I fear, an eminently thankless case and task. With small tangible reward for you, too, I fear."

Mr. Bathurst's momentary curtness vanished and one of his irresistible smiles lit up his features. "On the contrary, Sir Robert, I am now filled with extraordinary hopefulness. Within one week, I am confident enough to hope, I shall be in a position to have cleared up completely each of the crimes that I have been investigating."

Sir Robert was plainly incredulous. His face mirrored the condition. "What do you mean, exactly, by that statement?"

Anthony ticked off the points of his answer on the tips of his fingers. "I hope to give you, *one*, the name of the person who killed Leonard Pearson, *two* and *three*, why and how he was killed, *four*, the name of Heriot's slayer, *five* and *six*, the reason and manner of *his* killing."

"You will do that in one week from now?" Sir Robert gasped.

Mr. Bathurst's jaw was rigid. "I would do it now, save for a slight doubt concerning point No. 4. Heriot was murdered by one of three people. I should apportion the respective odds as evens, tens and one hundred. I want the week's grace to make absolutely sure concerning my even money chance."

His optimism was infectious and Sir Robert's incredulity was affected by it. The latter knew, that the man who stood in front of him, meant what he said without the shadow of a doubt.

"You will, of course, acquaint me, Bathurst, before you take any step that may be described as decisive? I think that you owe me that privilege, considering the terms upon which we met." He smiled.

"I promise you, sir, that you shall have full advice. In the circumstances, I shouldn't dream of taking any action without first consulting you." Bathurst returned the smile with which Sir Robert had favoured him. "That's an advantage, you see, sir, that you get from me that you wouldn't get from official Scotland Yard. As a rule, that is."

Sir Robert took out his cigarette-case and extended it to Anthony. "I realize that very deeply. Thank you. Smoke?"

Mr. Bathurst took the cigarette upon the invitation and lit it. "Thank you, Sir Robert." He turned to go, but hesitated on the threshold. "You will expect to hear from me, then, within a week. I am confident that I shall not disappoint you. You give me *carte blanche*, of course?"

"To what extent?"

"Well, it's just within the region of possibility that I might wish to entertain one or two rather distinguished people—amongst others—in the course of the next few days. My own flat's rather small. On the other hand, you have some most spacious rooms here. Might I—?"

"Any time you like, my dear Bathurst. Give me fair warning—that's all I ask, and I'll make the necessary arrangements." Sir Robert was really gracious.

"My thanks again. I knew you would. Some people object to small rooms, you know. That's why one has to exercise so much care in dealing with individual cases. One man's fad is liqueur brandy. Another's is a blue-veined Stilton. And so the world goes on. We soothe the fevered Gorgonzola by playing on the pianola. Or sing an entertaining air, to Roquefort and Camembert." Anthony grinned.

Sir Robert Frant stared in mute incomprehension, but immediately Mr. Bathurst found himself outside the house in Lancaster Gate, his mood of gaiety gave way to one of gravity. The cigarette that he held between his lips was a Mouraki! So the damn thing still persisted! He went over the whole of the circumstances in his mind once again, from cigarette to cigarette, and this time the result rather pleased him than otherwise. If he could but draw the trumps from the hand of Dr. Barrow-South within the next twenty-four hours, he felt convinced that half of the game, at least, would be in his hands. The other half, then, would be but a question of time. . . . He murmured the famous doctor's name to himself as he turned into Wimpole Street, and there was something like a caress in the inflexion of his voice. "Dr. Revill Barrow-South."

CHAPTER XXII
MR. BATHURST DRAWS THE TRUMPS

DR. REVILL Barrow-South regarded his visitor gravely. He drummed upon his table with his finger-tips.

"I have already explained the position twice, Mr. Bathurst," he announced primly. "Once—in a most unpleasant little room at a place called, I believe, Langley Broom, where the judge's body was found—and secondly at the Coroner's Inquest. I hardly expected that I should be called upon to reiterate my statements yet again. First a sergeant of police, then the Coroner, and now you. Can you assure me that this interview is at all necessary?" Dr. Barrow-South ceased his drumming and surveyed the tips of his fingers with a suave complacency.

Mr. Bathurst decided that the time had come for him to draw upon his vast resources of tact. He had to effect persuasion, without surrender of principle on the part of his *vis-à-vis*.

"The last thing I desire from you, sir, is anything in the nature of a reiteration of your statements. You have stated the main facts so clearly and so concisely that there is no need for it. But there are disturbing elements about the case, sir. Most disturbing. Consider the things found in the trunk. That black cap, for example. Your professional card, too. Nobody, of course, attaches the slightest importance to that, nobody of any consequence, that is. But there is—" Anthony spread out his hands eloquently and finished on a high note. "I seek the truth. And I think you can help me in two important directions. You—and you alone, sir."

Barrow-South, however, was moderately proof against flattery. He made no immediate concession; he chose the middle course.

"Perhaps. That, I should say, remains to be seen. Understand that I don't promise anything. However, we shall see. What are these directions that you describe as so—er—important? Name them, Mr. Bathurst—if you please."

"You were called, Doctor, to Langley Broom when the body of Mr. Justice Heriot was discovered. And you performed the autopsy of that body. Your findings told you that he had been killed by chloroform. That is so, is it not?"

Barrow-South inclined his head with an air of magnanimity. This man who had come to him certainly did things with an air. "Quite true."

Anthony leant forward with a light in his eyes. "In addition, there is this fact. The judge was under your professional attention. I sincerely hope, Doctor, that you will find no difficulty in answering what I am going to ask you next. I hope that you will realize, that the urgency of the matter more than counterbalances any compunction you may feel in the opposite direction." He paused to see the effect his words had upon the doctor.

Barrow-South hummed and hawed. "Ask on, Mr. Bathurst."

"Thank you, Doctor. I appreciate the kindness of your—er—intention." Anthony chose his words carefully. "How long would Mr. Justice Heriot have lived, assuming that his end had been a natural one?"

Anthony waited eagerly for the reply. It came at long length.

"Not more than six months. Probably not as long as that."

"Thank you again, Doctor. I will not ask you to betray any more confidences directly. You will understand what I mean in a moment."

Mr. Bathurst took a sheet of note-paper from his pocket. He scribbled four words across it with his fountain-pen. This done, he pushed the paper towards the doctor. Barrow-South, with some surprise showing on his face, looked at it and then readjusted his pince-nez that he might read it the better. A minute passed. The specialist said nothing. Then he peered over the top of his glasses, rubbed his chin and surveyed Anthony gravely. Mr. Bathurst met the gaze coolly, waiting silently. Eventually—word by word—the reply came that he desired.

"That is so. You are undeniably right in your assumption. I don't, of course, know the source of your information, but that is a matter over which—"

"Attribute it to the science of deduction, sir. I marshalled certain facts that I've been able to hit upon, and they—accumulatively—led me to that conclusion."

Barrow-South shrugged his shoulders—evidently unimpressed. Like Gallio, he cared for none of these things.

"Is there any more that I can do for you? Please come to the point as quickly as you can. My time can scarcely be called my own, these days."

"I realize that, sir. None better. My second point is this. Was the fact that you have just confessed, known to anybody other than yourself?"

Barrow-South's reply came instantly. "To no one."

"To no one?"

"To nobody whatever that mattered."

"What do you mean by that, sir?"

Barrow-South shrugged his shoulders again. "My answer must be what it was—to no one."

Anthony decided to tread warily. "May I ask if you are absolutely certain of that, sir?"

"You may, but, as I told you, my answer will be just the same."

Mr. Bathurst tacked accordingly. "Did Mr. Justice Heriot know it himself?"

Barrow-South fidgeted a little in his chair. "Actually—in so many definite and direct words—no. He may have suspected it. I should say that he did, remembering certain remarks that he made to me. But let me put it like this. An X-ray which I had taken of his throat, told me vastly more than I told him. It spoke to me particularly. I spoke to him very much more generally. I had formed an opinion, and I had had it confirmed. And now, Mr. Bathurst, if you don't mind, I think I'll—" The doctor made as though to rise from his seat and terminate the interview. Anthony Bathurst reached over the table and pulled the piece of notepaper, that he had used previously, towards him. Taking up his pen again, he wrote a sentence hastily, almost feverishly, under the four words that he had written before. Then he held it up for Barrow-South's inspection. Placed as it was, the specialist was almost forced to consider it. "Am I right, sir?" demanded Bathurst, with an eagerness he made no endeavour to hide.

"Oh, well, if it comes to that, I suppose you are. All the same, you understand that there is no disturbance of my position. It's tantamount to the same thing, and makes no difference whatever. From your point of view, I told nobody. I'm afraid that you'll have to be satisfied with that."

Anthony smiled at his earnestness. ' 'I know what you mean, sir. I thoroughly understand the position that you take up. And—"

"And what?" demanded the doctor.

"I'm more than satisfied. I won't trouble you any more, sir. Good-bye, and many thanks."

Mr. Bathurst closed the door behind him. He failed to notice the strange look on the face of Barrow-South.

On his way home, Anthony debated two things. The first was the terms of the advertisement that he must draw up—the second, whether he should interview Dick Lanchester before the gathering at Lancaster Gate took place, or leave it until afterwards. Apart from these two contingencies, he had but one more piece of ground over which to go. That particular piece concerned a matter of cabin-trunks, and Mr. Bathurst felt that he could very well afford to leave it to the very penultimate effort. Attached to it, there was but an iota of risk. On the point of turning a corner into Langham Place, he stopped sharply, as he caught sight of a well-known figure advancing towards him. On the whole, a most appropriate encounter. Fate was taking a hand in the game, for Anthony had a use for Sir Randall. Anthony made certain that the man whom he watched approaching, should observe him. He walked, therefore, right across the gentleman's path and waited for contact.

"Good afternoon, Sir Randall. I wonder if you remember me? How do you do?"

Sir Randall, a little perturbed perhaps, at the encounter, stared at the man who confronted him. It was obvious to Anthony that he was striving for the connection. For a time it seemed to elude him. Then his face cleared, and his customary geniality asserted itself.

"To be sure. My young friend, the sleuth! Well, well, it's strange that we should meet here."

"I don't know, sir. London's a big place, you know. Quite a few people pass this way in an hour or so. Why shouldn't you and I?"

Sir Randall Bowers chuckled with laughter.

"Ha, ha! That's your way of putting it. What are you after now? Still trying to find out who killed poor old Heriot? Or is it Pearson, the moneylender, that's occupying your attention? Don't tell me that it's both."

Mr. Bathurst was cheeriness itself. "Yes! Still persevering. A little of each, sir. However, I hope that neither will engage me for very much longer. In a week's time—shall we say—I anticipate bidding them both farewell. A long farewell to all their weightiness."

Sir Randall's face creased in mirth. "Giving them best— eh? Well, well, I can't say that I'm surprised. You and your leash-companions, the police, will be able to add yet two more to the lengthy and growing list of unsolved murder cases. Eleven since last Christmas. What have you to say about that? In a civilized country, too. Not that I'm blaming you, mind you. Far from it, my boy. The dice in each of these cases were loaded against you, right from the start. I did my best for you, too. By the way, my boy, did you try to follow up my clue of the Mouraki cigarette? The case will turn on a matter of those stubs, I'm certain."

Anthony assumed an expression that puzzled Sir Randall considerably.

"In a way, I agree with you. The Mouraki cigarette clue, however, Sir Randall, seems to me to be double-edged. I'm by no means sure that in the words of the royal Gertrude of Denmark, 'it doesn't protest too much'. When I think I'm finished with it, and that my conclusions concerning it, are sound and thoroughly water-tight, lo and behold, it pops up again, in an entirely unexpected place, with the result that I'm called upon to revise all my theories and solve yet another equation."

Sir Randall cocked his intelligent old head to one side.

"I don't quite know how to take that, Bathurst. Seems to me that you're giving me a pill that you've carefully gilded before I gulp it down. Trying to tell me that my help's been more of a hindrance than an aid—eh, my boy? I'm right there—eh? Come along. Get it off your chest. Out with it."

Anthony Bathurst, with the confidence born of experience, and nurtured by his knowledge of psychology, took a step forward and placed his hand on Sir Randall's shoulder.

"Sir Randall, you positively misjudge me. Such an interpretation of my words is erroneous. Nothing, indeed, was farther from my thoughts. It was through you, that I first got my line to the truth. It's been a nasty case, but daylight is peeping through the curtains at last. Let me take this opportunity of thanking you, Sir Randall."

Sir Randall gasped. That is to say, as nearly as he could.

"That's a piece of confounded and unfounded optimism. I gathered from your words and tone that you were intending to give the case up. Seems that I was wrong—eh?"

Anthony nodded in sympathy. "That's all right, sir. Don't let a little thing like that worry you. I shall have my man, never fear.

And nobody will be more surprised than he, when I put my hand on his shoulder, I assure you."

There was something here that Sir Randall Bowers could understand. "You're welcome to your opinion, Bathurst, of course. And I don't think any the worse of you for being so damned self-confident-—I rather like it, as a matter of fact—but—and it's a big 'but', my boy—I don't agree with you. And that's that. Straight from an old man's shoulder." Sir Randall wagged an admonitory finger.

Anthony surveyed him with a quizzical smile. "You're a sportsman, sir. That's well-known from Simla to the St. Lawrence. Everybody says so. I'm not a rich man—judged by your own standard—but I'll tell you what I'll do with you. I'll lay you a wager that I have my man for the Pearson murder, and also for the Heriot murder, within the space of the next seven days. Half a ton on it. £50. And I'll promise you that I won't keep the money—your money—for myself."

Sir Randall stared wonderingly, and a funny little look appeared in his eyes.

"My dear boy," he announced jocularly, "that *is* most certainly 'on'. It is as good as taking money from a blind man. You can pay me by cheque. Cross it on—"

Anthony smiled. "Not in notes, eh? Well, we shall see. I don't mind how you pay me, but I was hoping for a note on the Bank of England. By the way, how are your engagements next week? In the evenings, say?"

"Why?"

"I'm arranging a convenient evening for collection, that's all. Friday suit you?" His eyes twinkled.

"As well as any other," grunted Sir Randall.

"Book it up, then."

The old man glared at the instruction, then thrust out his hand. "Good-bye." Mr. Bathurst re-echoed the valediction and raised his hat with studied courtesy. Turning, he went on his way, and within the distance of a few yards, he had come to a decision regarding his next activity. The conversation in which he had just engaged with Sir Randall Bowers, had turned the scale. He would, therefore, call upon Pamela Frant's fiancé—Mr. Richard Lanchester.

CHAPTER XXIII
ANOTHER MOURAKI

RICHARD Lanchester, after listening lazily to what was being said, carefully filled his silver cigarette-case. His dark brows contracted with a frown. His eyes scanned the speaker's face.

"Show Mr. Bathurst up," he said curtly. "Though what the devil he wants with me now, I'm hanged if I know. All right, Lambert. Go ahead."

Lanchester nodded rather cavalierly upon Anthony's entry. His right hand grasped the chair from which he had risen.

"Afternoon, Bathurst. Pleased to see you, and all that. What's doing? Anything of any importance? Sit down, old man, of course."

"Oh—thanks. Sir Robert hasn't, I suppose, informed you of the arrangement that I made with him for an evening during next week? There's hardly been time, I'm afraid."

Lanchester looked puzzled. "No. Why?"

"It would have made a difference—that's all. I didn't want to waste time telling you things that you already knew. The fact is, Sir Robert and I are inviting one or two people to a little gathering at his place—next Friday evening. To tell the truth, I didn't settle on the actual night till a short time ago."

Lanchester was still cold and curt. "I follow all that. At the same time, however, I don't quite see how it affects me. Perhaps you would be good enough to explain."

Besides its coldness and curtness, Lanchester's tone was a little unpleasant. Very little, it is true, but just enough for Mr. Bathurst to notice it. He rarely missed indication of that kind.

"Only this. I want you to form one of the party. That must be my excuse for bringing the matter to your attention. All right? You'll come?"

Lanchester looked a trifle uncomfortable. "Surely it isn't necessary. What can—?"

"No," returned Mr. Bathurst sweetly. "Looking at it purely from one point of view, perhaps not. But it's about those murders, and I should have thought that, seeing that your future brother-in-law has been so closely involved, you would have eagerly welcomed an opportunity to arrive at the truth. You owe it to him, and to his sister, Miss Frant."

"The truth of what—exactly?"

"The truth of the Pearson murder, for one thing."

Lanchester affected consideration. "Agreed. Can you promise me the truth, though?"

Bathurst was still sweet. "I have every hope, Mr. Lanchester."

"Hope sometimes lets a man down pretty badly. I wish you could give me something more definite. Then I should know where I stood. As it is—" Lanchester broke off precipitately and shrugged his shoulders.

"Of course," added Mr. Bathurst, cheerfully, "there is the other consideration, as well."

Lanchester turned and stared. "What other consideration?"

"Murder Number Two." Mr. Bathurst's cheerfulness seemed to be on the increase. Pressed down and running over. "The murder of the late Mr. Justice Heriot," he supplemented.

Lanchester's stare turned into an expression of amazement. "Again, I don't understand. How does that concern next Friday's gathering? Hilary Frant wasn't accused of that, was he?" He failed to keep the sarcasm from his voice.

"Gracious, no! What on earth put that idea in your head?" Bathurst's parry was adroit. "Murder Number Two enters the arena next Friday evening in exactly the same manner as its predecessor in crime will. Which, being interpreted, means that I hope to bring it up for judgment. To present you—and the others—with a satisfactory solution. Do you understand now?"

"H'm. Been busy, haven't you?"

"More or less. . . . Afraid I've been more persevering than brilliant. So no medals, please."

Lanchester was grim. "Didn't intend to hand out any. You never find me counting poultry until the hatching stage's over. Not a bad plan to work on, either, in the long run."

"Excellent," agreed Mr. Bathurst, cordially. "How we do see eye to eye. I can count on you, then?"

"Oh, I suppose so. If Sir Robert Frant's familiar with the arrangement. Cigarette?"

Bathurst courteously accepted the invitation. It was not altogether unexpected to him. It was also, entirely without surprise, that he saw that the cigarette which he took from Lanchester's case was a Mouraki. He deliberately tapped it on the back of his hand. Lanchester affected not to notice Anthony's action. Taking a second cigarette from his own case, he struck a match and lit it. He turned to Bathurst and apologized for his apparent thoughtlessness.

"Oh, I say, I beg your pardon. I was thinking that you were alight. Take it off this—do you mind?"

Anthony went close to him, and was able to use the remainder of the flickering match.

"Thanks. A Mouraki, I see. Extraordinarily popular, these cigarettes are becoming. I seem to be finding them everywhere these days. Before the Frant trial, I'd scarcely even heard of them. Ran across one occasionally, I admit, but it was hardly anything more than that. A craze of the moment, possibly. Anyhow, I like them well enough." Anthony Bathurst spoke the words, with his eyes intent on the burning match. Not for a second did his gaze meet that of the man to whom the speech was addressed. Lanchester's reply, however, was definitely startling.

"My dear Bathurst," he declared, "I never listened to more comfortable words in my life. Rare and refreshing words, as music in my ears. I'm almost tempted to ask you to repeat them. Alas! if only they were true! I'd be shaking hands with myself all day long. Anyhow, I shall still regard you as the super-optimist. My faith is rehabilitated."

This time it was Anthony's turn to stare.

"Explain, please, my dear Lanchester! I'm not sure that I get you."

Lanchester opened his eyes as though too astonished for words.

"Surely, Bathurst, you of all people know to what I refer? I *make* Mourakis. Or, rather, my factory does the job. My father did, too, before me. Lanchester's 'Mourakis' and Lanchester's 'Columbines' are our two staples. Don't you know our advert? Or isn't it used enough? They don't sell, however, anything like as well as you're trying to tell me. My dear fellow, surely you knew my family manufactured them?"

A moment or two after he had left Dick Lanchester, Anthony Bathurst was laughing softly to himself. The laughter was long-lived. "Neat," he mused. "Very neat, indeed. If I hadn't been so sure about the whole bag of tricks it would have startled me. On the other hand, it's all beginning to fit. Why not?" He was still laughing when he surveyed mentally the panorama of clues that were by this time stretching out behind him. Once again he went through them one by one. The chauffeur, the cigarette, the chloroform, and the black cap. Then he thought of Angela Mansell and the blue-veined cheese of Leicestershire. What great events from little causes spring, and on what slender threads do men's fates hang. The pin-prick may kill as surely as the sword thrust. There only remained for him now, the one operation that he had described to himself as the very penultimate. It was quite a simple step, this; he had kept it in his mind, however, ever since Angela Mansell had first mooted it to him. The cabin trunk that at the present moment was still reclining in Heriot's flat, had been delivered at the flat, she had stated, and taken in, during her own absence, one afternoon,, by an attendant attached to one of the adjoining flats. Anthony Bathurst dearly wanted to have a word with that attendant if it could be managed, and he was better prepared for the interview now than he had ever been. He harboured a strong idea that he would be able to describe the bringer of that trunk so accurately that definite identification from that attendant would follow as a matter of course. His luck held in that. He was able to find Angela Mansell on the premises. The girl's face lit up with pleasure directly she recognized the identity of the caller. Mr. Bathurst, in one of his most charming moods, explained his requirements. Angela, resisting an inclination to idolatry, recalled the previous conversation at once.

"Yes, sir. It was as you say. I wasn't here when the trunk came. So Futchells—that's the porter who's attached to the next block of flats—took it in for us. There was nothing to pay on it, or anything like that. It was simply a case of taking the trunk upstairs and leaving it outside the door of the master's room. I found it there when I came back from my afternoon walk."

"That's it, Miss Mansell. That's the little incident to which I referred. Futchells, did you say the man's name was? Is he about now?"

"Oh, yes, sir. He always is about this time of the day. Shall I go down and tell him you'd like a little conversation with him? I will, sir, willingly."

Anthony smiled at her eagerness. "Ask the estimable Futchells whether he'd like to earn a little matter of ten shillings. Coin of the realm Georgius V. Tell him the rate of pay will be eminently satisfactory. I don't expect that I shall detain him more than a few minutes."

The sprightly Angela was out of the door in no time, and Anthony was privileged to listen to her flying feet down the staircase. There was this to be said of Miss Mansell. She was genuine, and she was sincere, never taking pains to assume a *figure d'occasion*, and when she placed herself in Anthony Bathurst's service she did so with the feeling that she was serving somebody in her late master's succession. Breathless almost, she arrived at the portly figure of the before-mentioned Futchells, and in a few staccato sentences stated her case.

"Yus," replied the porter. "I recalls the hoccasion very well. I don't mind telling yer that I've good cause to. That was the afternoon when 'Ogg sent out three winners with Gordon Richards on each one of 'em. There was I, bin followin' the ruddy stable since the commencement of the flat, and that afternoon—missed 'em all. It's always the same with me, when they roll up—'not on'. Same as when Grand Salute walked the 'Unt Cup." Futchells sighed. "What does 'e want with me, this 'ere friend of yours?"

Angela pulled at his arm. "Come and see, Futchells—and he's not a friend of mine. Lord, man, he's not my sort. What are you thinking of? He's a gentleman high up in the police service, I think."

The porter accepted the situation, grimaced, and followed her upstairs. He warmed to the "gentleman" at once.

"That's right, sir," he admitted, after Anthony had made his preliminary statement. "The girl's put you right. The trunk was brought along here, one 'arlequin and pantaloon, in a big saloon car. The chauffeur 'opped down from the front and asked me which was Judge 'Eriot's place. I told 'im, and told 'im also, in the same breath, that 'is Lordship wasn't at home. I said as 'ow he was down at Reading arrangin' a little matter of 'emp for some cove." He pointed to his neck and clucked with his tongue. "Beggin' your pardon for my little joke, sir. But I was always what you might call 'one of the boys'." Futchells grinned voluntarily as he made the explanation.

"What did he say when you told him that, Futchells?"

"Said 'e'd come from one of the big stores where the old pot and pan 'ad ordered the trunk a few days before."

Bathurst demurred. "Didn't it strike you, Futchells, when that story was put up to you, that if the trunk had come from, to use your own words, one of the big stores, it would have been delivered by one of the recognized carriers, and not by the agency of a private car?"

Futchells pushed his cap to the back of his fat head and scratched, as an exercise of self-encouragement. Eventually—after a wealth of scratching—he conceded Bathurst's point.

"Yes, now I come to think of it, I suppose you're right, guv'nor. All the same, I wasn't on my guard, as you might say. Wot was there to make me suspicious? He wasn't tellin' no funny tale." Futchells paused, to go on again more vigorously. "It wasn't as though the bloke was gettin' away with anythin', was it? It was the other way round. 'E was a-fetchin' something in—not takin' something out. See my meaning, sir?"

Anthony nodded. "All right. Go on. What happened after that?"

"Well, bein' obligin' like, I give 'im a 'and in with the trunk, knowin' as 'ow the girl 'ere was out, 'cos I'd seen 'er go, about a hour previous. We drops it down outside one of the rooms, and 'e clears orf. I can't think of anything else, sir."

"Right. Now it's my turn, Futchells. I want you to do a bit of thinking. Can you remember this chauffeur?"

Futchells resumed his occupation of scalp scarifying. "Well, sir—it's a month or so ago, and I wouldn't like to swear to anything particular that might—"

"I understand all that. And because of that I'm going to try to help you. But please understand this. Unless you're absolutely *positive* about anything, don't answer 'yes'. If you're doubtful, *say* you're doubtful. Don't answer 'yes' simply because you imagine you'll be pleasing me by so doing. Because you won't please me. You'll be doing the reverse. Do you get me?"

Futchells grinned again. He liked this fellow. Got a nice way about him. "Right you are, sir. Fire away."

"This chauffeur, whom you helped," said Bathurst, slowly and deliberately, "was a young man. Tall, slim, and with raven black hair. He was distinctly what you would describe as a 'smart' man physically. A good-looker. To how many of those statements can you truthfully answer 'yes'? Think, now, before you speak."

The man almost crowed with delight. "There ain't no need to do much thinkin', sir. True. O.K. every time. The young feller was all what you say. You must know 'im well to 'it 'im orf like that."

Mr. Bathurst rubbed his hands. At long last the way was clear for him.

"Just one more little point, Futchells, to make absolutely sure. He has a little personal habit to which he is inordinately addicted. Er—which he's rather fond of. He constantly snaps the thumb and second finger of his right hand. Probably he doesn't know when he's doing it. It's a peremptory sort of gesture. Tell me, my dear Futchells, if you saw him do it when he came delivering trunks?"

The face of the porter became as the roseate hues of early dawn and the brightness of the sky. "Blimey, sir, you've got it in one. That's the bloke, for sure. Twice he did that, when I was helping him upstairs with the article. You've got him right enough, to a T."

"He was alone in the car, of course."

"Solitary, sir. Outside 'im, the outfit was like Mother Hubbard's Mother Hubbard. I'm sorry, sir, that I wasn't more careful, but you see, you don't always know at the beginning what you know at the end. How often I've said, sir, what I'd give for a sight of to-morrow evening's paper to-day. Just once. Not more. Blimey, I wouldn't 'arf knock the bookies up a catcher."

"Don't reproach yourself too severely, Futchells. It's easy for any of us to be wise after the event, and to a certain extent, you know, you've repaired your omission." Mr. Bathurst effected the transfer of a piece of paper bearing the promise of the Bank of England, which the porter folded carefully and then placed in his pocket. Sensing that this was the beatific signal, indicating the termination of the interview, Futchells touched his cap and withdrew, a prey to mixed feelings. Anthony watched him go, and turned to Angela Mansell.

"I've good news for you, Miss Angela. I'm inclined to think that you've been worried by me for the very last time. What have you to say about that, eh? Cheers?"

The girl tossed her head perkily.

"That's surely not good news, sir. At least not to me. I'm sure it's a real pleasure for me to do anything for you, sir."

"Now you know, that's very nice of you, Angela. And I'm sure, too, that you mean it. All the same, I'm a good many sorts of a stormy petrel, and I nearly always have to pop up in the wake of trouble. Good-bye! Let me know when it comes off, and I'll send you a wedding present. *Not* a toast-rack. On no account."

Miss Mansell's cheeks pinked, and it must be recorded that she watched Anthony's departing figure with the chords of Romance stirring in her heart. What other man could she ever love . . . after this secret idolatry? Lady Fullgarney, Cecilia Mary Cameron, and another (the story of whom may one day be told), by no means, you see, are allowed to have matters entirely their own way.

Two turnings from his flat, Anthony heard the unusual strains of a barrel-organ. He found himself unable to remember the last occasion when he had heard that particular instrument of torture at work in that corner of London. Arrived at his own place, he was met by a rather flustered Emily.

"There's a letter come for you, sir," she greeted him. "I've put it on the table in your room."

Against her habit, for she was almost free from the vice of curiosity, Emily showed unmistakable signs of lingering. Anthony spotted this.

"Well, Emily, what is it? Anything else to tell me?"

She twisted her hands, "It's a peculiar sort of letter, sir. Not at all the usual kind. I hope everything's all right, sir." The last sentence came in a rush.

Mr. Bathurst took the hint. "Well, we'll see, Emily, if that's what you want me to do."

Taking the stairs two at a time, Anthony came to the door of his room and pushed it open. On the table by the window, he could see the note of Emily's history and foreboding. He went to it and picked it up. As far as he could see from externals, a dirty thumb-mark was its chief mark of distinction. It was addressed to "Mister Bathurst". Anthony fingered it wonderingly for a second or so before he probed for its message. Then his face changed, and he smiled as he read:

Important. This is a bit of genuine information for you from a *friend.* I don't want to see you come to any harm, so keep your nose out of a case what don't concern you a little bit. Otherwise—you'll have a nasty accident.

A FRIEND.

Mr. Bathurst scratched his cheek pensively. "A friend," he murmured, with a certain measure of criticism. "Twice a friend, too. I wonder! Perhaps—but somehow I don't think so. No, I don't really think so. Some of the sentiments expressed are hardly the handmaidens of amity." Mr. Bathurst walked to the window that overlooked the street, and stood there, looking out. "So somebody's the wind up at last," he said to himself. "Well, that somebody's had a long run, and must have been thinking for some time that the danger was over." He turned and rubbed his hands. "But I'll have my bird yet. The trap will close when the right time comes, as neatly as the 'Peacock's eye' came home in the shop of Stefanopoulos."

Anthony seated himself at his desk, took his pen and wrote. He wrote for some little while. Then he leant back and carefully re-read what he had written. One or two features dissatisfied him. A sentence was garnished here, a period rounded there, a redundancy penned, an inelegance deleted. The whole was placed in an envelope which Anthony addressed. "The Editor, *The Era*, Soho Square, W.C.2." A somewhat similar effort found itself addressed to the Editor of the *Morning Message*. "Ten days," he whispered to himself, "should be enough, I think, to do the trick. If not, I will tell Sir Robert, and postpone matters for another week. But I don't think that will be necessary." He sat at his desk, thinking hard, trying to visualize the end. "It will be the biggest surprise," he murmured, "that she has ever had in her life." Rising, he opened the door and called down the staircase: "Emily!"

Chapter XXIV
THE JAWS OF THE TRAP

EMILY was upstairs to him in a second. "Get in or on a bus, Emily, as soon as you can conveniently leave your job downstairs, and take this to Soho Square for me. After that, deliver this second one. A breath of air will do you good. Tell the *Era* people that I want theirs in this week's issue. Say it's frightfully urgent. The other's all right."

The girl responded with alacrity. "Very good, sir. I'll pop along with them as soon as I've finished the pastry for to-morrow. Mrs. Pedder will be downstairs, if you should want anything. As you say, sir, the outing will do me good."

Emily half-curtsied, and made her exit with the two letters. The curtain was slowly rising on the last act, and as he looked back over all that had gone before, Anthony could scarcely remember an investigation that had been less exciting or more arduous. A sordid crime, a meretricious trial, and then—the staggering passing of Heriot. His mind went back to the many murderers whom his genius had foiled, and as it trailed over them, he began to wonder if he were destined to bring the present case to the conclusion that he so ardently desired. It was just possible, he considered, that, if he were careless, things might take a nasty turn. Certain animals have the unpleasant habit of snapping fiercely at the bars of the trap that holds them, and a fiercely-struggling fish may snap the sorely-tried rod. The bars or rod, therefore, must be strong. In that case, having looked round the personnel of the cast, he decided to have Lanchester on hand and in absolute readiness for immediate action. He himself would instruct Lanchester (and perhaps Captain Hilary Frant in addition) where to be, and what to do, should the lean-jawed pike take a deal of landing. For the moment, there was no more to be done—only the gruesome job of waiting. The days dragged slowly by, and the week dwindled to its close. Mr. Bathurst's tempting announcement in the *Era*, duly delivered by the assiduous Emily, appeared and was read by hundreds. A somewhat similar paragraph in the *Message* reached thousands. Mr. Bathurst himself is to be included in this category, although his attention was directed from another angle. The new week came. Sunday, Monday, and Tuesday were barren, yielding nothing, but the morning of Wednesday found Mr. Bathurst's telephone-bell ringing insistently. A bustling Emily answered it, and realizing its importance, put down the receiver, and called to Mr. Bathurst himself. Anthony, his nerves tingling, answered the call in his dressing-gown.

"Yes? Bathurst speaking. Oh—is that you, Sir Robert? What . . . oh, good! Splendid. Came this morning, you say. Yes, I thought it would draw something. Well, you know how to reply. I arranged that with you, didn't I? Yes . . . yes . . . I want the piano in the lounge-hall just in the corner, as I wrote you. . . .

Yes . . . under that balcony that runs along the back. What? . . .
Let me think. . . . Edna, I fancy. Oh, and I say, I've an idea that's
come along more recently that I think may prove moderately
profitable—what? Oh . . . no . . . I think not. No . . . not to any
great consequence . . . don't worry over that. Leave it to me. If
things go according to plan, everything will be all right. Dick
Lanchester will be there. . . . I've seen him . . . he knows the
night. . . . I'll have another chat with him before it comes, and
have him in a certain place that I already have in my mind's eye
. . . so don't worry, Sir Robert. Good-bye."

Anthony replaced the receiver, and stood for a little while
thinking, his hands thrust into the pockets of his dressing-gown.
As far as he could see, there was no loophole through which his
plans might miscarry. Once again, it was simply a question of
waiting for the eventful evening to come, and hoping for the best.
His next step would be to see Lanchester and arrange about him
and Captain Frant. That done, he would ring Sir Austin Kemble
at the "Yard", so that that excellent scout, MacMorran, should
be on the spot when the ticklish moment came. Come to think of
it, there was no reason why he shouldn't fix up with the Commissioner now. When the call was put through, the Commissioner
of Police adopted an air of almost parental superiority. It was
obvious to Anthony, as he spoke, that upon this occasion, at
least, he had caused Sir Austin a certain amount of misgiving
and disappointment.

"MacMorran's been waiting to hear from you for some time,
Bathurst," he rumbled rather piteously into the telephone.
"Asked me the other day how much longer you expected him
to wait?"

"By Jove," murmured Bathurst, with commendable sweet-
ness, "now that's downright good of him. As a matter of interest,
Sir Austin, purely academic interest, I've been very much in the
same position with regard to him."

Sir Austin, tasting the salt of the satire, grunted guttural
sounds into an inoffensive instrument.

"You don't seem particularly enthusiastic, sir."

"No, I don't. And as for MacMorran . . ."

"Well, give him this message, Sir Austin. After all, he's one of the best of lads. It will revive his drooping spirits." Mr. Bathurst repeated a succession of sentences with infinite deliberation. The question that they drew from the Commissioner, he answered instantly.

"Absolutely, sir. Rely on me. There isn't the shadow of a doubt. . . . Circumstantial evidence, I know . . . all of it . . . but pretty deadly in the power of its accumulation. Beyond that, sir, a most telling piece of evidence . . . where . . . oh, safely tucked away somewhere, I assure you. In excellent hands. I'll produce it when the time's ripe, never fear. It's because of that last piece of evidence I'm arranging this little stunt on Friday evening. As you know—I'm a tremendous believer in self-betrayal. Right. Tell MacMorran seven o'clock, or a quarter-past. I'll have everything ready, never fear. Good-bye, Sir Austin, and thank you once again very much. With apologies for having been such a festering sore."

Mr. Bathurst tucked his hands even farther in the deep pockets of his dressing-gown and pulled the skirts thereof round him. His mood had changed. His eye caught the gramophone on the table by the window. The humour of his new mood caught him and held him temporarily captive. Walking to his store of records, he turned them over carefully. It was some little time before he came to the record that he wanted. But at length he found it, and with a smile playing round the corners of his mouth, he prepared the needle and started the gramophone. Emily, downstairs with Mrs. Pedder, engaged on a little matter of tarragon flavouring for one of Mr. Bathurst's favourite soups, cocked her head pleasedly a moment later as she hummed to the musical strains that reached her from above. . . . "I'm goin' to get you. . . . There's something tells me. . . . I'm goin' to get you. I'm goin' to get you."

"That means no good for somebody, Mrs. Pedder, I'll be bound, Take it from me," she vaticinated with upraised finger. "When the master's in that mood, I've always noticed it's before something important happens. I remember it was the same in that 'Orange Axe' case that he had on some time ago. Reminds me, too, of an old schoolfellow of mine. Name o' Gladys Minchen. Married a fellow, she did, who looked O.K. and all that, but who turned out a regular bad egg. Used to bash her on the head with whatever he could find to lay his hands on. From an umbrella to a saucepan-lid. After a time, though, when she'd been married to him some time, she used to get warnin' of when he was goin' for her. And however do you think, Mrs. Pedder? You'd never guess. Not in a hundred times."

Mrs. Pedder admitted her inefficiency at all games of skill or chance. "Why—he used to sing hymns for hours beforehand. It kind of worked him up. One of his favourites was 'The King of Love my Shepherd is'. That was the one Gladys got to be most scared of. Whenever he turned that on, she knew she was going to click for a proper good hiding. Funny how religion takes some people, isn't it?"

The lounge-hall of Sir Robert Frant's home in Lancaster Gate merits and needs some little description. On the right, as you entered, just at the side of a door that opened on to one of the reception-rooms, stood a magnificent specimen of an old grandfather's clock. The first part of the lounge-hall, by the entrance-door, was tiled in black and white. Where the tiles ceased, there were stretched two handsome Feraghan rugs, each eight feet in length. On the left of the entrance-door, Sir Robert Frant had had put into operation a really clever and original idea. One, which may well be described, as quite away from the ordinary. He had had placed there a "screen cupboard". The decoration had been by no less a celebrity than the Polish artist—Panyo de Lubil. Outwardly a screen, in reality, it was not a screen at all. One of the. "folds" of the screen, depicted a door-way. The cupboards, when discovered, were put, of course, to utilitarian end; one was in use for hats, another for coats and wearing apparel. At the foot of a third was built a tiny walnut cabinet for gloved and other similar smaller pieces of body wear. Sir Robert, to tell the strict truth, had copied the idea from an Italian friend of his who resided close by, the Marchese Grimaldi, and in turn, had himself found many imitators.

One of these "fold" cupboards had been emptied, under Mr. Bathurst's instructions, to conceal the bodily frame of Chief Inspector MacMorran of New Scotland Yard. Pamela Frant was seated at the grand piano, which Anthony had ordered to be placed specially under the balcony. At her side, a few yards away, sat a tall girl . . . dressed in black . . . Miss Revallon . . . she had known Leonard Pearson. Captain Hilary Frant and Dick Lanchester were in their appointed positions. They had been thoroughly rehearsed by Mr. Bathurst in their parts which they might be called upon to play. Maddison Frant had taken up a prominent position by the grandfather's clock. As in the case of the others, it had been assigned to him, with deliberate aforethought by the same master of the ceremonies, Anthony Lotherington Bathurst. Maddison Frant, however, would have admitted, had he been taxed, that he could find little fault with the location (as a location pure and simple) from his own particular point of view. Actually, it pleased him. He was, to a very great degree, what might be termed centre stage, and he felt within his heart that he was the custodian of great values. At the same time, with his curiously complex mind, he was sufficiently depressed to be acutely unhappy. The surroundings in which he found himself were unusual. They were alien to him, and he was soon wishing that he had refused to have anything to do with the wretched business, right from its inception. But that was impossible, for he was now irrevocably committed. He had put his hand to the plough. . . .

Seated comparatively close to Pamela at the piano, on the other side from Miss Revallon, were two other distinguished gentlemen. By name, Sir Robert Frant and Sir Randall Bowers.

Anthony Bathurst himself, almost hidden by the bulk of Pamela's "Steinway", leant over it, nevertheless, in an attitude of what looked, to a superficial observer, very nonchalant ease. That superficial observer, however, would have been grossly deceived. Underneath Mr. Bathurst's careless exterior and seemingly negligent demeanour, there was a magnificently-keen alertness. Every nerve was taut and tightened; every sense was at its brilliant best. For he was close, now, to the moment of his triumph. The grandfather's clock chimed the quarter-hour past the seventh and startled Maddison Frant from the disturbing reverie into which he had been falling. The sound of the chime—ominous, he thought—brought him suddenly back to the unpleasant realization of what was to follow, and he found himself watching the white-faced girl at Pamela's side. Sir Randall Bowers was just on the point of interjecting what he intended to be a humorous remark, when a sound from outside struck on their listening ears. Anthony raised his hand and put a finger to his lips. The noise of the bell rang shrill through the hall. At a sign from Anthony, Pamela began to play, and from the other members of the waiting circle came the pleasant buzz and hum of racy conversation. Through it, cut the sound of the deliberate steps of a manservant on his way to the door.

"Take it a little quicker, Miss de Vere. Do you mind?" boomed the voice of Maddison Frant. "We must remember that it is essential to have *pace* at this particular moment. Anything else would be suicidal. The scene on the mountains when the musician realizes that he's hopelessly and irretrievably lost, and that the shades of evening are falling fast, will slow it down considerably, you know, and we mustn't risk having too much of a good thing. We don't want a flop."

Pamela nodded in understanding, bent her head to the notes and played again. The Revallon girl seemed in a condition of fascination. Pamela Frant had played but little when Maddison, her uncle, checked her again.

"Pardon me for a moment. I'm wanted, I think." At an almost imperceptible nod from Mr. Bathurst, leaning across the piano top, the actor-manager turned to the grotesque figure that had entered somewhat irresolutely, to stand on the fringe of the circle . . . cap in hand.

"Mr. Maddison Frant?" inquired the stranger. His voice was coarse.

"Yes? I'm he. . . ."

"I've come in answer to the advert in the *Era*. You were expectin' me, I think. I wrote yer on Tuesday morning from Whillimoir, up in the north."

"Of course. Of course," returned Maddison Frant genially. "I expected you, naturally. I've your letter here somewhere. Ah, yes, here it is." He read the letter through and looked up again. "So you describe yourself as a 'speciality dancer'? I think I've heard of you."

At this development of mutual understanding, the figure advanced a few steps and looked round the circle.

"I'm just running over one or two numbers in my new production. That's the thing that I may want you for. I was in somewhat of a fix—I want a speciality dancer who's also a cripple. It's absolutely essential to the show. I was afraid that I should experience great difficulty in getting hold of the right man. That was the reason I advertised. Thought it was the only way. I appear to have been unusually fortunate." He smiled cordially at his visitor, and now that the stranger had come forward to stand in better view, all in the hall could see that his left leg had been amputated just above the knee and that he supported himself on an ugly-looking crutch. Apart from these distinctive features, his costume was strikingly bizarre and original. He wore a doublet of scarlet satin broidered with ornate gilt buttons, with similarly coloured knee-breeches, one of which had been cut to fit the mutilated limb, and hung loosely close to the crutch. Maddison Frant spoke across the room to his niece on the music-stool.

"Just play the 'Mountaineers Song' again, Miss De Vere, will you, please? Play it through to us so that this gentleman can get a proper idea of it . . . time and so on."

Pamela nodded gravely, and the music lilted through the apartment. The nerves of Sir Randall Bowers began to get hot and jangled. Edna Revallon stifled a gasp in her throat.

"Rather catchy, what?" suggested Maddison.

"Yes," returned the stranger curtly. "I suppose you want me to do a dance to it, don't you?"

"That's the idea, my friend. You see, it's like this. I'll explain it to you. Yussuf, the mountaineer, has lost a leg fighting for the Allies in the Great War, but his courageous spirit is still unquenched. Nothing will ever damp his ardour. Whenever he hears the music of this particular song that has been sung in his family for generations, it is too much for him. It overpowers him—it is completely irresistible—and he simply has to give way to the expression of his soul . . . and dance! Got the idea?"

"Why, yes, guv'nor. I mean, sir. If the young lady would be so kind as to play it through just once again, I might be able to show you what I can do. I am pretty useful with one leg and a 'swinger'."

"Of course. Just what I was about to ask you," returned Maddison Frant, the soul of urbanity.

"You won't mind me putting my cap down, will you, sir?"

Frant conceded the request with a graceful wave of the hand and, in acceptance of the concession, the crippled dancer swung himself along with his crutch and placed his cap on the chair nearest to him. Maddison Frant gestured to Pamela, and once again the air of the "Mountaineer's Song" was heard by those present. The dancer advanced again into the centre, facing the piano, Mr. Bathurst, and Edna Revallon (dazed by the sight of him), laid his crutch carefully on the Feraghan rug and suddenly, with both arms clasped behind his back, started his grotesque performance. Taking into consideration the man's physical disability, it was a performance of much merit. Using his crutch very much as the crossed swords are used in the sword-dance, the dancer pivoted on his one leg with an extraordinary degree of skill. Maddison Frant, back now in his position by the grandfather's clock, showed, by a series of benign inclinations of the head, his entire approval of the performance. Sensing the warmth of the reception, the heartened stranger improved perceptibly. His sense of rhythm became better and his body more of a harmonious whole. The music of the song ceased and the dancer swayed to the finale with a beauty and grace of movement that seemed almost incredible in a man whose body had suffered as his had. . . . Maddison Frant went towards him, rubbing his outstretched hands in undisguised admiration.

"Excellent," he murmured—"really excellent. I expected nothing anything like as good as that. I don't mind admitting as much to you. What do you think, gentlemen? Just the man we want, don't you think?" He appealed to the other men.

They expressed agreement, Sir Randall Bowers being particularly voluble. "You'd go a long way and fare much worse," he contributed.

Mr. Bathurst, however, had a point which he evidently desired to make to Maddison Frant. He came forward.

"Just a suggestion, sir, if you don't mind. One that occurred to me a moment or so ago."

"Certainly. By all means. Let's have it."

The famous actor met Mr. Bathurst a few yards from the piano and they conferred. Maddison listened with evident sympathy to the suggestion that Mr. Bathurst had to make to him.

"Yes," he said at length. "I think that's worth trying—Mr. Hagenheimer. As you say, the perspective of the picture would be better that way, and anything that was out of alignment would be easily discernible. The appeal to the eye is perhaps, in a number like this, more important even than the appeal to the ear. A point which is so often forgotten. We'll try your idea at once."

Anthony returned to his coign of vantage behind the piano and Maddison Frant motioned to the scarlet-clad dancer.

"I want to see you again," he declared. "That is to say—with the audience here where you were, and not up there. Try the dance from under the balcony—just by the side of my pianiste. The grandfather's clock will then be O.P. Again, Miss De Vere, please."

The dancer took up his new position after a series of curious hop-like thuds that sounded strangely throughout the room, and Pamela once again tinkled the notes of the "Mountaineer's Song"; Anthony Bathurst vacated his place and strolled out towards Maddison Frant. The cripple jumped in once more, and there reigned again, the movements of the dance bizarre. On this occasion, possibly, the execution was even better. Maddison Frant was quick to express his pleasure.

"You may regard yourself as engaged," he said, with a gesture of magnanimity. "That will do, Miss De Vere. And you, Miss Revallon, I shan't require you any more to-day, thank you."

Pamela bowed and made her exit. Edna Revallon followed her.

"My business manager will see you with regard to terms, now." Frant indicated Anthony. "He'll fix up your contract at once. Also, I should like your photograph for publicity purposes. He will see to that as well. Come along, gentlemen." At his hand-wave, Sir Robert Frant and Sir Randall Bowers followed Maddison into another room. Anthony Bathurst, in his new role, set about carrying out Maddison Frant's most recent instructions.

"We'll leave the contract question for a moment or two, if you don't mind. First of all, I'll make arrangements for that photo the guv'nor wants." He faced the dancer as he stood on his crutch under the balcony—not more than a dozen yards between them. "I'll tell you why he wants it. He wants it because I want it." His words were icily cold. "I want a photograph of the murderer of Leonard Pearson at Perry Hammer in Berkshire, on the night of Wednesday, April the 22nd."

The man's eyes blazed with an ungovernable fury. He took one step back, bracing himself to his full height as he did so.

"Oh—do yer—" he snarled, casting a quick glance round the apartment. The glance told him that he and his unknown accuser were alone. "You've got to catch me first." With a movement of bewildering celerity, he whipped the crutch from his armpit, whirled it to his shoulder, and with catlike quickness, flung it with an amazingly-obtained force, straight at Anthony Bathurst's head. As he did so, Mr. Bathurst dropped to the floor and the heavy crutch hurtled through the air and smashed against the screen-cupboard at the end of the hall. Simultaneously, there dropped upon the cripple-killer, from the balcony above him, two hefty forms, those of Dick Lanchester and Captain Hilary Frant. The job was after their own hearts. The three men struggled in a heaving and cursing mass as MacMorran came dashing from his hiding-place.

"There's your man, MacMorran," murmured Mr. Bathurst in tones of joyfulness. "The gentleman in scarlet at the bottom of that little ant-hill. Mr. George Alfred Stubbs, of Bethell's Buildings, Canning Town, lineal descendant of Long John Silver. He murdered Leonard Pearson in very much the same way as he tried to murder me. Put the bracelets on him and warn him in the usual way, will you? He's a thoroughly nasty piece of work, taking him all round."

MacMorran obeyed the order with alacrity. There was a gleam of steel bracelets. They held hairy wrists. At the same moment there returned Sir Robert, Sir Randall, and Maddison Frant.

"Thank you, Bathurst," said Sir Robert, with a simple gratitude. "I can never repay you. The Revallon girl thanks you, too. And thank you, too, Maddison."

CHAPTER XXV
THE KNOWLEDGE OF DR. BARROW-SOUTH

MADDISON Frant took his brother's hand and gripped it tightly.

"I'm going now, Robert," he said. "I can't spare any more time. I've a lot to do. But what little I've done for you, I'd do again gladly. Always remember that. *Au 'voir*, Bathurst."

"Au 'voir," returned Anthony lightly. The door closed on the actor, and Mr. Bathurst turned to the others. "Take me into a nice, comfortable room, Sir Robert," he said, addressing his host, "and I'll talk to you of the secret of Mr. Justice Heriot."

Sir Robert eyed him queerly. "You weren't content, then, with the knowledge that you had?"

Mr. Bathurst shook his head decisively. "Bless your life, no.. .. The mystery intrigued me so much, sir, that I wasn't content to rest until I had solved it. I'm a greedy devil, you know. Sir Randall Bowers here, will bear me out in the truth of that statement. Lead the way, Sir Robert."

Sir Robert Frant shrugged his shoulders resignedly and ushered the little knot of men into' the room that did duty as his library. He gestured them to take their respective seats.

"Now, Bathurst," he declared, "let's hear it, whatever it is, and then we'll devoutly and fervently hope that we've listened to the last of the whole wretched business. The dead shall bury their dead."

"I can't promise that, sir, but within a very short time from now, I shall have solved the Heriot mystery and given you the name of the murderer. That's my job. I will commence my story by going back a little, if you will allow me to do so."

Sir Robert pushed the box of cigarettes over to the others. "We'll smoke, at all events, while Bathurst talks. Cigarette, Hilary? You, Lanchester? Or would you prefer cigars?"

The two young men addressed, and Sir Randall also, took advantage of the first invitation. Anthony watched the last-named closely as he selected his cigarette.

"Mourakis, Sir Randall. Still running up against them, you see."

Sir Randall's reply was unintelligible, and he shifted uneasily in his chair. Anthony began his story.

"The key to the situation that culminated in the murder of Justice Heriot is in the hands of Dr. Barrow-South. Clever man that he undoubtedly is, meriting in every way his great and international reputation, on this occasion he has nevertheless made one great mistake. Great, because it is irreparable. I doubt whether he knows it at the moment; its commission has very probably passed from his mind. Directly taxed with it, he might even deny it, but his denials would be valueless. Because he *made* the mistake—it cannot be rectified now—and the error has helped to lead me to the truth."

He paused to note the tensity of the faces that were fixed on his. "We follow up these grains of human error, you know, when we go investigating. They're as manna to us in the wilderness of wandering. It happened like this. Heriot consulted Barrow-South, some time before Captain Frant here was to be tried for the Pearson murder, and eventually diagnosed that the poor old judge was a doomed man. Only a few months were left to him. He had that incurable malady—cancer of the throat. His speech was affected and the dread growth had him in its merciless grip. Unhappily, Dr. Barrow-South passed this knowledge on. That was the mistake he made to which I referred just now.

If he hadn't done so, I doubt if the murderers of Heriot would ever have been known. Perhaps, too, Pearson's killer might have remained unsuspected. However, that's merely conjecture, with which I desire little intimacy."

The breathing of his hearers grew heavy and hard; unheeding, Mr. Bathurst proceeded.

"Before I leave you this evening, I hope to detail the steps by which I apprehended Stubbs. And before that most important step, those which brought me to the other solution. In the meantime, however, I have another task. One, too, which has a bearing on the other two. Consider, please, the situation as I left it. The old judge' nodding at his coffin. Pearson dead—murdered. Captain Frant moderately close to the condemned cell. Dr. Barrow-South studying the malignant tumour in Heriot's throat. As eminent a person as Sir Randall Bowers describing Pearson's murder, in the daily Press, as justifiable homicide." Anthony uttered the baronet's name lightly. "Consider also the different facets of human psychology as they focussed themselves on this general state of affairs and found themselves, after a time, playing upon it. Playing upon it until *power* was evolved. Reflection, always, if strong enough, evolves power. Enough power in this case to galvanize the activity of antagonism. One man became obsessed by it. His worry and anxiety gave way to action. He planned. He schemed. Most intelligently and most cunningly. But it was imperative that he should have auxiliaries. The more he looked at his problem, testing it, weighing it scrupulously, the more his way out of it, pleased him and appealed to him. And by a strange conjuring of Fate, the forces he required for the effectiveness of his scheme were almost miraculously to his hand. They were by no means miscast, either. They fitted as the glove to the falconer's hand."

A knock sounded on the door as Anthony Bathurst uttered the last two words of his sentence.

"Come in," he called quietly. The door opened slowly at his bidding . . . the tardiness of the opening was almost agonizing to those who watched . . . they knew not what for . . . all that came to their quivering senses was the feeling that here on the threshold was revelation . . . startling, perhaps . . . but glaringly true . . . so true that it could never be questioned . . . a form appeared in the frame of the doorway.

"God!" cried Hilary Frant sharply. "It's Heriot himself."

As he spoke the pregnant words, the well-known figure of Mr. Justice Heriot, in full court robes, walked towards them. There was a gasp of incredulous astonishment from somebody, but one figure sat in his chair . . . stricken . . . a huddled heap of startled shock and thwarted hopes. Then he recovered to confront the truth—to look into the eyes of this . . . other Justice Heriot.

CHAPTER XXVI
THE SECRET OF JUSTICE HERIOT

THE figure of Justice Heriot took a seat between Sir Robert Frant and Dick Lanchester. Mr. Bathurst, completely dominant master now of the whole ceremony, took up the reins again. He returned to the last words that he had spoken before the interruption and repeated them.

"They fitted as the glove to the falconer's hand." Anthony surveyed his company with that quick, comprehensive glance of his that always took in so much.

"Three of these gloves were required. A pair and a half, let us say. But he himself was one. There were but two others, then, to be obtained. One pair. He obtained this desired pair with moderate ease. Each of them listened to the story as he told it to them. Although a piece of special pleading, I will not deny that it held a tremendous amount of common-sense. There were risks attached to it, of course, but the value of the prize was dear to all three of them. Very, very dear. As to the moral issue, I will not enter upon a discussion of it. 'Let him who is without sin among us . . .' The audacity of the venture rather takes my breath away, but it succeeded, perhaps by *reason* of that very audacity, which, we find, is very often the case. Although audacious, however, it was not excessively difficult of execution. Sir Robert—in a way—I congratulate you. *You* killed the judge, I presume, by chloroform, or some similar preparation? Barrow-South was right? Yes?"

Sir Robert pulled himself together in his chair to face the unforgiving minute—and nodded silently.

Anthony proceeded. "You, Lanchester, would, of course, make an excellent chauffeur. And—er—carrier of cabin-trunks. And you, sir, played the judge with your own masterly touch. The performance had a wealth of intimate detail and showed signs of infinite understanding. Your make-up and voice alike were almost perfect."

The figure in the court robes replied to Anthony, and the voice now was the voice of Maddison Frant. It held a tinge of defiance.

"Thank you, Bathurst. Allow me also to congratulate you. As I told you a few days ago, I did it for my brother's sake."

"Shall I tell the whole story, Sir Robert, or would you prefer the task?" Anthony's mood altered to one of comparative sternness.

"I would prefer that you did it, Bathurst," returned Sir Robert quietly.

"Very good, then. If I make a mistake anywhere, correct me, please. When you, Sir Robert, heard from Dr. Barrow-South, that the man who was about to preside over the trial of your son, for Pearson's murder, had cancer of the throat that would prove fatal within a very short time, your brain began to play with an idea. Heriot was by no means noted for his velvet glove. Rather was he famed, the world over, for the iron hand within it." Bathurst turned to the others. "And Captain Hilary Frant, his father considered, had scarcely a leg to stand on. Every point of his defence even could be turned by the Prosecution, if it so chose to do, into damning evidence against him. Sir Robert could already see the condemned cell . . . three yards of cord, and a sliding board . . . the hangman with his gardener's gloves . . . the roof of glass . . . and the pit of shame. . . . He could also hear the stroke of nine and see the headlines of the midday papers. . . . 'Execution of Captain Frant . . . Perry Hammer murderer pays the penalty of his crime . . .' and all the usual stock and stark sentences that are used by the more sensational Press to garnish the execution dish for greedy readers. He determined, at all costs, to prevent this. At the risk of his own reputation . . . of his own life. He would grasp the bludgeon of Fate in his bare hands and turn it from the head of his son to the head of another. For he already had the first two tricks of the game in his hand. I will return to that. He began to argue with himself. He used a satisfying brand of persuasive pleading. After all, he reasoned to himself, it was not murder that he contemplated. Far from it. On the other hand, he would exercise the exquisite quality of mercy. He would give Heriot a painless passing instead of the terrible one that Nature was about to bestow upon him. Mr. Maddison Frant, whom, we have with us, the great character actor whose powers of make-up have helped to place him at the pinnacle of 'the' profession, would play the judge at the Autumn Assizes. *And, as that judge, he would sum up so favourably to the accused that the jury would be almost certain to return a verdict of not guilty.* They are invariably so quick to take that lead. Consider, then, the plan when perfected. Handwriting, appearance, and mannerisms could be carefully cultivated, and the great difficulty to be contended in the ordinary way *was already circumvented*. The difficulty of Heriot's voice. Note that, all of you! It was affected by his trouble, and *any difference would pass more or less unnoticed*. The other trick that he held, to which I made very brief reference, consisted of this fact. Besides discussing Heriot's symptoms with him, Dr. Barrow-South had also given away the vital information that Heriot would be stopping over at Erleigh, with Lord and Lady Madden, during the time of the trial. This eased matters considerably, and the great scheme grew and developed, until the time came for its fruition. The first thing to do was to 'phone Lord and Lady Madden on the afternoon that Heriot was expected, to the effect that he was unable to come. 'Something vital' had occurred to make him change his plans. Maddison 'phoned the message from a public call-box, I should say, purporting, of course, to be Heriot himself. Lancaster's car, number-plate changed, no doubt, ran to Reading and was outside the station when Heriot's train, carrying Heriot, arrived. 'Erleigh Court,' says Lanchester, a very spick-and-span chauffeur, door of the car open in the usual way, and in steps the unsuspecting Justice Heriot, with his suit-case and personal accoutrements. Mr. Lanchester jumps to the driving-seat, to the manner born, and off goes the car with the victim inside. En route for Erleigh Court? No! For his last ride! The Judge is on his final journey, 'songs all sung and deeds all done'. Were you inside the car when he got in, Sir Robert?"

Sir Robert Frant shook his head. His face twitched.

"No. I was a little distance ahead of them. In another car, with Maddison driving."

"Thank you. I wasn't sure on that point. I merely conjecture the next move also. But I suggest that the Judge was induced to alight at a convenient place where there was little or no danger of being overlooked. He was old, and naturally therefore, a comparatively easy prey. The fatal drug was all ready in Sir Robert's skilled hands, the two brothers did their work, the trunk that they had brought with them was at hand, and the first big step had been successfully taken. Heriot had been removed and Maddison was equipped with his robes, appointments, and clothes. Sir Robert then drove in *his* car—the one that Maddison had been driving—to the hotel at Reading where he was staying, the 'Sicilian'. The trunk, containing the dead body of Heriot, accompanied him. But Maddison Frant, due to appear at the theatre that evening, was driven back to town by Lanchester, who returned to Reading that evening and, I think, each evening afterwards. Each morning, he went back for his passenger, who, when he left his house on the first morning after the murder, the day that the Assizes opened, was already made up as Heriot, assumed the judicial robes in the car, and proved himself sufficiently able throughout the various cases over which he presided, to play the part successfully that Sir Robert had assigned to him." Mr. Bathurst turned to the trio of conspirators. "Am I right, gentlemen?"

Lanchester took it upon himself to reply to Anthony's question. His tone, although superficially courteous, held a trace of almost insolent sullenness. The position in which he found himself was far from his liking, and he grudged Bathurst this mastery of the situation.

"As near as makes no odds."

Mr. Bathurst gestured his thanks. "Each evening, or late afternoon it might be, when the court adjourned, Maddison Frant walked straight to Lanchester's car and was driven back to town for the evening performance at his theatre. This was a master move. In a way, you see, the fact that he was appearing in the evening gave a definite 'alibi' suggestion. You remember, Sir Randall, the occasion when you waved to him, and also the incident of the dropped Mouraki?"

Sir Randall smiled and nodded. "Wasn't far out, was I?"

Dick Lanchester grinned grimly. "I remember it, too. Directly after it happened. I half-turned, as soon as I had chucked the beastly thing away, and spotted Sir Randall here doing the retriever act. I've cursed my carelessness ever since."

"I fancied you knew something of that little incident, Lanchester," replied Anthony Bathurst—"that was how I eventually explained to myself that astonishing plague of Mourakis that swarmed on to me. Mourakis to right of me, Mourakis to left of me. By the way, Lanchester, I must offer you my most appreciative congratulations on your final explanation of that business. A very neat touch indeed, that. Fortified, too, of course, by the highly interesting fact that it happened to be true. It was as neat a touch as Mr. Maddison Frant's eulogy of the pseudo Heriot's summing-up." Bathurst smiled.

"What happened *after* the trial, Bathurst?" interposed Sir Randall Bowers. "The trial of Captain Frant, I mean."

"I'm coming to that, sir. All that was needed, then, was to dispose effectively of Heriot's body. So the corpse, robes, clothes, and black cap, which Maddison, for some reason, had retained, were arranged in a cabin-trunk at the 'Sicilian' and subsequently left, in the darkness, somewhere on the lonely road at Langley Broom. The idea was this. The trunk, of course, would be made the subject of a hue and cry—and traced back to Mr. Justice Heriot himself. Maddison purchased it on the first occasion that he appeared in public in the role—a few days before the Assizes were due to commence. Made up, this time, in what I will call Heriot's mufti. I shall have something else to say about this trunk a little later." He glanced round at Maddison. "What made you finesse with the black cap, Mr. Frant?"

The actor's reply was surprising, but eminently characteristic. "It appealed to my sense of the theatre. I couldn't rid myself of the image of Collier's picture. It haunted me throughout the whole proceedings."

There was silence for a little while.

"You've explained the plan, as you described it, Bathurst. Now, however, I should like you to go deeper. After all, to a certain extent, I'm paying the piper. I should, therefore, be entitled to call the tune." The speaker was Sir Randall Bowers.

CHAPTER XXVII
PIECES OF THE PATTERN

"SIR Randall Bowers," returned Mr. Bathurst, "I shall be delighted to deliver the full basket. This was the manner of my deductions. I will deal first with the Heriot case, then with the facts of the Pearson murder, which latter may be said to be the foundation of the whole edifice. Look at it how I might, several things about Heriot began to be put in the 'surprising' class. Naturally, I didn't give him a deal of thought until after he had been murdered. His killing though, was a distinct challenge to me to sit up and take notice. The spotlight of the drama, as it were, was turned right on to him . . . to show him up. Then, the more closely I looked at things generally, the more 'surprises' bobbed up and literally yelled for me to take a closer look at them. I will detail them one by one, in the order in which they presented themselves to me. Seriatim, then. 'A.' That extraordinary (for Heriot, the 'hanging Judge') 'summing up'. Every point for the defence was cultivated assiduously. The defence was complimented for its scrupulous fairness. The points for the Prosecution, on the contrary, were lightly skated over. Result, then, of my intensive study—of Heriot at the trial—it was *unlike*

Heriot'. Note that! Moving on, then. 'B.' The motor-car that Heriot used to take him from the Courts of Justice and also to purchase a cabin-trunk from the firm of Orridge, Debenham & Co. Consider! An interview with Heriot's confidential maid, by name Miss Angela Mansell, elicits the rather astounding confirmation (under the circumstances) of something that I had heard before, that he positively hated the motor-car as a means of transport. Avoided it, whenever he could. Sir Randall Bowers had told me this before Angela. She gave me complete corroboration. Again I found myself wondering. Anyhow, there we were again. The use of the motor-car was *'unlike Heriot'*. See where I'm getting? The idea that's coming to me? Was the Heriot, whom I had seen trying Captain Frant, the same Heriot whose body had been found in the lane near Langley Broom? It wanted probing. It got it."

At this point Anthony broke off. He seemed to be feeling for his next words. This was unusual for him. When they came, they were slower . . . more deliberate.

"When I had started my probing, I met with a set-back. I was getting used to that kind of thing by then. It was a nasty set-back. Brought me up with a jolt and a jerk. Worried me for a time, no end. The real Heriot had idiosyncrasies—fads if you like it. And mannerisms. You know what I mean . . . like we all have. Like Lanchester, for instance. He snaps his second finger and thumb together. Right hand. He did when he took the first trunk back to Heriot's flat."

Lanchester stared. Bathurst went on again.

"Heriot loved dark red roses, had a penchant for taking iodine drops during the morning . . . at certain seasons of the year . . . leant forward at a witness . . . elbow on desk and pen in hand . . . pen pointing at the witness. Used to finger his neck . . . when he looked at the accused in the dock. *And the Heriot at the trial had done all these things.* Was it likely that an impostor could *possibly* have reproduced so faithfully these pieces of personality? There was also another point in regard to this that gave me serious pause. Heriot's malady of the throat! There it was. One couldn't mistake it. Not overdone, never made too obtrusive, but all the same, showing just enough for people to hear the disaffection in the voice." He swung round on to Maddison. "Splendidly done, sir, if you will allow me to say so."

Maddison Frant waved his hand in deprecation. Anthony acknowledged it and proceeded.

"Then, happily for me, I remembered something. Something of immense importance. A paragraph concerning the precarious state of the Judge's health had appeared in the Press a little time before the Frant trial. On the other hand, this statement was not exact . . . it was more general than particular. 'Complete loss of voice' . . . but no details as to why. The Heriot of the trial had not completely lost his voice . . . although his voice was seriously impaired. If, therefore, my idea that somebody had impersonated Heriot were true, it must have been somebody with a fairly close knowledge of him. And yet . . . there were these contradictions. I was in doubt. That doubt began to be dispelled by a most unexpected agency. That agency was one number of a monthly magazine."

A startled exclamation left the lips of Maddison Frant. His brother sat bolt upright in his chair. The actor was unable to restrain himself.

"You clever, clever devil. How on earth did you . . . ?"

"No merit of mine there, so spare my blushes. I am indebted to that certain Miss Angela Mansell for that piece of information. I had no idea of the existence, even, of the interview, and got on to it by pure chance. Still, it served my purpose admirably. It showed me how the impersonator of Heriot could have picked up those little personal mannerisms against which I had been hitting my head. By the way, sir . . . you went wrong there. Did you know?"

Maddison Frant frowned. "How do you mean?"

"The *Piccadilly* told the public much of the private life of Justice Heriot . . . but not all. You couldn't obtain all that in the space of a magazine interview. Ever heard of the Mitre Restaurant in Reading?"

"Naturally. My lunch was sent in from there, during the trial, at the midday adjournments."

"That's it. And you never once sent the Cheddar back and asked them to send you the Stilton. I know, because I've checked up on the point."

The two brothers and Sir Randall Bowers made no attempt to conceal their amazement. "What in the name of . . . ?"

Anthony smiled sweetly. "Just as you were unaware of Heriot's aversion to the motor-car as a means of transport, so were you equally oblivious to his passion for a blue-veined Stilton. A passion that caused him to eat no other cheese. As a fount of information, my Angela, you see, outdid your *Piccadilly*. Regard then, my conclusions. Somebody had copied faithfully the personal touches that had been made public, but others, that had not been mentioned, were conspicuous by their absence. But—and a big but this—mark it well—*that somebody* had inside knowledge with regard to the condition of Heriot's throat. I had a simultaneous equation, you see, demanding values in the form of identifications for three unknown quantities, x, y and z. A chauffeur with a Daimler car, an impersonator, and an anaesthetist." He looked slyly at Sir Robert. "I had them already in my cast. There they were—all three of them. Lanchester, expert car driver, Mr. Maddison Frant, a famous actor, and his brother, an eminent doctor, skilled in the performance of dangerous operations. Miss Frant, I think, knew nothing of the conspiracy. There was the motive there, as well, to make the look of my combination even more attractive. Any lingering doubt that I might have still harboured was pretty well dispelled when I discovered from a highly authentic source that Sir Robert had heard of Heriot's throat trouble, and when I was able, too, to identify Lanchester as the chauffeur who had carried the second trunk to Heriot's flat in Strathpeffer Mansions. Don't ask me who told me of Heriot's condition, Sir Robert. I can't tell you. It's a secret of the consulting-room. Mine."

Mr. Bathurst grinned at the pungency of his sally. He continued:

"The existence of that second trunk puzzled me considerably for quite a long time. I was unable to explain to myself satisfactorily the presence of this second trunk in the crime. What in the name of goodness had made it necessary? Eventually I cottoned on to an idea. Lanchester here, will tell me, if I'm right or not." He began to rub his hands. "It's really extraordinary how one knot very often rubs out another knot. One ragged end joins up with another, and . . . as it were . . . they merge. Now, one of my nasty knots in the Heriot case, that is to say, if my theory of the killing were the correct one, was the delay between the end of the trial and the finding of the body. If you remember, it wasn't discovered until the late afternoon, or early evening of the day *after* the trial. I explain that like this. If Heriot had been found directly after the trial of Captain Frant, Dr. Barrow-South, or whatever doctor performed the autopsy, would have declared immediately 'this body had been dead some hours', and the eyes of the authorities would have been at once opened to the impersonation. As it was, however, Dr. Barrow-Smith *accepted the fact* that Heriot had been alive twenty-seven hours previously. There was such strong evidence for him to do that. The Judge had taken the Frant trial . . . everybody knew that. . . . The result was that he didn't go deep enough to discover that the old man had been dead for a considerably longer time than he thought. How often, the things that we take for granted, prove a pitfall to us. This brings me again to the trunk matter."

His eyes sought Lanchester again.

"Whilst I was considering this question . . . and conjuring up the ghastly scene in Sir Robert's room at the Sicilian hotel . . . the body of the judge being packed away in the trunk . . . in his robes and the black cap . . . all the whole paraphernalia had to be kept there until the trial was ended . . . I began to toy with a theory that would fit the appearance of trunk No. 2. I'll take a chance now, and launch it on you. The trunk in Heriot's flat . . . that we're calling trunk No. 2 . . . is in reality trunk No. 1." He paused, but no answer or comment was forthcoming from the group of men to whom he spoke. "By trunk No. 1, I mean the trunk purchased by Mr. Maddison Frant in his guise of Heriot in ordinary clothes. It was taken to Reading, and did duty . . . inadequately . . . it wasn't quite big enough, you see, to take the body comfortably. . . . there had been a risk carrying it in the car to the 'Sicilian' just after the killing . . . this risk must on no account be repeated on that last journey to Langley Broom. Lanchester came back to town, bought another and larger one, at the same shop as previously, took the first one back to the judge's flat, and returned to Reading with the real trunk No. 2. Am I right?" Bathurst chuckled at the acquiescence that greeted him. "I thought so. I measured the one at Heriot's, and compared it with Inspector MacMorran's notes of the one at Langley Broom."

Sir Randall Bowers leant forward with a question. "Who dropped Barrow-South's card in the trunk, and why?"

Anthony turned to the others and pointedly awaited their reply.

"It was an accident," explained Sir Robert. "We knew nothing of it. It must have dropped from a pocket of his ordinary clothes."

"That, then, I think, finishes the Heriot tangle. Oh—by the way—there's one tiny point." Anthony paused. "The car, I suppose, was not driven down the road to Langley Broom. There were no tracks that I could—"

"No," returned Lanchester. "Too risky. We ran along the top, and two of us carried the trunk down the turning. It was damnably dark—not a soul in sight. Didn't take us five minutes the whole job."

Sir Robert rose, and went straight over to Anthony. "I must know, Bathurst," he said quickly, "before we go any further, what do you propose to do? There is Sir Randall, too. . . ." Anthony turned to Sir Randall Bowers. "You heard Sir Robert's question, sir. What's the answer?"

The old man's face crinkled into a smile.

"'Pon my soul, Bathurst. You're asking me to compound a felony. Me at my time of life, too. And considering my career."

"I remember your letter to the *Morning Message*, Sir Randall. Also your general outlook that has taken you where you are. After all, you know—"

"I quite agree, Bathurst. Cancer's a beastly thing, and the end's tough and horrible. . . . The pain . . . I wouldn't see a rat suffer from it. I expect you knew that, you young devil, when you invited me to come along here. I'm with you, my boy, in whatever you decide."

"Sir Robert," declared Mr. Bathurst, with a touch of gaiety, "you hear what Sir Randall says? In that case, then, I have but one more duty to carry out, for I also am content to let things remain as they are. That duty is to tell you the story of the murder of Leonard Pearson."

CHAPTER XXVIII
DEATH IN THE WOOD

"LEONARD Pearson, although he deserved all he got, was, nevertheless, unlucky to get it when he did. After Captain Frant had left the library, Pearson sat there for a time with £1,000 in notes in front of him. The weakness of the case for the Crown, if there were one, always seemed to me, to centre round that pile of notes. Captain Frant's evidence that he had had the notes, received some measure of confirmation, it will be remembered, from a bookmaker named Skerritt, amongst others. I was late on the case, as you know, but it struck me as a most remarkable thing that those notes had vanished. I went to Perry Hammer, in the first instance, therefore, with the strong idea that a third party had intervened in the affair after Captain Frant had left Pearson in the library. I went with the intention, too, of looking for data that would fortify that 'third-party' theory."

He paused to light a cigarette that he took from Sir Robert's box; it was eloquent testimony to his power of holding an audience that nobody spoke during the operation. When he proceeded, he spoke very quietly.

"Those data, gentlemen, were very soon to come. I will tell you. I elicited the fact from the servants, that the front of the house, when lit up, was visible from the road. With this in mind, I argued to myself that this 'third party' might have been the object of a chance attraction. Somebody passing by the house on the main road had been tempted, we will say, by what had suddenly caught his eye. He had skirted the house, worked round to the back, made his way to the french-doors, and seen Pearson *and the pile of bank-notes.* I clung tightly to this possibility, and what I saw in Pearson's room when I gave it the look-over, set my nerves a-tingling. I little thought, at that minute, when I trailed the scent for the first time, that I should be so long in reaching my quarry. Pearson had been struck down from behind. But there was a standing-mirror on his table, always placed, so Murray, his butler, informed me, on his master's right hand."

"That's quite true," broke in Hilary Frant. "I can confirm that statement. I remember seeing it there."

"Pearson's assassin, therefore, must have come behind him, *on Pearson's right.* Had he approached from the left Pearson must have seen him *reflected* in the mirror on the table! I then took a chance. A long shot (I like 'em rather). I imagined the unknown murderer standing in the french-doors, which Captain Frant had obligingly left open when he cleared out. On the right of them. On the right of them as he watched Pearson in front of him. And it occurred to me that he might have clutched at the right-hand portiere as he stood there . . . waiting to strike the blow that killed Pearson. If he had . . . it is conceivable that he might have torn it a little . . . a man's weight used in that way will often do that. I inquired. I was lucky. It was as I had surmised."

Bathurst stopped again and flicked the ash from his burning cigarette. Again, there was a hushed silence.

"Regard the quandary that faced me now. Complicated, too, by another fragment of evidence. One of the maids had heard three 'thuds' in Pearson's room on the night of the murder. Remember that, please. How was I to find my man? A pretty ticklish problem, gentlemen, you will admit. I resolved to move via those notes, of which nobody, mark you, had the numbers. The 'fifties' were my big chance. Could I discover any £50 notes that had found their way about that time into unusual banking accounts? Notes, let me suggest, that might have been changed for somebody. Sir Austin Kemble, the Commissioner of Police at the Yard, put some of his wonderful machinery at my disposal, and I soon got on the track of two notes. One, the first of which I got news, had been paid in by the licensee of an inn, known as the 'Blue Tambourine', just outside Reading. Yes—Reading, of all places. Hallelujah! I went down there. And there, gentlemen, I came to a dead stop. To a blank wall. The man who had paid it in to his account, the man, that is, who had no doubt changed that note for somebody, would give no more evidence in this life. For the reason that he was dead. Burnt to death in the Anthurium Cinema fire—in the town of Reading itself. Mrs. Lane, his widow, could tell me nothing. She had no idea from whom her husband could have obtained that (to me) precious note. So, you see, my first real clue fizzled out at once, and I returned to town, I'm afraid, rather crestfallen. To run, however, into the clue of note the second. Canning Town, the locality this time, gentlemen, A bacon shop in Canning Town. This note had been changed here for a customer named Rose Stubbs. . . . Bimson, the bacon-man, had been rather worried about it . . . but she was a regular customer who wanted the money badly. After all, it wasn't his business, he told me . . . the note was good. I repaired to Mrs. Stubbs and interviewed her. She had a very strange story to tell me. You will never guess what it was."

Bathurst gazed round the assembled company as though inviting comment. None came.

"She had received this note on the morning of the 24th of April, from an anonymous donor . . . in a letter . . . this letter came in an envelope that had borne the *Reading* post-mark. The handwriting of the address was unknown to her. She had, unfortunately for me, destroyed this envelope . . . months ago, remember. Had I seen it, I think I could have identified the writing. That's by the way, however. Think though of the date and the district. Once again, beautifully to the point, weren't they? I inquired of Mrs. Stubbs concerning her lord and master. You shall hear what she told me of him, and be able to compare it with what you saw of the gentleman a little while ago. He was a crippled dancer, she said, who worked with a man named. Bill Holly. Stubbs had a crutch. Holly had an organ. Stubbs danced to it. Considering his physical handicap, she told me, his dancing was amazingly clever. Moreover, he worked between London and Oxford. And more startlingly still, *he had disappeared*. Instead of coming home for the week-end, as was his invariable custom, he had seemingly vanished into thin air! I came away from Mrs. Stubbs, feeling sure that her nomadic husband could tell me a good deal, if he so chose, of the facts of the Perry Hammer murder. The fact that he used a wooden crutch, I argued, might explain the thuds that had been heard in Pearson's room. But I was unable to find my friend of the steps. When the trial of Captain Frant intervened, I was very much afraid that I should never find him. Why?" This in answer to Maddison Frant. "Because I felt moderately certain that he was dead. Why were there *no more* £50 notes coming through in the district? What had happened to him? This was the progressive line of the argument that I used to persuade myself that Stubbs had been gathered to his forefathers. Stubbs, I decided, had gone to the 'Blue Tambourine', it was a house that he was in the habit of using, and Lane, a very kind and easygoing landlord (I had his widow's word for that), had changed one of his notes for him. *But Lane had died in the cinema fire.* Wasn't it extremely likely that Stubbs had perished with him? Several of the bodies, you will remember, were so badly burned as to be unidentifiable. After the trial, however, with its rather surprising verdict (Captain Frant himself will admit that, I think, on the evidence), I determined to probe to the bottom and make as certain as I could of the demise of Mr. Stubbs. I went to Mrs. Lane again at the 'Blue Tambourine'. This time, however, with a hand that contained a trump or two. I was able to describe Stubbs to her. She knew him at once. He had been in the inn between the murder and the fire. Also, on this second visit, my luck was right in. Not that it helped me a lot. I had the felicity to meet Mr. William Holly. I poked a considerable breeze into that gentleman. Made him spill his beer. He informed me, on recovery, that his erstwhile business partner, Mr. Stubbs, had 'hopped it'. The date that he placed on the dissolution of partnership was most significant. He was trying to save his own skin . . . *because he knew how Pearson had been murdered.* The police will hug friend Holly to their bosom before the week is out, and I'm open to bet that he'll turn King's Evidence. I've met his sort before . . . a pronounced yellow streak."

Bathurst laughed and turned to Sir Robert Frant.

"I'm afraid, you know, that Holly will term me ungrateful. He was kind enough to send me a letter of warning that it would be more healthy for me to mind my own business. Ah, well . . . I shan't be the first person to be misjudged. Where was I? Oh . . . at the 'Tambourine'. My next place of call was the Anthurium Super Cinema. Not only did I trace Stubbs as far as there, but also *found his crutch*. The crutch with which he had killed Pearson. Hardly burned at all . . . but with a slight stain on the arm-rest that has since been found to be mammalian blood. By Jove! how that find warmed the cockles of my heart. Twenty to one, I said to myself, that Stubbs is alive. Cleared to another part of the country . . . abroad, perhaps. The fire gave him his great chance, you see, and he seized it with both hands. I think this is what happened. Conjecture, of course, but the circumstantial evidence that we have backs it up. Lane, his companion for the evening, tried to save Stubbs. Carried him towards the exit. For a time the cripple clung to his crutch . . . then, in the fierce struggle . . . and pandemonium of panic, he dropped it. Lane fell exhausted. Stubbs, either crawling on all three or assisted by others, was flung, buffeted and bruised, to safety. You have seen yourselves that he wasn't altogether helpless without it. Thinking it over, afterwards, he decided not to claim his lost crutch. George Alfred Stubbs was dead. He would remain dead. Dead until the sea vomits those on whom it has fed . . . dead for ever. He bought a stick and went North . . . the reverse direction to Jess Oakroyd. When he got there and settled down to enjoy his little fortune, he bought a new crutch. The one that he tried on me just now."

Lanchester broke in with a question. "How did you lure him here, Bathurst? I'm not quite clear as to—"

"By means of a tempting advertisement, which I hoped might catch his eye. His deformity was such, and his work so unique, that he was well-known on the road, and I thought that if he didn't see it himself, somebody might call his attention to it. I used the *Era* for the advertisement, and in the *Morning Message* I had a daily paragraph, setting out the special kind of dancer that was wanted for Frant's new production. The *Message* gets everywhere, you know, and the second chance came off. The paragraph in question hinted at big money for the man who could fulfil the unusual conditions, and I can assure you that those conditions were so carefully outlined that they fitted our man to the proverbial 'T'. The money he took from Pearson's table wouldn't last for ever . . . he knew that . . . and rose to my bait, as you know. I'm sorry for his wife . . . I can't measure her surprise when she hears of the arrest . . . a very decent little woman. Sir Randall's going to help her, though. A present of £50 will cheer her considerably." Anthony's eyes twinkled. "You lose, you know, sir."

"Give me the address," Bowers said gruffly. "I'll send it along to her to-morrow."

"Speaking of that, Bathurst," declared Sir Robert, "there was one thing that you said just now that I didn't quite understand. I understood you to say that the note that this man's wife received in April was sent to her anonymously. Also that she didn't know the handwriting on the envelope. Yes?"

"Yes," replied Bathurst, imperturbably.

"You said, though, that you think you know whose writing it was. I'm afraid that I don't quite—"

"I'm fairly sure, Sir Robert, that the handwriting was Lane's, late landlord of the 'Blue Tambourine', Reading. Stubbs got him to do the job for him." Anthony looked round the company. "No other point, is there?"

"Was the crutch flung at Pearson?" inquired Captain Frant.

"Probably not, I think. Held in the hand all the time, but whirled round at full length, so that Pearson could be struck with tremendous force and strength."

As Mr. Bathurst had predicted, Holly turned King's Evidence. This contingency, added to the fact that seven more £50 notes were found in the possession of the prisoner, and that he was proved to have been in Perry Hammer on the night of the crime, turned the scales against him. It was on a wet morning in February that he awoke for the last time . . . cursing to the end the man whose genius had brought him to the gallows. They called for him about five minutes to nine. . . .

Bathurst himself, is disinclined to discuss the inner details of the Perry Hammer murder.

"There's one thing that I regret about it," he always says, when it crops up for conversation. "I was late on the case. The scent was within an ace of being cold when I got there. The result is that I am constantly asking myself a question . . . would Heriot have died, when and how he did, if Cardinal Vespucci had not lost his historical agate on the platform of the railway-station at Milan?"

For an answer to this question he never waits. Because he knows, within his heart, that he alone has the power to supply the answer that would be generally accepted as satisfactory and convincing. After all, you know, somebody must pay the penalty when a reputation is international. And the Cardinal recovered his agate!

THE END